THE DAILY DOCTOR

365¼ WHONIVERSAL MEDITATIONS ON LIFE AND HOW TO LIVE IT

SIMON GUERRIER
& PETER ANGHELIDES

BOOKS

BBC Books, an imprint of Ebury Publishing
20 Vauxhall Bridge Road
London SW1V 2SA

BBC Books is part of the Penguin Random House group of companies
whose addresses can be found at global.penguinrandomhouse.com

Doctor Who is produced in Wales by Bad Wolf with BBC Studios Productions.

Executive Producers: Russell T Davies, Julie Gardner,
Jane Tranter, Phil Collinson & Joel Collins.

First published by BBC Books in 2023

www.penguin.co.uk

A CIP catalogue record for this book is available from the British Library

ISBN 9781785947988

Commissioning Editor: Albert DePetrillo
Project Editor: Steve Cole
Design: seagulls.net
Production: Antony Heller

Printed and bound in Great Britain by Clays Ltd, Elcograf S.p.A.

The authorised representative in the EEA is Penguin Random House Ireland,
Morrison Chambers, 32 Nassau Street, Dublin D02 YH68.

CONTENTS

INTRODUCTION
TRAVEL WITHOUT THE TARDIS

THE DOCTOR
Think about me when you're living your life
one day after another, all in a neat pattern.
Think about the homeless traveller and his old
police box, with his days like crazy paving.

Dragonfire by Ian Briggs (1987)

• • • • • •

The Seventh Doctor encourages Melanie Bush to remember him when she leaves the TARDIS for the final time. It's a sad, sweet moment. Of course she will think of the Doctor and those extraordinary adventures in time and space. How could she not? After all, the pair of us think about little else.

You probably think about it as well. The Doctor, travelling in the TARDIS – and what it would be like being there, too.

Maybe you know where you'd like to go; the historical figures you'd like to meet or distant worlds you'd like to explore. The Doctors' friends have met Kublai Khan and Ada Lovelace, Rosa Parks and William Shakespeare. The TARDIS has visited a living sun, a diamond planet and a world of giant, psychologically manipulative crabs.

But exploring is just one reason it would be great to board the TARDIS. We'd also have the most extraordinary companion and guide.

The Doctor has traversed all of time of space, from the Big Bang (which was accidentally caused by a fuel tank jettisoned by the time-travelling space station Terminus) to the final five minutes of the universe (where Ashildr sat watching the last stars die). The Doctor has laughed and larked about and fallen in love; fought battles, sometimes at great personal loss; suffered and survived; soaked it all up and learned from it.

Often brilliant, sometimes baffling, always inspiring. Thousands of years old, with lifetimes of knowledge picked up along the way. Wouldn't it be wonderful to have that experience to call upon whenever we get stuck in life? To know that wisdom, guidance and perspective was immediately to hand.

When Mel left, she knew how to contact the Doctor again, should she ever have the need. 'I'll send you a postcard,' she said. 'I'll put it in a bottle and throw it into space. It'll reach you – in time.'

But instead, let's see if we can bottle some of the Doctors' advice. The useful stuff they've already shared with us. And while we're at it, why not also share insights from the Doctors' brilliant friends?

That, of course, is what this book sets out to do, including at least one quotation from each of the Doctor's TV adventures to date. Whether you're facing a major crisis or the flotsam of an ordinary day, we trust that the Doctors' philosophy will bring you succour. The quotations are in random order, except for when they're not, which we hope produces something of the effect of travelling in the TARDIS and flitting back and forth in time.

Each quotation explains the situation in which it appears in the story, and perhaps some broader context in *Doctor Who*. Then we suggest how it offers an insight, or inspires one, that you might apply in a practical way. We don't need tips and tricks about foiling alien invasions or how to communicate with an enormous, glowing Tythonian trapped deep underground; that's not the sort of stuff we expect you'll have to deal with very often in life. (Although, if you do, look out for a distinctive, five-sided shield of metal, which is actually a communicator.)

But when it comes to love and loss, planning and negotiating, caring for ourselves and others… well, perhaps the Doctor's take on these matters can aid us in our own course through the times to come.

You have two options for how to use this book.

Be like Mel, living her life day by day in a neat pattern, and read the entries in sequence. One quotation per day, for each day of the year.

Or you can be like the Doctor, with days like crazy paving, and flip through this book in any order.

Obviously, we can't know – or guess – what might be going on in your life, or the scale of the challenges you face on any particular day. But if the quotation doesn't fit, it may at least divert you for a while. It might spark your own ideas about the way we can draw on knowledge and experience to improve things. In fact, that's something we've learned from going back over the whole history of *Doctor Who*. For all the monsters and explosions and weird goings-on, what often makes a difference is an ordinary person deciding to take action.

But we're not in control of where it will take you. That's all down to you now. Enjoy the adventure.

As the Doctor once said, 'The future lies this way...'

Simon and Peter, June 2023

JANUARY

1 JANUARY

LET'S GET STARTED

HARRY SULLIVAN
Where are we going?

THE DOCTOR
Er... forward.

Genesis of the Daleks by Terry Nation (1975)

• • • • • •

The start of a new year. You probably made resolutions. You'll do that *thing* or make that *change* or be that *better person*. That's all a bit daunting. Where exactly do you start?

The Time Lords once gave the Doctor a *really* daunting task. They sent him back in time to the planet Skaro where he had either to stop the Daleks being created, affect their development to make them less aggressive creatures, or discover some inherent weakness. Having agreed to this, the Doctor found himself in the midst of a battlefield, bombarded by heavy artillery.

He had no idea of the dangers awaiting him and his friends. He had no idea where to start looking for the Daleks. He didn't yet know how limited his options would be, leaving him with a huge moral dilemma about obeying the Time Lords' instruction. All he could do, for now, was take the first step forward.

Whatever you want to achieve this year, don't be daunted by the challenge. Don't worry about the details or the exact destination. Be mindful of the direction to head in – and get moving.

2 JANUARY

SHARING IS CARING

THE DOCTOR
He is the least important because we can all make fire.

An Unearthly Child by Anthony Coburn (1963)

• • • • • •

In the very first *Doctor Who* story, the TARDIS lands on a chilly desolate landscape thousands of years ago, where a tribe of early humans endure a miserable existence. Their leaders have always kept the method of making fire a closely guarded secret as a means to hold on to power – but the last leader has died without passing on that secret.

After the Doctor is seen striking a match, rival members of the tribe variously kidnap, imprison and threaten him to 'make fire come from his fingers' for them. By controlling this 'firemaker', they advance their own claims to be leader.

Of course, that attitude is exactly why the tribe is in such trouble in the first place. The Doctor is keen to share the knowledge openly and empower *everyone* in the tribe. In articulating this idea, he seems to find common cause with new companions Barbara and Ian – they weren't getting on before but now they work together. Sharing isn't just giving something away; you gain from it as well.

3 JANUARY

BEING OBSERVANT

THE DOCTOR
Go to the TARDIS and bring these things back for me, will you?

DODO CHAPLET
How will I know where to find them?

THE DOCTOR
Well, open your eyes, my dear child.
Otherwise, you won't be any use to me, will you?

The Ark by Paul Erickson and Lesley Scott (1966)

• • • • • •

Dodo Chaplet thinks her first TARDIS trip has brought her to Whipsnade Zoo, and expects to see the American Bison and the tea bar. In fact, the TARDIS has brought them to a futuristic spaceship, and what Dodo has brought is a cold – which turns into a plague for the vulnerable locals.

The Doctor comforts Dodo when she becomes tearful, but his expectations of his travelling companions remain high. While devising a cure, he gives Dodo a list of items to collect. And although she's barely been in the TARDIS before, he expects her to find what he needs.

Dodo locates the items promptly. Earlier, she'd been observant enough to recognise that the spaceship contains flowers from America, birds from Africa, a snake from Brazil, and an Indian elephant – proving that you don't need someone to spell everything out for you if you're paying attention to your surroundings. It pays to keep your eyes open, whatever the situation.

4 JANUARY

DOING IT YOURSELF

DEREK MOBERLEY
But I'm not a surgeon.
What about you? You're a doctor...

THE DOCTOR
You must help yourselves.

The Seeds of Doom by Robert Banks Stewart (1976)

• • • • • •

At a research base in Antarctica, Charles Winlett is infected by an alien plant and begins to transform into a monstrous Krynoid. The only chance to save his life is to stop the spread of infection – by cutting off the man's arm!

The other researchers turn to the Doctor for help with the amputation but he coolly declines their entreaties. His friend Sarah Jane Smith tells them that the Doctor isn't a medical professional. But that doesn't seem to be the reason for his refusal.

The Doctor has often flouted the Time Lords' rules which strictly forbid interference in the affairs of other peoples and planets. In Antarctica, however, he chooses to abide by that rule because it's important that humanity is able to act for itself. He is being cruel to be kind.

We often want to help when asked, but sometimes the best way for someone to learn and become independent is when we take a step back and leave them to the challenge unaided.

5 JANUARY

JUST SAY YES

THE DOCTOR
Won't somebody please say 'Yes'?

Meglos by John Flanagan and Andrew McCulloch (1980)

• • • • • •

The Doctor returns to the verdant planet Tigella for the first time in fifty years – and is promptly arrested and sentenced to death. The Deons tie him up and plan to squash him under a large stone slab.

They do this because the huge, heavy Dodecahedron that provides the Tigellans with power, and which the Deons worship, has disappeared. The Doctor is the prime suspect for this improbable crime because he was the last person seen coming out of the Power Room where the object stood. Except that the Doctor hasn't even been there!

The Doctor's friend Romana soon learns the truth: a malevolent cactus called Meglos is impersonating the Doctor, and it was he who stole the Dodecahedron from the Power Room. Romana and her allies present their evidence to the Deons and argue about who is really to blame – but, as the Doctor points out, the slab is still poised to fall on him.

It's important to discuss matters, debate the merits of evidence and pick over detail. But don't let that prevent you from making a decision!

6 JANUARY

CHERISH LIFE

ROSANNA CALVIERRI
One city to save an entire species.
Was that so much to ask?

THE DOCTOR
I told you, you can't go back and change time.
You mourn, but you live. I know, Rosanna. I did it.

The Vampires of Venice by Toby Whithouse (2010)

· · · · · ·

The Doctor prevents Rosanna Calvierri from sinking Venice, and thwarts her plan to turn it into a replacement for her aquatic home world, Saturnyne. Rosanna has taken human form, so she can work above water to convert enough human women into breeding partners for her ten thousand male children who are swimming in the Venetian canals.

Faced with her defeat, Rosanna berates the Doctor for not allowing her to trade one city for her whole race – especially as she knows the fate of the Doctor's own people. Before he can stop her, she throws herself to a dreadful watery death.

We fear mortality because it thwarts our desire to achieve more in the future. But because it is an inevitable part of life, we can look back on our time without regret. Knowing our end will come enables us to cherish every moment of the life we have.

7 JANUARY

HAVE FAITH IN OTHER PEOPLE

PETE TYLER
Doctor, help us.

THE DOCTOR
What, close the breach? Stop the Cybermen?
Defeat the Daleks? Do you believe I can do that?

PETE TYLER
Yes.

THE DOCTOR
Maybe that's all I need. Off we go, then!

Doomsday by Russell T Davies (2006)

• • • • • •

Five million Cybermen cross from a parallel world to the Earth in this dimension, seeking to conquer and upgrade the people here. But they clash with an army of Daleks and battle soon rages in the skies above London – with humans caught in the crossfire. Yet the breach between dimensions has its own dangerous effect and the parallel Earth is starting to boil.

Not surprisingly, the Doctor is feeling daunted by the sheer scale of the multiple threats facing both Earths. But Pete Tyler has faith in the Doctor's ability to solve the crisis – and that belief is enough to boost the Doctor's spirits and inspire him take action.

Pete can't have known that his words would have such a dramatic effect. But it often doesn't take much to inspire someone. A kind word. A bit of recognition. A demonstration of faith in them. Today, do what you can to boost the confidence of someone else around you.

8 JANUARY

LOOK UP

THE DOCTOR
The deep and lovely dark.
We'd never see the stars without it.

Listen by Steven Moffat (2014)

· · · · · ·

A week into January and maybe you're feeling that it's already gone on too long. Christmas feels like forever ago now, we're back to work and school, and it's all a bit cold and miserable.

But no need to get downhearted. As the Doctor says, the dark is when we get to see the stars at their best and brightest. In the depths of winter there is plenty to relish – a warm meal, a cup of tea, a fire – and they all feel much more welcoming now than at any other time of the year. Take comfort where you can.

In fact, if it's clear, go out and look at the sky as dusk falls. There can be extraordinary sunsets in winter. Watch the Moon come into view, see Venus shine strongly among the scatter of fainter lights that are everywhere in that night sky. Let your eyes adjust to them. Drink them in.

And if's too cold and wet and overcast, go back inside and have a hot drink. Doesn't that feel better?

9 JANUARY

RESPONDING TO DISAPPOINTMENT

THE DOCTOR

You betrayed me. Betrayed my trust, you betrayed
our friendship, you betrayed everything that
I've ever stood for. You let me down!

CLARA OSWALD

Then why are you helping me?

THE DOCTOR

Why? Do you think I care for you so little that
betraying me would make a difference?

Dark Water by Steven Moffat (2014)

• • • • • •

You cannot change the past, though Clara Oswald wants to. Grief-stricken after her boyfriend's death, she tries to force the Twelfth Doctor to bring him back. The Doctor insists it would be a paradox loop that would disintegrate Clara's timeline: if he changed the events that brought Clara to this point, she would never then come to ask him to make the change.

Clara thinks she has entrapped the Doctor, but he's only allowed her to think that. He wants to see how her betrayal would play out. She believes that the Doctor must now send her away and is astonished when he absolves her.

Betrayal by someone you love will provoke surprise, anger, sorrow, maybe grief for the loss of your relationship. Were they careless, weak, or deliberate and malicious? You cannot change the past. You can only decide how you respond, and whether you will forgive.

10 JANUARY

COMPASSION WHEN TESTED

THE DOCTOR
You know, I'll never understand the people of Earth.
I have spent the day using, abusing, even trying
to kill you. If you'd have behaved as I have,
I should have been pleased at your demise.

PERI BROWN
It's called compassion, Doctor.

The Twin Dilemma by Anthony Steven (1984)

• • • • • •

The newly regenerated Sixth Doctor is liable to sudden, dramatic changes of mood. At one point, he even attacks his poor companion, Peri. Horrified by his own actions, he heads to the desolate asteroid Titan 3, to live a repentant life as a hermit. Poor Peri has no choice but to go with him.

Soon they are caught up in a sinister alien plot, and find themselves trapped in a base which has been set to self-destruct. With typical quick thinking, the Doctor finds a way to transmat Peri to safety, but the base apparently explodes before he can join her back in the TARDIS.

The Doctor is amazed by Peri's relief when he then turns up alive; it's not at all what he deserves. But her compassion transcends such small concerns. Don't take pleasure in the suffering of others, no matter what they might have done.

11 JANUARY

CONSIDER ALTERNATIVES

DREAM LORD

You ran away with a handsome hero. Would you really give him up for a bumbling country doctor who thinks the only thing he needs to be interesting is a ponytail? But maybe it's better than loving and losing the Doctor. Pick a world, and this nightmare will all be over. They'll listen to you. It's you they're waiting for. Amy's men. Amy's choice.

Amy's Choice by Simon Nye (2010)

• • • • • •

The Doctor visits Amy Pond and Rory Williams in their cottage in rural Leadworth. He's not convinced he can save them from the killer Eknodines infiltrating the village.

The Doctor is in a powerless TARDIS with Amy Pond and Rory Williams. He's not convinced he can save them from the fatal effect of an approaching cold sun.

The mysterious Dream Lord taunts Amy that she must choose which reality to live in.

But neither is real – they're imagining both, under the influence of a mind parasite that fell into the TARDIS time rotor.

Difficult decisions rarely come down to simple alternatives. When faced with no good choice out of a pair, consider carefully before you pick the lesser of two evils. There may be a completely different better option available.

12 JANUARY

LOVE COMES FIRST

AMY POND

Look at you pair. It's always you and her, isn't it?
Long after the rest of us have gone. A boy and
his box, off to see the universe.

THE DOCTOR

Well, you say that as if it's a bad thing.
But honestly, it's the best thing there is.

The Doctor's Wife by Neil Gaiman (2011)

· · · · · ·

Amy Pond and husband Rory Williams find the Doctor chatting to his TARDIS as he makes repairs. Someone else who knows him well says he's like a nine-year-old trying to rebuild a motorbike in his bedroom.

That someone else is the TARDIS herself. The Doctor encounters her personification after an alien entity removes the TARDIS matrix and puts it into a flesh body.

Whoever travels with the Doctor also travels with the TARDIS. He thinks he took her from his home world, but the TARDIS knows it was she who stole him away to see the universe. The TARDIS doesn't always take him where he wants to go, but she always takes him where he needs to be.

Amy and Rory. The Doctor and the TARDIS. When you meet the person destined to be your partner, you should put them and your relationship above all else.

13 JANUARY

MAKE FRUIT NOT WAR

THE DOCTOR
Bananas are good.

The Doctor Dances by Steven Moffat (2005)

• • • • • •

During the worst of the London Blitz in 1941, the Ninth Doctor and his friend Rose Tyler meet a rogue time agent from the 51st century who calls himself Captain Jack Harkness. Jack is self-confident and amoral, and mocks the Doctor's lowly sonic screwdriver as a small and simple tool.

Instead, Jack brandishes a chunky sonic blaster – or 'squareness gun' as Rose calls it, because it makes square holes in objects. The blaster is a product of the weapon factories on Villengard in Jack's own time. The Doctor says he visited once and vaporised the whole complex. There's now a banana grove where it once stood.

Later, the Doctor deftly swaps Jack's blaster for a banana, preventing him from shooting an eerie, possessed child. It's a neat example of the Doctor's whole attitude: preferring a healthy bit of fruit to a deadly weapon. Bananas are a good source of potassium, the Doctor tells Jack. They're also rich in other nutrition such as riboflavin, niacin and fibre.

So, today, take the Doctor's advice: why not have a banana?

14 JANUARY

THOUGHTFUL GIFTS

DELIVERY BOT
Delivery for the Doctor

THE DOCTOR
Ah! It's the Kerblam Man!

Kerblam! by Pete McTighe (2018)

• • • • • •

A space postman delivering to the TARDIS? The Doctor's fam think they've seen it all, now. The teleport pulse they tried unsuccessfully to evade was an incoming delivery from Kerblam, the biggest retailer in the galaxy.

The cheery delivery bot materialises inside the TARDIS, ready to hand over a box printed in familiar colours. The Doctor doesn't remember ordering anything but is elated by the unexpected appearance of the Kerblam Man. She's even more delighted by her parcel's contents: a distinctive red fez that she immediately pops on her head.

Instead of cash or a gift card, delight recipients with more thoughtful presents. It takes more time, and more consideration, but wouldn't you like to receive a gift you weren't expecting but that is just what you want? When it comes to treating others, treat them as you would treat yourself. You'll bring some extra feelgood factor to your day as well as theirs.

15 JANUARY

NOT KNOWING WHAT YOU'RE LOOKING FOR

DEXETER
The specimen is useless.
Nothing. No aggression,
none of the characteristic traits. Useless.

THE DOCTOR
Oh, come on. Depends on your point of view.

DEXETER
I'm speaking scientifically.

THE DOCTOR
So am I.

Full Circle by Andrew Smith (1980)

• • • • • •

Every fifty years on the planet Alzarius, the coming of 'mistfall' precedes sightings of giant crab-like spiders, while marshmen emerge from the swamps and attack the humanoid settlers living nearby.

The settlers have an instinctive fear of marshmen, retreating from their presence and regarding them with awe. Decider Dexeter thinks that a scientific understanding of the creatures will free his people from fear. But he's disappointed when his experiments on a marsh-child show no innate aggression.

The Doctor is vehemently opposed to such cruel experiments, and also sees that the results show something far odder and more disturbing. Spiders, marshmen and settlers are all one species, changing from one to another in a regular cycle!

There's no point asking a question if you think you already know the answer. Let yourself be open to the weird, the wonderful and the unexpected. That's how we break the cycle and move on.

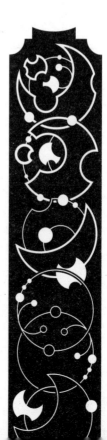

16 JANUARY

PAIN'S PURPOSE

THE DOCTOR
Pain is a gift. Without the capacity for pain,
we can't feel the hurt we inflict.

Death in Heaven by Steven Moffat (2014)

• • • • • •

Danny Pink has suffered. He was knocked down and killed by a car just when he was making plans with girlfriend Clara Oswald. His mind was uploaded to the Nethersphere, a virtual reality in which former lives are edited and rearranged so that they can be downloaded again into their Cyber-converted former bodies.

In his newly resurrected Cyber form, Danny faces an astonished Clara in a graveyard. He wants Clara to activate his inhibitor, to delete the emotions he feels on seeing her again. The Doctor warns Clara that doing so will complete Danny's conversion into an emotionless Cyberman, unable to feel his own or other people's emotions. But unless the inhibitor is activated, Danny cannot access the Cybermen systems to warn the Doctor what they are planning.

Pain is essential to survival. It's our alarm system to protect us from harm. Physical pain warns us against hurting ourselves. Emotional pain means we can empathise with others, and prevent us from hurting them. Suffering makes us resilient and compassionate.

17 JANUARY

LAST, BEST HOPE

SARAH JANE SMITH
Things are bad, aren't they?

THE DOCTOR
Yes. ... Desperately bad but we can
only do our best and hope.

The Masque of Mandragora by Louis Marks (1976)

• • • • • •

The Mandragora Helix is a powerful, living energy source with a malign controlling intelligence. When it gets aboard the TARDIS, the Doctor unwittingly transports it to 15th century San Martino in Italy, at the time of the Renaissance.

There, young Duke Giuliano is keen to engage with new ideas about science and learning that will ultimately transform the world. But his wicked uncle, Count Federico, plots to assassinate Giuliano and take over his estates. Federico thinks he can exploit the power of the Mandragora Helix to do this.

Instead, the Mandragora energy aims to eliminate humanity's ambition and sense of purpose, turning people into idle, mindless sheep. The helix is so powerful, the odds so stacked in its favour, that the Doctor can only guess at ways to defeat it.

Nevertheless, he persists and remains hopeful. That positive attitude, that determination to dig in and do his best, is what vanquishes the Mandragora Helix. Don't give up. Stay positive and keep going – you might well be surprised at what you can achieve.

18 JANUARY

ON JUDGING OTHERS

THE DOCTOR
I don't think I've ever misjudged anybody
quite as badly as I did Lytton.

Attack of the Cybermen by Paula Moore (1985)

• • • • • •

The satellite Riften 5, in orbit round planet Vita 15, is occupied by mercenaries such as Lytton, who once worked for the Daleks as a commander of troopers attempting to rescue Davros from imprisonment.

The troopers were ruthless, gunning down escaped prisoners and an innocent passerby – and though Lytton reprimanded them, it was for the loss of 'valuable specimens'. A year later, the Doctor encountered Lytton again, this time working for the Cybermen.

But in fact Lytton was really working to *betray* the Cybermen, on behalf of the oppressed Cryons of Telos! He wasn't the cold, cruel cynic he appeared – and he'd never worked for the Daleks out of choice.

Lytton's efforts to help the Cryons succeeded, but he was captured, tortured and converted into a partial Cyberman himself. The Doctor battled valiantly but could not save this enigmatic, conflicted but ultimately good man.

We can often be quick to judge people when we don't know or fully understand what motivates them. The least we can do though is admit it when we're wrong.

19 JANUARY

TRUSTED ADVISORS

THE KNIGHTMARE
What do you say, Dad? I should kill him.
He'll be dead in a minute. What difference does it make?

THE DOCTOR
Kill him and you make an enemy of me.

The Woman Who Lived by Catherine Tregenna (2015)

• • • • • •

Ashildr has lived for more than eight hundred years. She didn't ask to be made immortal. She believes she's waited longer than she should ever have lived, and lost more than she can ever remember. Over the centuries she's taken on many roles, and developed an indifference to human suffering.

In the mid 17th century she's left Ashildr far behind. She styles herself as the Knightmare, a highwayman who fears no hangman in Christendom. Rival footpad Sam Swift the Quick doesn't like the Knightmare stealing his patch. He and his pair of colleagues ambush her and the Doctor, who Sam thinks is his rival's father.

The Knightmare swiftly overpowers all three. Only the Doctor's words prevent Sam dying by a shot from his own captured pistol.

Good advice is helpful. It educates you and can change your perspective. Mentors, coaches, colleagues, teachers, friends, parents: when making an irrevocable decision, sound out the opinion of someone you respect.

20 JANUARY

PLAY TO YOUR STRENGTHS

ELLIOT NORTHOVER
I can't do the words. I'm dyslexic.

THE DOCTOR
Oh, that's all right, I can't make a decent meringue.
Draw like your life depends on it, Elliot.

The Hungry Earth by Chris Chibnall (2010)

• • • • • •

Schoolboy Elliot Northover finds it hard to read because of his dyslexia. The Doctor asks him to draw a map of the village as they investigate the mysterious shifting earth around Cwmtaff. When Elliot worries about the words, the Doctor reassures him that no one is good at everything.

Elliot already knows from his father that he's not struggling alone. He has his own strategies: he learned inductive reasoning from listening to audiobooks of Sherlock Holmes stories. He's already earned the Doctor's trust and shown that he can handle difficulties.

So the Doctor offers Elliot a personal example and sets him a bold challenge. He also provides him with role models: dyslexia never stopped Da Vinci or Einstein, so it's not going to stop Elliot.

Lack of aptitude in one thing doesn't have to be a limitation. You have ways to cope, and you have motivation from your other interests and abilities. Instead of worrying about your perceived weaknesses, play to your strengths.

21 JANUARY

WHAT ARE YOU WORKING TOWARDS?

THE DOCTOR
Greed and ambition, that's all it is.
Wait till they find out what their precious
production figures have cost them.

The Power of the Daleks by David Whitaker (1966)

• • • • • •

We all have goals. Sometimes we set them ourselves, sometimes other people set them for us. But they're always the same sort of thing. Work harder. Be more productive. Do more with less, in quicker time.

Well, let Lesterson be a warning. He was a scientist on the planet Vulcan, thrilled by the prospect of being able to double his colony's mining output overnight. But you'd think a scientist might ask more questions about how this was actually possible, and about what it might cost. After all, this mining was all going to be done by Daleks – and they can't exactly wield a pickaxe.

It's not just that Lesterson focused on the end result rather than the way it would be achieved. The greed and ambition of the human settlers on Vulcan meant they lost sight of what's truly important: the quality of their lives together.

22 JANUARY

USE YOUR TIME WISELY

MISSY
Apparently, you think you're going to die tomorrow.

THE DOCTOR
Well, I've got some good news about that. It's still today.

The Magician's Apprentice by Steven Moffat (2015)

· · · · · ·

Time Lords meditate before they die, contemplating the absolute in repentance and acceptance. Clara Oswald knows the Doctor's more likely to throw a party. She and Missy track him to medieval Essex, where he's concluding a three-week jamboree while hiding from his arch-enemy, Davros.

Missy confronts the Doctor with his confession dial, which, according to ancient tradition, Time Lords send to their closest friend on the eve of their final day. It's his Last Will and Testament.

Clara's annoyed the Doctor chose Missy as his closest friend. Missy is more put out that the Doctor thinks of Davros as his arch-enemy. The Doctor's too busy partying to worry about his fate.

Change is inevitable. Jobs, relationships and life may not last forever. So what's next? If you can try again, persevere. If there's nothing you can do, acknowledge your feelings and accept it – but don't be consumed by it. Be kind to yourself. There are other things you can be doing instead with the time you have.

23 JANUARY

WHAT'S THEIR MOTIVATION?

THE DOCTOR
The way you look after all those kids... It's because you lost
somebody, isn't it? You're doing all this to make up for it.

The Empty Child by Steven Moffat (2005)

* * * * * *

As the bombs rain down on London in 1941, young Nancy leads a
ragtag gang of homeless children in search of a good meal. When the
air-raid sirens go off, people rush from their houses to the bomb shelters in their gardens – and Nancy is good at spotting which of these
abandoned homes have the best supplies of food.

On the trail of a crashed Chula warship, the Doctor is impressed
by Nancy and joins the homeless children for dinner. Nancy insists on
good table manners – everyone has to wait patiently for her to carve
the roast, chew their food properly and remember to say 'thank you'.
The Doctor's shrewd enough to ask why Nancy works so hard to look
after these children.

He doesn't challenge Nancy for stealing food but questions the
roots of her behaviour. That leads him to understand a personal tragedy
behind Nancy's brave words and actions. As a result, the Doctor is able
to help her acknowledge and move on from what's happened to her –
and deal with the crashed warship at the same time.

Don't be quick to judge people; show active interest in them and
what they do, and you'll both benefit.

24 JANUARY

COUGHS AND SNEEZES SPREAD DISEASES

THE DOCTOR
You have a handkerchief, I hope?
Well then use it, my child!

The Ark by Paul Erickson and Lesley Scott (1966)

• • • • • •

In the far future, humanity survives the destruction of Earth by escaping on a huge spaceship – the Ark. Also on the ship are samples of animal and plant life, including lizards and an elephant. Plus there are alien creatures working to serve humanity – the one-eyed, mop-haired Monoids.

Dodo Chaplet, on her first trip in the TARDIS, thinks this is all very exciting. But she's also got a bit of a cold and soon the whole ship is infected. What's more, these people of the distant future don't have much immunity to such ancient bugs. All of humanity is soon at risk, disturbing the whole balance of power.

It doesn't take much to help cut down the spread of disease, and that can make a big difference to people with lower immunity (and is a courtesy to everyone else). Cover your mouth when you cough or sneeze. Carry a handkerchief. Wash your hands regularly and thoroughly.

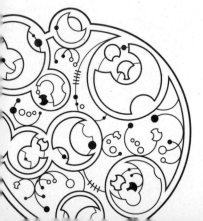

25 JANUARY

SUPERSTITION

THE DOCTOR
We're all the same. We want certainty, security, to believe
that people are evil or heroic. But that's not how people are.
You want to know the secrets of existence? Start with the
mysteries of the heart. I can show you everything if you stop
being afraid of what you don't understand. If you trust me.

The Witchfinders by Joy Wilkinson (2018)

● ● ● ● ● ●

Is any sufficiently advanced technology indistinguishable from magic?
King James has the Doctor tied up because he believes she's a witch.
He's seen her use her magic wand when facing mud creatures. No
doubt he'd be surprised to learn she made it herself in Sheffield.

The king believes his quest for goodness and knowledge, beauty
and art are rational. The Doctor tells him that his witch hunts are
killing and scapegoating and stirring up hate. He's hurting his own
people because he's scared to face up to the darkness inside himself.

Listen to your heart when you're listening to others. Superstition
is no basis for a life well lived. Nor is labelling people for who they
are, rather than what they do. Nobody is entirely devil or angel,
coward or hero.

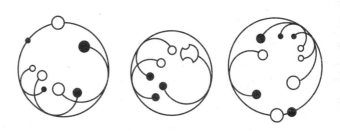

26 JANUARY

WATCH OUT FOR YOUR FRIENDS

CLARA OSWALD

No! Doctor, no! I'm not dead,
I'm in here! Can you hear me?

I'm your friend. I'm your friend!

No, please, don't.

DALEK

I am a Dalek. I am alive.
Mercy. Mercy.

I am your enemy. Your enemy.

Mercy. Mercy.

THE DOCTOR

You shouldn't be able to say that. That word shouldn't exist in
your vocabulary. How did Davros teach you to say that?

The Witch's Familiar by Steven Moffat (2015)

• • • • • •

The Dalek sewers are revolting. The decaying remains of ancient Daleks surge from underground to destroy their city on Skaro. Fleeing the destruction with Missy, the Doctor is confronted by a lone Dalek – but it will not kill him.

Missy has trapped Clara Oswald inside its casing. She lies to the Doctor that this Dalek has killed Clara, and he should destroy it. The Dalek casing mistranslates Clara's words. If she says 'I love you' it says 'Exterminate'. The more Clara protests, the more it seems like a mad Dalek, proud of what it has done.

Until it says the one word that Daleks do not use, because they do not understand it.

You know your friends and family. You'll spot if they're having more than just a difficult day, and the warning signs that they are struggling emotionally. Trust your instincts. Take a risk in being honest about what you notice and why you're concerned.

27 JANUARY

SEE NOT RULE

THE MASTER
One must rule or serve. That's a basic law of life.
Why do you hesitate, Doctor? Surely it's not loyalty to the
Time Lords, who exiled you on one insignificant planet?

THE DOCTOR
You'll never understand, will you?
I want to see the universe, not rule it.

Colony in Space by Malcolm Hulke (1971)

· · · · · ·

The planet Uxarieus is a barren, rocky world in 2472 but was once home to a great civilisation whose genetically engineered 'super race' developed an incredibly powerful Doomsday Weapon. What we know as the Crab Nebula is the cloud of cosmic matter that was once a sun – until the weapon was tested on it, completely obliterating it in the process.

The Master is keen to unearth this great weapon and use it for further conquest but he can't understand why the Doctor wouldn't want to join him. He says they could use the power of the weapon for good, to end wars and suffering across the universe.

But the Doctor knows the weapon can only bring death and destruction – as it did to the civilisation who built it. You can't control everything, and trying to do so can cause real damage. Sometimes you need to let go and see what happens.

28 JANUARY

LET THEM KNOW

THE DOCTOR
Psst! You are wonderful.

ROMANA
Me, 'wonderful'? I suppose I am.
I've never really thought about it.

State of Decay by Terrance Dicks (1980)

· · · · · ·

On a planet in another universe the Doctor is at a low ebb. He's discovered that a giant vampire – an age-old enemy of the Time Lords – is planning its return. The vampire is such a powerful, terrifying adversary the Doctor doesn't know how to stop it.

But his friend Romana remembers she once read back on Gallifrey that emergency instructions for just this sort of crisis are installed in all Type 40 TARDISes – the same model number as the Doctor's! With this information, they'll have a decent chance of beating this awesome foe.

No longer morose, the Doctor tells Romana how he feels. They both brighten and then set off to get the job done.

Everyone likes to feel appreciated. If you like someone's work, let them know. If you like *them*, let them know. It doesn't mean they owe you any kind of response – look how Romana plays down the Doctor's compliment – but let them know anyway.

29 JANUARY

GUNS THAT DON'T KILL PEOPLE

ROSE TYLER
Doctor, they've got guns.

THE DOCTOR
And I haven't – which makes me the better person,
don't you think? They can shoot me dead but
the moral high ground is mine.

Army of Ghosts by Russell T Davies (2006)

• • • • • •

The TARDIS materialises inside Torchwood Tower in Canary Wharf, London, amid numerous relics and specimens of alien incursions. Armed troops immediately surround the time ship, but the Doctor goes out to meet them cheerfully and of course refuses to carry any weapons himself.

In fact, the Doctor very, very rarely *ever* wields a gun, let alone dares to use it. When necessary, the Doctor is an excellent shot – expertly shooting out the lock of a door in *The Visitation* (1982) or hitting a distant, floating gravity globe in *The Time of Angels* (2010). But in both cases, the gun is used as a tool – just as the Doctor uses the sonic screwdriver – not as a weapon.

When he faces the weapons-toting troops of Torchwood, the Doctor's response is to make a flippant joke. Yet he sticks to his moral code even when the odds seem frighteningly stacked against him. Whatever challenge you face, be the better person.

30 JANUARY

THERE'S HELP WHEN YOU NEED IT MOST

THE DOCTOR

The way I see it, every life is a pile of good things and bad things. Hey. The good things don't always soften the bad things. But, vice versa, the bad things don't necessarily spoil the good things or make them unimportant.

Vincent and the Doctor by Richard Curtis (2010)

• • • • • •

The Doctor and Amy Pond visit Vincent van Gogh near the end of his life in 1890. They see the world through Vincent's eyes: a night sky is not dark and black without character, it is deep blue, with lighter blue and stars bursting through. And they see how his depressive illness affects his moods and behaviour.

They show Vincent the future legacy of his work. He weeps tears of joy and says he's met the first doctor ever actually to make a difference to his life. Amy is shattered when she discovers this does not prevent Vincent's death by suicide: they've made no difference. The Doctor hugs her and explains that they definitely added to Vincent's pile of good things.

A quarter of us will suffer from mental illness during our lifetimes. If you're in emotional distress or struggling to cope and you need someone to talk to, groups like the Samaritans and Befrienders Worldwide listen. They won't judge or tell you what to do. Call them any time, day or night for free, or check out their help and advice online.

31 JANUARY

WHAT DO THEY GET?

THE DOCTOR
Wait! I came to this planet because I needed a new
source of energy supply. My TARDIS depends for its
function upon a rare and precious mineral of Varos:
Zeiton-7. I can show you new prosperity.

Vengeance on Varos by Philip Martin (1985)

• • • • • •

The torture and execution of prisoners in the Punishment Dome on planet Varos is broadcast live to the planet's population to both entertain and scare them, keeping them in order. The Doctor and his friend Peri are horrified by the situation and try to stop the broadcasts.

First they appeal to those in charge on moral grounds – arguing that such brutal treatment isn't right. The Governor of Varos acknowledges the cruelty but doesn't think he has the power to change it – where would they even start?

Yet, as the Doctor faces execution, he reveals that the Governor of Varos is being cheated in a deal to supply a mineral ore that is plentiful on this planet but rare everywhere else. That galvanises people, not least because they see exactly what needs to be changed.

To get people's support in making meaningful change, it helps to identify a tangible challenge and a clear solution.

FEBRUARY

1 FEBRUARY

WANDERING FREE

THE DOCTOR
I am a citizen of the universe and a gentleman to boot.

The Daleks' Master Plan
by Terry Nation and Dennis Spooner (1965–66)

• • • • • •

One Christmas in the 1960s, the police in Liverpool catch a suspicious-looking old man lurking inside a police box that wasn't there before. When asked if he's from England or Scotland, the old man says no. When asks if he's Welsh, the Doctor says that the police inspector's ideas are too narrow and small.

In fact, we don't discover the Doctor's origins until much later in the series. We learn that the Doctor is a Time Lord in *The War Games* (1969) and that the name of his home planet is Gallifrey in *The Time Warrior* (1973–74), before *The Timeless Children* (2020) reveals that this may not be who the Doctor is at all...

A lot of our identity is shaped by where we're from – our family, home town and country. But the Doctor seems to think what's more important is where we're going and how we'll get there. 'Travel broadens the mind,' he tells the police inspector. There's dignity enough in such an open quest for knowledge. That's who the Doctor is.

2 FEBRUARY

BE CONSISTENT

AMY POND

Listen. The Doctor's been part of my life for so long now,
and he's never let me down. Even when I thought he had,
when I was a kid and he left me, he came back. He saved me.
And now he's going to save you. But don't tell him I said that,
because the smugness would be terrifying.

The God Complex by Toby Whithouse (2011)

• • • • • •

Saying nice things about your friends in front of them may feel
embarrassing for you and for them. Whereas saying unkind things
behind their backs is heartless and cowardly.

Amy Pond is talking to a coward in the facsimile of a 1980s Earth
hotel. Gibbis is a Tivolian, and terrified by the threat of the deadly
unknown creature that's stalking them. Amy reassures him about why
she trusts the Doctor to keep them safe. She doesn't want the Doctor
to overhear her, even though her words are caring, warm, and sincere.

How do you talk about an absent friend, colleague or relative?
Would you say it if they could hear you? Because it's probably how
the person you're speaking with will think you talk about them when
they're not around.

3 FEBRUARY

YOU CAN'T GO BACK

THE DOCTOR
My entire planet died, my whole family. Do you think it
never occurred to me to go back and save them?

Father's Day by Paul Cornell (2005)

• • • • • •

Rose Tyler's father Pete is killed in a road accident on 7 November 1987, when Rose is just a baby. More than anything, it's the fact he died alone that haunts Rose ever after.

The Doctor takes grown-up Rose back in time so that she can at least be by her father's side in his final moments... but when she sees the car approaching her dad, she can't help but run out in front of it to save Pete's life! Yet her delight is short-lived. By changing history, Rose creates a wound in time which attracts huge and deadly creatures that want to consume everything within the damaged area – the whole of Earth.

Rose learns that it's dangerous to tamper with history, even for the best of reasons. We're not like the Doctor and can't go back in time to try to put things right. But we can still learn lessons from Rose. Don't act rashly. And, as the Doctor warns her, be careful what you wish for.

4 FEBRUARY

BURNING THE CANDLE AT BOTH ENDS

THE DOCTOR
Well, Jamie, the experiment's nearly over. I've had no sleep.
I've been up all night, but it's been worth it.

The Evil of the Daleks by David Whitaker (1967)

• • • • • •

Jamie McCrimmon is furious. He thinks that the Doctor conspired with the Daleks and their servants to put him in deadly danger. While being tested as a guinea pig, Jamie exhibits a whole battery of emotions so that the Daleks can distil the human factor for use in their evil plans.

In truth, the Doctor knows the human factor contains elements like mercy. He uses Jamie's captured emotions to humanise three Daleks – an activity he spent the whole night achieving. The Doctor sometimes says that sleep is for tortoises, but even Time Lords need a nap if they've regenerated or had a big lunch.

We all sometimes pull an all-nighter: an urgent project deadline, revising for an exam, nursing a baby. But sleep deprivation reduces endurance, increases pain sensitivity, impairs your immune system, raises stress and anxiety, spoils your concentration, prompts poor decisions, and makes you irritable – so always look to maximise rest breaks where you can.

5 FEBRUARY

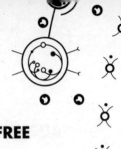

THE TRUTH CAN SET YOU FREE

THE DOCTOR
Did I ever tell you the story about how I was once
captured by the Medusoids? They're a sort of
hairy jellyfish with claws, teeth and a leg.

They put me under one of these mind probe things,
you see, and tried to get me to tell them where I was
going. So I said I was on my way to meet a giant rabbit,
a pink elephant and a purple horse with yellow spots.

Well, the poor old machine just couldn't believe it
and had a nervous breakdown. They put me under
another one of these mind probe things and
the same thing happened.

JO GRANT
But you weren't telling the truth. I mean, you weren't
really going to meet a giant rabbit, a pink elephant
and a... what was it?

THE DOCTOR
A purple horse with yellow spots. Yes, I was.
You see, they were all delegates for the
Third Intergalactic Peace Conference.

JO GRANT
How did you get away from these things?

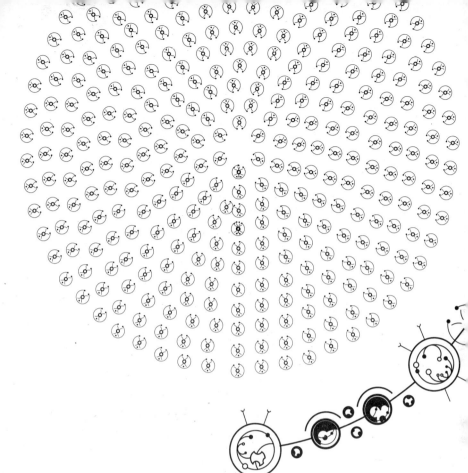

Well, they had to turn me loose eventually.
They ran out of mind probes.

Frontier in Space by Malcolm Hulke (1973)

· · · · · ·

Telling the truth can quite literally set you free!

6 FEBRUARY

FAREWELL WELL

THE DOCTOR
There's something else – K-9.
He'll be all right with you behind the mirrors.

ROMANA
I'll take care of him.

THE DOCTOR
I'll miss you. You were the noblest Romana of them all.

Warriors' Gate by Stephen Gallagher (1981)

• • • • • •

Having been trapped for a long time in E-Space, the Doctor finally has a chance to escape back into our own universe – so he is surprised when his friend Romana wants to stay behind. But after all their adventures together she can't bear the thought of returning home to Gallifrey. Besides, there is work to be done in E-Space, freeing the Tharils from enslavement on many worlds.

Romana and the Doctor have been great friends and he clearly feels her loss. But he also respects her decision – and is rather proud of her, too. What's more, he's generous in parting with Romana and gives her his robot dog, K-9. It's both a kind and practical gift because K-9 will be of great help to Romana in the challenges that lie ahead.

It's not always easy to part company with someone you care about but you can soften the blow with a kind word or thoughtful gift. Take solace in the good times you had together.

7 FEBRUARY

PERFECT PRESENTATION

THE DOCTOR
I'm very sorry for your loss. I'll do all I can to solve the death
of your friend slash family member slash pet.

Under the Lake by Toby Whithouse (2015)

• • • • • •

Clara Oswald knows the Twelfth Doctor can be tactless when his enthusiasm outweighs the need to recognise the emotions of humans around him. So, she has written some flash cards for him to train with. They include:

- I completely understand why it was difficult not to get captured.
- I didn't mean to imply that I don't care.
- No one is going to get eaten / vapourised / exterminated / upgraded / possessed / mortally wounded / turned to jelly. We'll all get out of this unharmed.

The crew of an underwater base in 2119 Caithness, Scotland, are perturbed when his excited explanation about ghosts disregards their grief at the recent loss of their colleague, Captain Jonathan Moran.

If you have a speech to deliver, creating prompt cards can be helpful. It's a terrible idea for a heartfelt personal message, but ideal in a school or business presentation.

8 FEBRUARY

ACTIVE LISTENING

SEAN

You are so on the team. Next week we've got the Crown
and Anchor. We're going to annihilate them.

THE DOCTOR

Annihilate? No. No violence, do you understand me?
Not while I'm around. Not today, not ever. I'm the Doctor,
the Oncoming Storm... and you basically meant beat
them in a football match, didn't you?

The Lodger by Gareth Roberts (2010)

• • • • • •

The Doctor plays football in the park for The King's Arms, a pub team in Colchester. His friend and temporary landlord Craig Owens is put out that the Doctor is so unexpectedly adept on the pitch, as they thrash The Rising Sun's team.

It's a brief distraction for the Doctor, who is trying to remain incognito while investigating temporal anomalies in the area. His instinct is to react to footballer Sean's comment about 'annihilating' the opposition in the way he usually thinks, rather than how Sean intended.

Listen actively to understand better and become a better communicator. Resist the impulse to interrupt with comments or questions. The other person will feel you're hearing their message, and the conversation will be more enjoyable for you both.

9 FEBRUARY

SENSE IN RETROSPECT

THE DOCTOR

History sometimes gives us a terrible shock and that is
because we don't quite fully understand. Why should we?
After all, we're all too small to realise its final pattern.

The Massacre of St Bartholomew's Eve by John Lucarotti (1966)

• • • • • •

The TARDIS lands in Paris in 1592, where the Doctor and his young friend Steven are soon caught up between warring religious factions. Steven befriends a serving girl, Anne Chaplet, but when events in the city turn especially violent, the Doctor tells Anne to go home. Steven and the Doctor leave in the TARDIS where the Doctor reveals that some ten thousand people will die in the massacre he and Steven just fled.

Steven is furious that the Doctor left Anne in such potential danger but the Doctor insists (not for the first time) that history cannot be changed... The Doctor believes he's made the right albeit difficult choice – but will come to rethink this kind of decision.

It's hard to understand events as they're happening. Dramas and crises can be overwhelming. But later, looking back, we can gain perspective to make sense of what happened – and learn from the experience.

10 FEBRUARY

TWO-WAY CONVERSATIONS

ERIC KLIEG

How did you know in the first place?

THE DOCTOR

Oh, I use my own special technique.

ERIC KLIEG

Oh really, Doctor? And may we know what that is?

THE DOCTOR

Keeping my eyes open and my mouth shut.

The Tomb of the Cybermen by Kit Pedler and Gerry Davis (1967)

• • • • • •

Professor Parry leads an expedition to Telos, searching for the last remains of the Cybermen. He suspects the Doctor is a rival archaeologist, but allows him to join them when the Doctor helps open the doors to the ancient Cyberman city.

The pompous Parry thinks people hang on his every word. He suggests they have reached a dead end. The Doctor, who has been quietly studying the room, politely contradicts him – and opens a hidden door. The expedition's snooty logician Eric Klieg wants to know what advance information the Doctor had about the symbology logic device that opened the door.

Resist the temptation to be the centre of attention just by talking. Constant chatter, or just waiting for an opportunity to interrupt the conversation, distracts you from really taking in what is going on around you.

11 FEBRUARY

HANDLE FEAR

SARAH JANE SMITH
It's destructive! It's killing people!

THE DOCTOR
An alien lifeforce, shipwrecked on a strange planet. Crystalline, regenerates through irradiation. It's probably afraid.

The Hand of Fear by Bob Baker and Dave Martin (1976)

• • • • • •

When Sarah accidentally comes into contact with an ancient, stone hand she becomes possessed by an alien intelligence. She marches briskly into the Nunton nuclear power station, blasting the guards and any other personnel who try to get in her way.

The Doctor intercedes and Sarah regains her senses. Then a technician called Driscoll becomes possessed by the intelligence. He walks straight into the reactor core and is vaporised in an instant, and there's a huge nuclear explosion. But the energy released is absorbed by the stone hand which regenerates into a full humanoid body – Eldrad, the silicon-based Kastrian.

Eldrad has killed people and continues to lash out. However, when the Doctor talks to her calmly and offers to take her home, Eldrad accepts. She's still dangerous yet the Doctor prevents her from harming anyone else.

When people are threatened or afraid, they can potentially lash out, but we can all learn from the Doctor whose behaviour often seems mindful of the old proverb: 'A gentle answer turns away wrath, but a harsh word stirs up anger'.

12 FEBRUARY

WHEN NICE ISN'T NICE

THE DOCTOR

Absolutely incredible: a TARDIS linked to a Stattenheim remote control! The Rani is a genius. Shame I can't stand her. I wonder if I was particularly nice to her, she might…? No.

The Mark of the Rani by Pip and Jane Baker (1985)

• • • • • •

In the 1810s, groups of textile workers in England are destroying new machines that they believe are doing them out of work. These workers are known as 'Luddites', named after their supposed leader, Ned Ludd.

Around the village of Killingworth, these attacks have become particularly violent. The Doctor learns that the Luddites' aggression is the result of scientific experiments being carried out on workers by his old schoolmate from Gallifrey, the Rani. She's callously removed the chemical from people's brains which enables them able to sleep.

The Doctor sets out to thwart the Rani but can't deny her technical brilliance. He's so impressed by the remote-control system she's made for her TARDIS that he briefly considers trying to charm her into sharing her technology. But of course he immediately dismisses the idea.

Don't be nice to someone, or overlook the harm they do, just because of what you think you can gain from them.

13 FEBRUARY

PARTING THOUGHTS

THE DOCTOR

I'm your friend. But friends help each other face up to
their problems, not avoid them. You are the maddest,
most beautiful thing I've ever experienced, and I haven't
even scratched the surface. I wish I could stay. But if
either of us are gonna survive, you're gonna have to let
me go and keep on being brilliant by yourself.

It Takes You Away by Ed Hime (2018)

• • • • • •

The Doctor is face-to-face with a Time Lord fairy tale. The Solitract
consciousness is desperate to find friends, but in doing so it is collapsing
the universe.

She offers to stay in the Solitract plane; she has lived longer, seen
more, loved more and lost more than the humans the Solitract found,
and she can share that. Though it means the Doctor leaving her other
friends behind in the universe.

However, it turns out that even this arrangement will destabilise
things and kill them both. The Solitract may want them to be together,
but it can never work.

Leaving your parental home, changing jobs, ending a relationship
– sometimes you have to make a break for the best. Do it with good
will and you can hopefully remain friends, even if it's no longer the
same as it was before – or as it might have been.

14 FEBRUARY

LET LOVE GO

THE DOCTOR
One day I shall come back... Until then, there must be no regrets, no tears, no anxieties. Just go forward in all your beliefs and prove to me that I am not mistaken in mine. Goodbye, Susan.

The Dalek Invasion of Earth by Terry Nation (1964)

• • • • • •

Parting from loved ones is difficult. The Doctor has had close relationships with those travelling in the TARDIS and when they leave it can be heartbreaking – hearts-breaking for the Doctor. Hardest of all was the time the Doctor locked his own granddaughter out of the TARDIS.

Susan always longed for the security of life in one time and place. The five months she spent as a school pupil in London, 1963, were the happiest of her life. But she would never choose to leave her grandfather. So he made the decision for her.

She'd outgrown him, fallen in love and now had a life of her own to live. No matter the strength of our feelings or how the loss will hurt us, we can't hold back those we love. Enable them, encourage them and – if need be – let them go. That is real love.

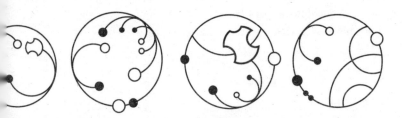

15 FEBRUARY

SPARKING MEMORIES

THE DOCTOR

People fall out of the world sometimes, but they always
leave traces. Little things we can't quite account for.
Faces in photographs, luggage, half eaten meals,
rings. Nothing is ever forgotten, not completely. And if
something can be remembered, it can come back.

The Pandorica Opens by Steven Moffat (2010)

• • • • • •

Amy Pond has found her engagement ring. Her fiancé Rory Williams left it in the TARDIS for safekeeping. She doesn't recognise it, because he's no longer in her memory. He was swallowed by a crack in time, and forgotten by everyone except the Doctor.

Amy finds the ring in the Doctor's pocket and can't understand how it makes her feel a loss she cannot explain. When Rory is brought back in the form of a centurion by the Nestene Consciousness, he's based on Amy's childhood interest in Romans and a photo of Rory in fancy dress – and she remembers him at last.

We can't literally bring back people who have died. But we can bring them back to our minds through photos, letters, clothes, perfume, souvenirs, places; they make happy memories so much more vivid.

16 FEBRUARY

BAD PLAYERS

THE DOCTOR
Oh, my dear friend, don't waste our time on trivial formalities.
You have been defeated, so now leave us alone.

The Celestial Toymaker by Brian Hayles (1966)

• • • • • •

The Doctor, Steven and Dodo find themselves in the domain of the mysterious Toymaker, a mercurial being with extraordinary, god-like powers. The Toymaker likes to play games and sets a series of challenges. As the Doctor and his friends win each contest, a part of the Toymaker's world vanishes...

But there's a game within this game — the Toymaker has set a diabolical trap. If the Doctor plays the winning move in the last of the challenges, the final part of the Toymaker's world will vanish, and the Doctor and his friends with it! If the Toymaker can't win, he always destroys his opponent. To escape this awful fate, the Doctor must be especially cunning.

Contests of one kind or another can be stimulating and fun. Games, debates and challenges all test our skills and resources. But some people don't play fairly, especially if they don't get their own way. If so, be like the Doctor and back away...

17 FEBRUARY

BEING LET DOWN

THE DOCTOR

The Time Traveller panics. He can't bear the thought of a world without the music of Beethoven! Luckily, he'd brought all his Beethoven sheet music for Ludwig to sign. So, he copies out all the symphonies and concertos and gets them published. He becomes Beethoven. And history continues with barely a feather ruffled.

Before the Flood by Toby Whithouse (2015)

• • • • • •

The Doctor tells a story about a Time Traveller with a passion for the works of Ludwig van Beethoven. When he travels in time to meet his 18th century hero, no one has heard of the composer. Fortunately, the Time Traveller is a big a fan and he can fix that.

This never really happened. The Doctor's actually met Beethoven. Nice chap, very intense, loved an arm-wrestle.

There are times when things fail because the person you've relied on is getting it wrong. They may lack the necessary skill or confidence or motivation. Or they may even not show up on the job. You can offer them help, coaching, training – or at the end of the day, you may just have to step up and do it yourself.

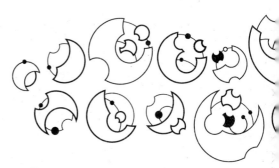

18 FEBRUARY

NEGOTIATE WITH UNDERSTANDING

ELDANE
Are you authorised to negotiate on behalf of humanity?

THE DOCTOR
Me? No. But they are.

NASREEN CHAUDRY
What?

AMY POND
No, we're not.

THE DOCTOR
Course you are. Amy Pond and Nasreen Chaudhry,
speaking for the planet? Humanity couldn't have better
ambassadors. Come on, who has more fun than us?

Cold Blood by Chris Chibnall (2010)

· · · · · ·

Winston Churchill once said that 'meeting jaw to jaw is better than war'. A strategic discussion can resolve a problem to the satisfaction of both sides.

The deepest drilling project in human history has disturbed an extended Silurian hibernation. Hawkish warrior Alaya declares war and wants to wipe out humanity. But when the Doctor reaches the buried Silurian city, their leader Eldane is prepared to negotiate instead.

The Silurians know the Doctor isn't from Earth. The Doctor understands that diplomacy requires human and Silurian participation. Who better to help forge an agreement than a geologist involved in the drill project and a woman who has experience of alien life?

Good negotiators don't just talk, they listen patiently. They can think clearly and rapidly under pressure and uncertainty, consider options and make decisions. By understanding the other side's fears and needs, they can find compromise and agreement.

19 FEBRUARY

WORDS TO ASPIRE TO

CLARA
You told me the name you chose was a promise.
What was the promise?

THE ELEVENTH DOCTOR
Never cruel or cowardly...

THE WAR DOCTOR
Never give up, never give in.

The Day of the Doctor by Steven Moffat (2013)

• • • • • •

On the last day of the horrific Time War between the Daleks and the Doctor's people, all time and space stood on the brink of complete obliteration. The Doctor could stand it no more and prepared to use a powerful weapon that would annihilate his own people and their mortal enemy – but save the rest of the universe.

It was the most terrible decision, but one he had to make. And yet, as his hand closed over the button, he was reminded of a promise.

We all make mistakes. We all have our off days – or even many in a row. The Doctor has lived a very long life, peppered with regrets. Sometimes the Doctor is downcast and feels defeated. But that's when the promise matters most. The promise is something to hold on to on those gloomiest of days.

We're imperfect beings. We can't get it right all the time. But we can try to be better. In remembering the promise of his chosen title, the Doctor saved more than his own people. He also saved himself.

20 FEBRUARY

BEING GOOD IS BEST

THE DOCTOR
I only take the best. I've got Rose.

The Long Game by Russell T Davies (2005)

· · · · · ·

The Doctor takes Rose Tyler and their new friend Adam Mitchell to what's meant to be a fantastic period in future history: the Fourth Great and Bountiful Human Empire in the year 200,000. It's a time when Earth and its five moons are the hub of a galactic domain stretching across a million planets and as many species.

Yet while the Doctor and Rose enjoy the sights and wonders aboard space station Satellite 5, Adam is determined to help himself to its advanced technology. He sends a message back home to 2012 full of details about what he has learned, so that he can later exploit the information for profit.

Unsurprisingly, the Doctor is not happy about this and he ends Adam's travels in space and time. But note what the Doctor says about Rose – he refers to her as 'the best' because she hasn't been selfish or sought to profit from her travels.

In the Doctor's eyes, if you show respect, and enjoy things for their own sake rather than material gain, then you meet the standard.

21 FEBRUARY

USING TOOLS

THE DOCTOR
I'm not wild about computers myself, but they are a tool.
If you have a tool, it's stupid not to use it.

Inferno by Don Houghton (1970)

• • • • • •

Professor Stahlman believes he can penetrate the Earth's crust and tap a vast new storehouse of energy that has lain dormant since the beginning of time. The scheme is complex, using a robot drill with its built-in power source fed by cables from a nuclear reactor.

Stahlman thinks his project is being stifled by an overabundance of experts and advisors like the Doctor; he believes that the computer is oversensitive and its data unreliable. The Doctor recognises that Stahlman's self-interest is clouding his judgement and advises that the computer's warnings are heeded.

We rely on computers as tools to handle complex systems quickly and accurately and to automate laborious work. To get the best answers, we must understand the questions we ask them and the data we provide them – whether it's a pocket calculator or an AI system, if you put garbage in you'll get garbage out.

22 FEBRUARY

(DATA) BANK JOB

THE DOCTOR
Do you think this stuff is sophisticated?
There are worlds out there where this kind of
equipment would be considered prehistoric junk.

The Deadly Assassin by Robert Holmes (1976)

● ● ● ● ● ●

While travelling in the TARDIS, the Doctor has a prophetic vision of the president of the High Council of Time Lords being gunned down in cold blood. The Doctor immediately races home to Gallifrey to prevent the murder, but fails to do so and is then blamed for committing the heinous crime himself!

In trying to prove his innocence, the Doctor discovers that his arch-enemy, the Master, has infiltrated the amplified panatropic computations of the Time Lords' Matrix databank. These trillions of electrochemical cells contain the knowledge of all dead Time Lords and are used to predict the future. The Master somehow hacked this complex system and beamed the prediction of the president's murder into the Doctor's mind, thereby luring him into a trap.

The Time Lords are complacent about their data security, as the Doctor has discovered on several occasions. Even sophisticated systems like theirs can be superseded by advances in technology and prove vulnerable to those looking to exploit potential weaknesses.

Learn from the Time Lords' mistakes and be careful with what you store digitally. Keep your data – and yourself – safe.

23 FEBRUARY

MAKE AN IMPRESSION

THE DOCTOR
I thought if you could hear me, I could hang on
somehow. Silly me. Silly old Doctor. When you wake
up, you'll have a mum and dad, and you won't even
remember me. Well, you'll remember me a little. I'll be
a story in your head. But that's OK. We're all stories
in the end. Just make it a good one, eh?

The Big Bang by Steven Moffat (2010)

• • • • • •

The universe resets itself, and the Doctor rewinds as his time stream unravels and erases. The cracks in time can only close properly when he is on the other side, and Amy Pond is the only one who can remember him.

He speaks softly to seven-year-old Amelia as she sleeps in her childhood bed. Talking to her of the TARDIS – somehow both brand new and ancient, that he borrowed from his own people. The bluest blue box. She will remember it, and bring back the Doctor, at her wedding.

We are each the hero of our own story, and characters in other people's. The impression we make on them in life is what keeps us in their hearts throughout our lives and beyond.

24 FEBRUARY

SPEAKING THE SAME LANGUAGE

THE DOCTOR
[*SPEAKING IN HOKKIEN*]
This unworthy person welcomes you
and delights in your safe arrival.

The Mind of Evil by Don Houghton (1971)

• • • • • •

The Master's latest diabolical scheme has the whole world once again on the brink of war. A Chinese delegation arrives in London for negotiations, but they're unimpressed by what they find. That is until the Doctor speaks a few words to delegate Fu Peng in his own language.

As the Doctor admits, his grasp of the Hokkien language is a little rusty, but Fu Peng still appreciates the courtesy and welcome implicit in the Doctor's gesture because so few other westerners have made a similar effort. They soon become good friends and start discussing what to have for dinner (dried squid and stewed jellyfish).

On later occasions, the Doctor shows similar courtesy in knowing the correct way to greet the king of planet Peladon, the emperor of the Draconians and an abbot from Tibet. Preparation, thought and good manners often make a strong impression. You don't need to be expert in how people prefer to be addressed, but a little effort can go a long way.

25 FEBRUARY

STEPPING OUT

THE DOCTOR

I should have brought wellies. That could have been another precaution. Always bring wellies. I love wellies. In fact, I think I half-invented them.

The Battle of Ranskoor Av Kolos by Chris Chibnall (2018)

• • • • • •

On the planet Ranskoor Av Kolos, the Doctor has purloined a rucksack full of Captain Paltraki's equipment. She says she is taking necessary precautions, but then immediately squelches into a murky puddle.

The Third Doctor hides his TARDIS key in his elastic-sided boots. The Eleventh Doctor mocks the Tenth Doctor for wearing sandshoes. The Fourth Doctor rocks brogues and boots as required. And the Master may claim he dresses fashionably, but it's the Eighth Doctor who chooses the perfect pair of shoes for that occasion.

The Doctors' travelling companions could learn from all this. There's a lot of running when you're on adventures across the universe, and in the wrong pair of shoes it's all too easy to twist your ankle.

Wearing the right footwear is essential. Go for something that's practical, comfortable and durable. It's worth splashing out on a decent pair.

26 FEBRUARY

GENIUS OR STUPID

THE SECOND DOCTOR

Dastari, I have no doubt you could augment an
earwig to the point where it understood nuclear
physics – but it'd still be a very stupid thing to do!

The Two Doctors by Robert Holmes (1985)

• • • • • •

Professor Joinson Dastari is Head of Projects at Space Station Camera
in the Third Zone, a pioneer in genetic engineering and, according to
the Doctor, has enough letters after his name for two alphabets. He's
exceedingly clever, as demonstrated by his fascinating work on rho
mesons as the unstable factor in short-lived pin galaxies (which only
exist for one quintillionth of a second).

But even someone as bright as Dastari can be spectacularly dim. In
technologically augmenting the Androgum known as Chessene o' the
Franzine Grig, he unwittingly creates a formidable villain. Then there's
the fact that he sides with the Sontarans because they will support his
experiments, not considering what evil they might do with it. Dimmer
still, he attempts to pit his wits against two incarnations of the Doctor
at the same time!

Even very intelligent, talented and experienced people can
make mistakes or do daft things. Judge people by their actions not
their accolades.

27 FEBRUARY

WHO YOU WORK WITH

THE MASTER
Together?

THE DOCTOR
One last hope.

Logopolis by Christopher H Bidmead (1981)

• • • • • •

Having murdered Tremas, the father of the Doctor's friend Nyssa, the evil Master later murders Vanessa, the aunt of the Doctor's friend Tegan. Next, the Master meddles in the essential work done by mathematicians on the planet Logopolis. But his misjudgement here leaves the whole universe in peril – even endangering himself.

The Doctor realises that there is only one way to put things right and save the universe: he must collaborate with the Master.

The Doctor's friends are understandably horrified by the idea, but the Doctor shakes the Master's hand and they start working together to do what must be done. The Doctor would probably argue that we can't always choose who we work with and that we don't have to like them or condone their behaviour. But any such alliance should really only be entered into as a last resort.

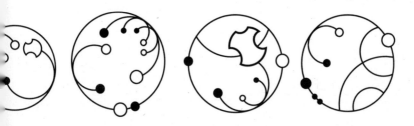

28 FEBRUARY

LIVE A FULL LIFE AT ANY AGE

THE DOCTOR
Some people live more in 20 years than others do in 80.
It's not the time that matters, it's the person

The Lazarus Experiment by Stephen Greenhorn (2007)

. . . . . .

On the roof of his laboratory building, Professor Richard Lazarus admires the view across London as he breathes in the night air. He is 76 years old, but he looks like he's only 40. He claims his experiments will change what it means to be human – and he's started with himself.

Lazarus says that one lifetime's been too short for him. How much more could he achieve in twice that time, or three times, or four? The Doctor is old enough to know that a longer life isn't always a better one. The scientist's transformation is not a gift but a curse.

A full life doesn't have to be a long life. Quality isn't determined by quantity. That can be some comfort when a talented person dies young – celebrate what they achieved, not a lost future. It's also recognition that you're not defined by how old you are today. No matter what your age and your previous accomplishments, you can still achieve new things in your life.

Of course, the Doctor's words do not hold true if you have a leap-year birthday on 29 February – then you're technically 20 years old, even when you're 80!

MARCH

1 MARCH

NO GOOD WAR

THE DOCTOR

When you get back to Skaro, you'll all be national heroes. Everybody will want to hear about your adventures. So be careful how you tell that story, will you? Don't glamorise it. Don't make war sound like an exciting and thrilling game. Tell them about the members of your mission that will not be returning, like Miro and Vaber and Marat. Tell them about the fear, otherwise your people might relish the idea of war. We don't want that.

Planet of the Daleks by Terry Nation (1973)

• • • • • •

There's an army of 10,000 Daleks hidden beneath the surface of the planet Spiridon. This would surely threaten the rest of the galaxy if these Daleks had not all been frozen to death by the Doctor, Jo and a group of brave Thals.

The Thals — who are from the same planet as the Daleks — head home victorious, but the Doctor counsels them to take care in retelling what happened. Death and destruction make for exciting stories but are not to be relished in real life. In fact, it's rather like a Dalek to think otherwise.

2 MARCH

CALLING A BLUFF

NOLLARR
You are not Odin, and that is not Odin's sign.

THE DOCTOR
Oh, and you would know that how, exactly?
Have you met Odin? Do you know what Odin looks like?

ODIN
Oh, my people. I am Odin. And now your
day of reward has finally dawned.

The Girl Who Died by Jamie Mathieson and Steven Moffat (2015)

• • • • • •

The Doctor's in no mood for Vikings, but has little choice when a raiding party seize him and Clara Oswald and cart them off on a two-day journey in a longboat. The Doctor plans to convince them that he is a supernatural being by performing his usual amazing trick with a yellow yo-yo.

Viking Warrior Nollarr is unimpressed – not least because Odin promptly manifests himself in the sky above them. Merciless Mire soldiers immediately teleport into view, indifferent to the cowering villagers and ready to harvest half the village, starting with the strongest and fittest.

Be cautious not to boast about things you cannot do. There'll come a point when you're caught out on something, like threatening to resign your job, when the other person calls your bluff – and you'll be faced with an unnecessary bad choice or an embarrassed climb-down.

3 MARCH

DON'T PICK UP A GUN

THE DOCTOR
People keep giving me guns and I do wish they wouldn't.

The Gunfighters by Donald Cotton (1966)

• • • • • •

When the TARDIS arrives in Arizona in October 1881, the Doctor – who just wants help with his toothache – is mistaken for notorious criminal Doc Holliday. It's initially funny that, for various convoluted reasons, people keep handing guns to the Doctor. But it also adds to the tension.

Many viewers probably knew Holliday's name, not least because the real-life story inspired successful movies such as *My Darling Clementine* (1946) and *Gunfight at the O.K. Corral* (1957). Even if they didn't know the fate of the real Holliday, the *Doctor Who* story leaves us in no doubt that there's trouble to come. And the more the Doctor is seen wielding a gun, the more likely it is he'll become embroiled in the violence...

Except every time he's given a gun, he puts it down again or gives it away. It's true in other stories too: the Doctor refuses to take a gun, or wields one very reluctantly when there don't seem to be any alternatives.

You might not have a gun, but you can still hurt people in other ways – through anger, malicious gossip, a cruel joke. But you can always choose not to.

4 MARCH

DEMONIC INFLUENCE

THE DOCTOR
If this is trial by combat, your Majesty, there's clearly a
victor and a vanquished. Must blood be shed?

The King's Demons by Terence Dudley (1983)

• • • • • •

On 4 March 1215, the TARDIS materialises during a joust outside
Fitzwilliam Castle in the presence of King John. Locals and horses
are perturbed by this strange arrival, but the king assures them that
there is no cause for alarm. When the Doctor and his friends Tegan
and Turlough emerge from the police box, the king welcomes them
as his 'demons'.

The Doctor notices the king's odd behaviour and recognises the
date. He says it's very well documented that on this same day King John
should be in London, taking a solemn oath to take the cross as a crusader.

One duellist, impetuous young Hugh Fitzwilliam, is knocked
from his horse by the king's champion, Sir Gilles – who then moves
in for the kill. The Doctor uses his own status as a 'demon' to inter-
cede, which offends Hugh's honour and the customs of the age. But the
Doctor also saves the young man's life.

Use whatever power you have, however limited it might be, to
help others when you can.

71

5 MARCH

THE OPTIMIST'S JOURNEY

THE DOCTOR
None of us know for sure what's out there.
That's why we keep looking. Keep your faith.
Travel hopefully. The universe'll surprise you. Constantly.

The Battle of Ranskoor Av Kolos by Chris Chibnall (2018)

• • • • • •

Life doesn't always work out as you anticipate. The Doctor thought she'd seen the last of the dangerous Tzim-Sha when she banished him from Earth. But he's spent centuries waiting on the planet Ranskoor Av Kolos.

Graham O'Brien always thought he'd kill Tzim-Sha, as revenge for his wife's death. But when facing Tzim-Sha, he thinks of what his grandson said and spares the Stenza warrior.

The Doctor bids farewell to the planet's inhabitants: Captain Greston Paltraki and the ageless telepathic Ux. Paltraki hadn't known his future – he couldn't even remember his own name after being bombarded by violent psychotropic waves. And training for the Ux was 'building doubt' – the more they learn, the less they realise they know. They'd expected to see their Creator, but it was Tzim-Sha all along.

Don't fear that things won't work out as you expect. That needn't be a bad thing. Don't be frozen in the present, unable to decide. Travel hopefully. Change is part of your journey.

6 MARCH

GIVE THEM ENOUGH ROPE

THE BORAD
No! You've tricked me!

THE DOCTOR
You tricked yourself.

Timelash by Glen McCoy (1985)

• • • • • •

In a dark and dingy vault, the Doctor confronts the Borad, ruthless dictator of the planet Karfel. The Borad was once a humanoid scientist, Megelen, who persisted with unethical experiments on the native Morlox creatures. When one experiment went horribly wrong, he became a half-human, half-Morlox creature himself.

You'd think this might have made the Borad more risk averse, but he acts arrogantly – and rashly in the Doctor's presence. He even threatens to fire a time acceleration beam that will age the Doctor to death!

However, the Doctor is wearing a Kontron crystal that he's modified into a ten-second time break. He warns the Borad that this will absorb the deadly energy and then, after ten seconds, beam it back where it came. The Borad thinks he has cleverly seen through what he believes is just the Doctor bluffing and fires the killer beam.

There's an old phrase that pride comes before a fall. Yes, the Doctor has played a trick. But it's the Borad's over-confidence and hubris that brings about his own destruction.

7 MARCH

VISITING TIME

THE DOCTOR
You've got a choice. Sit by their bedside for 24 hours
and watch them die, or sit in here for 24 hours and
watch them live. Which would you choose?

The Girl Who Waited by Tom MacRae (2011)

• • • • • •

Apalapucia was voted number two planet in the top ten greatest destinations for the discerning intergalactic traveller. Sunsets, spires, soaring silver colonnades. And unfortunately, when the TARDIS arrives, under planet-wide quarantine after an outbreak of the deadly One Day Plague.

The Twostreams medical facility runs rooms at different speeds so that its 40 thousand residents can have visitors watch them live, rather than die.

It's natural to worry about visiting people who are ill. Don't worry so much about the words you say, just that your message comes from the heart. You don't have to fill every moment of your visit with talk. Listen. Focus on the person, not your next appointment. Your presence makes a difference.

8 MARCH

LESSONS FROM HISTORY

THE DOCTOR
The whole story is obviously absurd.
Probably invented by Homer as some good
dramatic device! No, I think it would be
completely impractical.

The Myth Makers by Donald Cotton (1965)

• • • • • •

The TARDIS lands on the plains outside the legendary city of Troy where the Doctor intercedes in a desperate fight between mythical heroes Achilles and Hector. They think the Doctor, having apparently appeared out of the air, must be the great god Zeus – and he's soon embroiled in their war.

The Doctor's friend Steven knows his history, and the famous story of how the 10-year siege of Troy was ended – as recounted in *Aeneid* by the Roman poet Virgil in about 25 BCE (and briefly mentioned in Homer's *Odyssey* of about 750 BCE). But the Doctor dismisses the idea of hiding soldiers in a huge wooden horse that the Trojans will supposedly take into their city. At least, he dismisses it at first...

History and fiction can help guide us through life's problems. Sometimes, a bold or obviously absurd idea is exactly what's needed to break an impasse. Oh, and as Virgil said, beware of ancient Greeks, even when they're bearing gifts!

9 MARCH

CRISIS SHOWS US WHO WE ARE

THE DOCTOR
Rose, before I go I just want to tell you: you were fantastic.
Absolutely fantastic. And you know what? So was I!

The Parting of the Ways by Russell T Davies (2005)

• • • • • •

The Ninth Doctor is dying. He's absorbed all the energy of the Time Vortex to save his friend Rose Tyler, and every cell in his body is now rapidly being killed off. Oh, he could cheat death yet again and change into someone else, but he'll never see Rose with the same eyes, the same daft old face.

She doesn't understand. She can't even remember what he's done or that he's saved her. He doesn't seem to mind, and grins warmly back at her. While his hearts might be breaking, there he is, cracking jokes, putting Rose at her ease as best he can, explaining what's to come. He puts her first, right up to the end. Yes, he *is* fantastic.

We all face moments of crisis and tragedy at some point in our lives. They're awful to live through – and yet also very revealing. How we meet such moments shows who we really are.

10 MARCH

GOOD COMPANY

THE DOCTOR
Need a lift anywhere?

DAN LEWIS
Why, where you going?

YASMIN
No idea.

THE DOCTOR
Wanna come?

Flux: The Vanquishers by Chris Chibnall (2021)

• • • • • •

Dan can't return home. Not since his house was destroyed by an implosion bomb left by a dog-faced alien. Now his girlfriend has turned down his offer for a date because he's arrived late (again).

To be fair, he has been busy. He's assaulted Sontarans in the docks with a wok; unflinchingly faced Weeping Angels; broken into an Aztec temple; trekked up a mountain in Nepal. Oh, and he went into space with the dog-faced alien.

All that time, he's travelled with his trusted new friends Yasmin Khan and the Doctor. Together they have fought foes and saved the world. When they open the doors to the TARDIS for him, what's he going to say?

Getting a lift may be just getting from A to B. Or it can mean having your spirits raised by being with good friends. Remember, when someone you know offers to take you somewhere, that the company can be more important than the journey.

11 MARCH

BE PREPARED

THE DOCTOR
My dear Litefoot, I've got a lantern and a pair of waders,
and possibly the most fearsome piece of hand artillery
in all England. What could possibly go wrong?

The Talons of Weng-Chiang by Robert Holmes (1977)

• • • • • •

Nine women have gone missing in late Victorian London. Emma
Buller's husband Joseph last saw her at the Palace Theatre – but when
he tries to investigate, he is horribly murdered. The Doctor and Leela
investigate this crime with the aid of pathologist Professor George
Litefoot and the theatre's owner, Henry Gordon Jago.

Deducing that Joseph Buller was savaged by a giant rat living in
the sewers between the theatre and the River Thames, the Doctor
borrows a long-barrelled, Chinese-style firing piece from Litefoot and
sets out to dispose of the creature.

Litefoot warns that the gun has not been fired in fifty years
but the Doctor seems confident it will still work as it was made in
Birmingham! With the right kit and steely determination, he enters
the sewers... just in time to save Leela from the rat.

Whatever task you set out to do, it's always much easier to accomplish it if you have the right tools.

12 MARCH

FIX YOUR OWN MESS

XOANON
We are all free thanks to you, Doctor.

THE DOCTOR
Oh well, it was the least I could do in the circumstances.
After all, I did start the trouble in the first place.

The Face of Evil by Chris Boucher (1977)

• • • • • •

The Doctor tries to help a spaceship stranded on a distant world. He hopes to repair it by making a direct link between its damaged data core and the compatible centres of his own brain. However, instead of taking only the information needed to renew itself, this advanced computer takes *everything* – a copy of the Doctor's whole personality! It then develops its own, separate identity.

The crazed computer, now calling itself 'Xoanon', begins a tyrannical regime lasting generations. But, returning to the spaceship many years later, the Doctor realises his mistake and reconnects to Xoanon. Even though he knows this will be painful, it's the only way to free the descendants of the crew.

We all make mistakes or get things wrong. It's tempting to deny that it's our fault or argue that we acted with the best of intentions. But that doesn't help solve the problem. Own your errors and, if you can, put them right.

13 MARCH

HONING SKILLS

THE DOCTOR
You're immortal, not indestructible.
You can be hurt, killed even.

ASHILDR
Ten thousand hours is all it takes to master any skill.
Over a hundred thousand hours and you're the best there's
ever been. I don't need to be indestructible. I'm superb.

The Woman Who Lived by Catherine Tregenna (2015)

● ● ● ● ● ●

The Doctor once chose to bring the Viking Ashildr back from death. In making her immortal, he condemned her to everlasting life.

He meets her again eight hundred years later in England, 1651, where she masquerades as a highwayman. Over the centuries she's developed many talents: surgeon, scientist, inventor, composer… it's a fantastic CV. She learned to use the longbow at the Battle of Agincourt, where she could shoot six arrows a minute and got so close to the enemy that she penetrated armour.

To hone a skill, you need more than time and practice. Shooting a longbow alone for a week won't improve your ability as much as practising for a day with an expert to coach you. If you repeatedly use poor technique, you'll make it harder to unlearn those instincts and develop the best form. Focus on quality as much as quantity when you're learning.

14 MARCH

MONSTERS FIGHTING MONSTERS

DALEK
You would make a good Dalek.

Dalek by Robert Shearman (2005)

• • • • • •

In a bunker deep under Utah in 2012, Henry van Statten – the man who owns the internet – hordes top secret alien relics. On display in his collection are the arm of a Slitheen and the head of a Cyberman. He also possesses a real, living Dalek.

This is, apparently, the last of the Daleks, just as the Doctor is the last of the Time Lords. But whereas the Doctor's friend Rose Tyler feels sympathy for both of these remaining survivors of the Time War, the Doctor wants the Dalek destroyed. The Doctor is angry and frightened in the presence of his old foe. And, as the Dalek taunts him, this leads him to behave like everything he professes to hate.

In doing so, the Dalek is unwittingly paraphrasing a well-known line of reasoning proposed by the German philosopher Friedrich Nietzsche (1844–1900) in his 1886 book *Beyond Good and Evil*. Nietzsche said that those who fight monsters must take care to ensure that in the process they do not become monsters themselves.

15 MARCH

DON'T JUDGE BY APPEARANCES

THE DOCTOR
Importance lies in the character and to what use you put
this intelligence. We respect you as we respect all life.

Galaxy 4 by William Emms (1965)

• • • • • •

Two spaceships meet above an unnamed planet in Galaxy 4, fire
on each other and then crash. The Doctor and his friends meet the
survivors on the planet's unstable surface: the humanoid Drahvins and
the enormous green Rills, who have slimy claws and breathe stinking
ammonia gas.

The Doctor's friend Steven thinks the tall, beautiful Drahvins are
'a lovely surprise', but soon discovers they're an austere, authoritarian
people who kill their surplus men to save on food. The Rills, meanwhile, are considerate and benign creatures, victims of an unprovoked
attack that they nevertheless understand.

'To the Drahvins we are ugly,' notes one of the Rills, 'so they
become frightened.' The Doctor and his friends admit they were
initially shocked by the Rills' appearance but learn to see them as they
really are: wonderful beings.

First impressions can be important but can also be deceptive.
A person's actions, their attitude, their mind, will show you who they
really are.

16 MARCH

OVERNIGHT SUCCESS

THE DOCTOR
Changing the world takes time. You have to be patient.

Nikola Tesla's Night of Terror by Nina Métivier (2020)

• • • • • •

Inventor Nikola Tesla will change the world. But first, he must save it. The Doctor needs his help to defeat the Queen of the Skithra.

Tesla despairs of prospering and selling his ideas. He was robbed on his journey to America and arrived with only four cents in his pocket. He still remained excited and optimistic about his prospects. But he now faces competition from his rival, Thomas Edison, reluctant investors, street protests and bad press.

The Doctor knows Tesla is destined to die penniless, but that the vision of wireless energy in a connected world started with him. She does not tell him this and encourages him not to give up because such things require dedication and persistence.

Overnight success is rare; it's usually just that everyone else suddenly notices something appears to be a success. More often than not, perfecting an invention or achievement or skill is the result of much trial and effort, research and practice, as well as building a market or an audience. It comes from commitment and perseverance. So whatever you're trying to do, however you're working to better yourself – keep it up.

17 MARCH

HANDLING INSULTS

SVILD

May death rain down on you both.

THE DOCTOR

Well, it's nice to meet you, too. Hurry along.

Flux: War of the Sontarans by Chris Chibnall (2021)

• • • • • •

Svild has suffered the ultimate shame for a Sontaran foot soldier — capture by the enemy instead of death in combat. He's shackled in Mary Seacole's hospital, refusing treatment and noisily asserting his rights to silence.

Even when the Doctor releases Svild's bonds and discharges the patient, he still has no gratitude for his treatment and storms out, snarling further imprecations.

There's no denying that words can hurt like weapons. But if you react in kind, you lose the high ground; Svild is unaware of this, which is perhaps how he came to be hit by a cannonball in the first place.

When people insult you, they're looking for the gratification of provoking a reaction. That might be your angry response or your embarrassed silence. Deny them that satisfaction. You can quietly ignore them and walk away. You can ask them to repeat it for clarification so they and others can hear how ridiculous or rude it is. Or you can respond in a polite, unperturbed manner that shows you will not allow them to goad or control you.

18 MARCH

TIME AND SPACE TO HEAL

ADRIC
And the regeneration?

THE DOCTOR
I don't know. I can feel it isn't going to be as
smooth as on other occasions. Sooner we get
to this Zero Room place the better, eh?

Castrovalva by Christopher H Bidmead (1982)

• • • • • •

Regeneration damages the nervous system, especially the dendrites which receive signals from other cells. The nervous system is a very delicate network of logic junctions called 'synapses', and in their weakened state they act rather like radio receivers, picking up all sorts of jumbled signals which overwhelm the Doctor's senses.

Luckily, the TARDIS contains a 'Zero Room', a big, empty, pinkish-grey space which for some reason smells like roses. Balanced to zero energy with respect to the world outside it, the Zero Room is a neutral, isolated environment – its stark simplicity exactly what the Fifth Doctor needs so that he can sleep and heal himself.

Even when the Zero Room is jettisoned from the TARDIS, the Doctor's friend Nyssa constructs a smaller 'Zero Cabinet' to speed up his recovery.

When you're sick, stressed or tired, it's important that you make time to heal, ideally somewhere quiet and calm where you can conserve your energy.

19 MARCH

KEEP ON WITH THE JOB

PERI BROWN
[OVER SPEAKER SYSTEM]
You murdered him! Why did you have to –

The sound abruptly cuts off. The Doctor, listening, is pained.
Then he rallies himself, continues – and runs into two Daleks.

THE DOCTOR
Ah, there you are. They went that way...

Revelation of the Daleks by Eric Saward (1985)

• • • • • •

At the Tranquil Repose funeral home on the planet Necros, dying people are held in suspended animation until cures can be found for them. The evil Davros sees these people as a resource to be exploited. The best will be turned into Daleks; the rest into food.

As the Doctor races to stop this monstrous enterprise, over the funeral home's speaker system he hears what sounds like his friend Peri being exterminated.

The Doctor allows himself a silent moment to grieve. Then, heroically, he presses on with his vital mission. When he's then confronted by Daleks himself, he quickly thinks on his feet.

Even though we don't come across as many life-or-death situations as the Doctor (thankfully!), sometimes when a task is really important we need to put our feelings aside until later, after we've got the job done – however difficult that might be at the time.

20 MARCH

DON'T REVISIT OLD PAIN

THE DOCTOR
Do you ever remember it?
Two thousand years, waiting for Amy?
The last Centurion. Not the sort of thing anyone forgets.

RORY WILLIAMS
But I don't remember it all the time.
It's like this door in my head. I can keep it shut.

Day of the Moon by Steven Moffat (2011)

• • • • • •

The longer you live, the more you have to remember – and to forget. Abiding memories are from heightened emotion – joy, grief, achievement, pain, love. You best recall what you repeat as stories and anecdotes, though memories evolve and change with each imperfectly recalled retelling. For some painful memories, the only person you tell may be yourself.

Rory Williams has more to remember than most. Erased from current history, he returns as an Auton duplicate in Roman times. He survives 1,894 years as a Centurion, waiting for true love Amy Pond until at last he is made human again. Two millennia of love and loss are finally redeemed at their wedding.

It can hurt to relive some things in your thoughts. Events. Emotions. People. Avoid the temptation to continually revisit that old pain. You don't have to forget, but you can choose not to dwell on it.

21 MARCH

RELATIONSHIPS EVOLVE

THE DOCTOR
I'd like to see a butterfly fit into a
chrysalis case after it's spread its wings.

POLLY
Then you did change!

THE DOCTOR
Life depends on change and renewal.

The Power of the Daleks by David Whitaker (1966)

• • • • • •

Ben Jackson is baffled and suspicious when he discovers a man he's never seen before on the TARDIS floor. Moments earlier, his friend the Doctor stumbled in through the doors. Now this total stranger is in his place. The clincher for Ben is that the ring the Doctor always wore doesn't fit this man's finger. What has he done to the Doctor?

Polly thinks she knows. The Doctor said his old body was 'wearing a bit thin', so he has got himself a new one. It may seem impossible, but before travelling with the Doctor they'd have been saying that about a lot of things.

Not all friendships are lifelong, no matter how much we want them to be. People evolve and change from the moment we first meet – their tastes, appearance, experiences, health, beliefs. And we evolve, too. We can still change together, if we accept it.

22 MARCH

FEEL GOOD, FIGHT EVIL

THE DOCTOR
There's something very satisfying in
destroying something that's evil!

The Savages by Ian Stuart Black (1966)

• • • • • •

On an unnamed planet in the distant future, the rich and sophisticated Elders know all about the Doctor, having watching his exploits as the 'traveller from beyond time' on their machines. But these machines are also responsible for propping up the cruel imbalance of power on this future world. The Doctor is horrified at the treatment of a whole class of people the rulers dismiss as mere 'savages'. This, the Doctor concludes, is evil.

It's a serious, cruel injustice, and the Doctor is equally serious in challenging the system. He and his friends Dodo and Steven lead a revolt to smash the wicked system. But they find enormous satisfaction – even delight – in doing so.

Addressing wrongs can take courage. Often you need support from other people to achieve real change. But find like-minded people and you can make a difference – and you might enjoy the experience, too. So, what wrong do you think needs righting, and who do you know that feels the same way?

23 MARCH

FRIENDS WHO GROUND YOU

NARDOLE
Look at you, avoiding the subject.

THE DOCTOR
I'm not avoiding anything, I'm just trying to save a planet.

NARDOLE
Which is what you always do
when the conversation turns serious.

The Return of Doctor Mysterio by Steven Moffat (2016)

• • • • • •

Nardole collects the Doctor in the TARDIS after a confrontation with aliens from the Shoal of the Winter Harmony. The aliens are animated human cadavers plotting to take over the Earth — and are from a race the Doctor first encountered with River Song.

So many things remind him of River, with whom he has just spent his final night before her imminent death. He also first met Nardole alongside River. Nardole believes the Doctor brought him into the TARDIS because he was worried about being alone after losing River. He observes that the Doctor is distancing himself from those feelings.

It's OK to have distractions when you're sad, so long as you're not burying your emotions. For us, it'll be something like golf or baking or Pokémon. For the Doctor, his hobby is saving the world. It's sad when things end, but everything begins again too, and that's happy. And it's good to have a friend who can remind us of that.

24 MARCH

KEEP IN TOUCH

THE DOCTOR

Me and you are off to Australia to see my old mate from MI6.
I say old mate. I've met him once, but he seemed very nice.
We text, though. Does that count?

Spyfall Part One by Chris Chibnall (2020)

* * * * * *

The Doctor meets loads of friends and acquaintances. She doesn't mind dropping their names into conversation, especially if they're famous, like Audrey Hepburn or Pythagoras.

It's a wonder she can remember them all. She'd say that everyone is important, not just those who are celebrities. When investigating attacks on spies around the world, she tells her friends that she knows Agent O, a 'horizon watcher' at MI6 whom the agency fired.

Former champion sprinter Agent O is now on the run. Fortunately, the Doctor can reach him via WhatsApp, and decipher his cryptic clues about his location in the Australian Outback. Too bad that, when she finally catches up with him, she discovers that the Master has killed Agent O and replaced him.

Social media means fewer excuses these days for losing contact with old friends, former colleagues or relatives. Who have you not spoken to in a while? Drop them a message now and see how they're getting on.

25 MARCH

LOOK FOR THE LOGICAL

THE DOCTOR
It's not a curse. Curse means game over.
Curse means we're helpless. We are not helpless.
Captain, what's our next move?

The Curse of the Black Spot by Stephen Thompson (2011)

• • • • • •

Logar the Fire God. Professor Clegg's psychometry. A Cyberman army of ghosts. Again and again, the Doctor challenges the belief that objects, actions or situations can have irrational or superstitious origins. 'Cursed' is big with humans, he believes, because it means bad things are happening but they can't be bothered to find an explanation.

The crew of Captain Avery's becalmed pirate ship blame a siren for the curse on their boat that condemns them to die as she picks off the weak and injured. One touch of her hand and you're dead.

The Doctor discovers that the black spot in their palms isn't a curse, it's a tissue sample. The siren is really a virtual doctor, and her song is anaesthetic.

There can be comfort in excusing your problems with things that are outside of human control. But there is also debilitating despair and fear. Look for the logical and you will empower yourself to make your own choices.

26 MARCH

OTHER PEOPLE'S ADVANTAGES

STEVEN
I take it you both come from the same place, Doctor?

THE DOCTOR
Yes, I regret that we do – but I would
say that I am 50 years earlier.

The Time Meddler by Dennis Spooner (1965)

• • • • • •

In Northumbria in 1066, the Doctor and his friends meet a meddling monk who turns out to have a TARDIS of his own! In fact, this Monk hails from the Doctor's home world but his technology is more advanced.

The Doctor can't help cooing over the Monk's Mark IV TARDIS and its automatic drift control which means it can safely suspend itself in space. The ship works more reliably than the Doctor's TARDIS – it changes shape to blend in with its surroundings and goes exactly wherever in time and space it is directed. At least, it does until the Doctor tampers with its workings.

The thing is, despite the Monk's advances, the Doctor still confounds him. They're about as smart and wily as each other, but the Doctor is helped by his friends and earns the trust of those around him.

You might feel that others have certain advantages over you, but concentrate on what matters most: strong and meaningful relationships with people.

27 MARCH

STYLE COUNSEL

THE DOCTOR
Oh, I see you've accessorised it.

OSGOOD
Yes.

THE DOCTOR
The old question marks.

OSGOOD
You used to wear question marks.

THE DOCTOR
Oh, I know, yes, I did

The Zygon Invasion by Peter Harness (2015)

• • • • • •

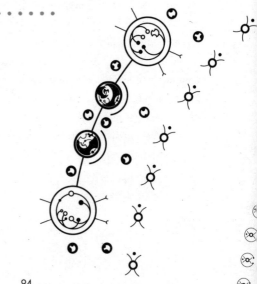

Petronella Osgood is a smart and capable UNIT scientist, and a big fan of the Doctor. She knows he often worked for the organisation – and in a variety of faces and styles.

Along with her white lab coat, Osgood wears clothes reminiscent of the Doctor's previous appearances. She was giddy with excitement on first meeting the Eleventh Doctor, when he complimented her on her long multicoloured scarf.

Travelling together in the presidential plane, the Twelfth Doctor observes that Osgood's shirt collar sports the question mark motif that was a feature of four earlier Doctors. But she won't tell him whether she is the Zygon who has been dressing as Osgood dressed like the Doctor. Whoever she is, the Doctor says he's proud to know her.

Whether it's business casual at work or at social events outside, people love to adopt their own style. It may be unique, or a mix-and-match. A film character or a band T-shirt. Vintage or modern. Bold or demure. Whether it's to your taste or not, accept that it's how they choose to express themselves.

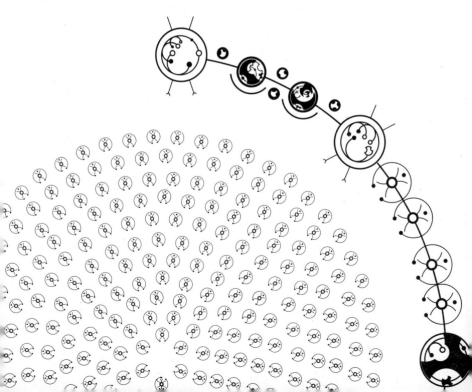

28 MARCH

TAKE NOBODY'S WORD FOR IT

BALAZAR
It is said the Immortal eats them.

THE DOCTOR
Never believe what is said, Balazar, only what you know.

The Trial of a Time Lord Parts One to Four (aka 'The Mysterious Planet')
by Robert Holmes (1986)

• • • • • •

Millions of years in the future on a planet known as Ravalox, an oppressed society lives underground in 'Marb Station'. Here, they are in awe of the so-called Immortal, a being that saved them from a fireball some 500 years previously, but who now resides unseen in a castle deep within the system of tunnels.

The Doctor is curious about the Immortal because, in all those centuries, the Immortal has reportedly never emerged from its castle. The only people to enter its domain and actually encounter the Immortal are the pairs of youths who pass an intelligence test – but they never return.

Balazar thinks this is because the Immortal eats the young geniuses but the Doctor wants better evidence before coming to any conclusion. Investigating, he discovers a much stranger truth and brings freedom to Marb Station.

Don't simply accept what people tell you. Question received wisdom to check that it really is right. That's how we make progress.

29 MARCH

I DON'T BLAME YOU

JO GRANT
I just wanted to say how sorry I am.
The bomb. I might have killed you all.

THE DOCTOR
Oh, that was nothing to do with you, my dear.

Terror of the Autons by Robert Holmes (1971)

• • • • • •

Poor Jo Grant. Her first day at UNIT does not go well. Keen to make a good impression, she wrecks a delicate experiment the Doctor is conducting, then gets captured and hypnotised by the wicked Master who tries to make her detonate a bomb to kill her new colleagues.

The Doctor was initially hesitant about taking on this young, inexperienced woman as his assistant, but he's soon won over by her kind heart and enthusiasm for the job in hand. When the Doctor sees how upset Jo is about what she tried to do, he assures her it wasn't her fault.

It's not just that he doesn't blame Jo for blundering into trouble. The Doctor's forgiveness, his trust in Jo, helps build her self-confidence. It's not long before she faces the Master again – but this time she resists his attempts to control her.

Focusing on other people's faults doesn't help them. Acceptance, forgiveness, encouragement – that's how you build them up.

30 MARCH

SPEAK TRUTH TO POWER

COUNTESS SCARLIONI
Discretion and charm. I couldn't live without it,
especially in matters concerning the Count.

THE DOCTOR
There is such a thing as discretion.
There's also such a thing as wilful blindness.

City of Death by David Agnew (1979)

• • • • • •

Countess Scarlioni lives with her wealthy art dealer husband in a luxurious Parisian chateau full of antique furniture and fabulous *objets d'art*. She thinks what caught her consort's eye is her ability to overlook him being a master criminal.

Her life of luxury prevents her admitting she doesn't truly know him. Otherwise, she'd see he's not a suave, sophisticated, well-connected member of the European aristocracy but a green-skinned alien disguised in a face mask and a tailored suit. The Doctor knows the truth about her husband's true identity, but she evades his questions about the Count.

A loved one, a colleague, a boss, or a public figure we admire – it can be hard to accept when someone we thought we knew is hurting others (or themselves) or breaking the law. There is a time to speak up, or speak out, when that happens. Don't simply turn away.

31 MARCH

DIFFICULT DECISIONS

THE DOCTOR
This is my life, Jackie. It's not fun, it's not smart, it's just standing
up and making a decision because nobody else will.

ROSE TYLER
Then what're you waiting for?

THE DOCTOR
I could save the world but lose you.

HARRIET JONES, MP FOR FLYDALE NORTH
Except it's not your decision, Doctor. It's mine.

World War Three by Russell T Davies (2005)

• • • • • •

The Slitheen family from Raxacoricofallapatorius contrive a diabolical
scheme to start a nuclear war on Earth. After killing everyone and
reducing the planet to molten waste, they can then sell radioactive
chunks as a fuel source for other aliens' spacecraft.

The Doctor has an ingenious plan to prevent this – but hesitates
because there's a risk that he, Rose Tyler and their friend Harriet Jones
will be seriously hurt or even killed. When he explains his dilemma,
both Rose and Harriet are keen for him to act. Harriet even takes charge.

Sometimes doing the right thing involves an element of risk. There
can be repercussions for you – and those around you. When faced with
such a decision, you can feel very alone. But have courage and you'll
inspire other people, too.

APRIL

1 APRIL

NOW PAY ATTENTION

THE VALEYARD
Another murder?

THE DOCTOR
Yes – and if you had been watching,
you would know who was the intended victim.

The Trial of a Time Lord Parts Nine to Twelve (aka 'Terror of the Vervoids')
by Pip and Jane Baker (1986)

• • • • • •

In the year 2986, the intergalactic liner *Hyperion 3* is on a scheduled flight to Earth from the planet Mogar, on the Perseus arm of our galaxy. Not everyone onboard is who they appear, and the Doctor and Melanie Bush are soon caught up in a real-life murder mystery.

These events are observed by a courtroom of Time Lords who have the Doctor on trial. The sardonic Valeyard, prosecuting the case, makes peevish comments throughout. But if he, like the Doctor, paid closer attention to the passengers, he'd have spotted a fateful clue.

Mogarians wear full spacesuits to survive in the oxygen-rich atmosphere. They also don't speak English and use translator systems. The Doctor spots that one Mogarian doesn't switch on his translator before speaking, so isn't what he seems...

The Valeyard might have seen this if he wasn't too busy making smart remarks. You'll observe more with your eyes open and your mouth shut.

2 APRIL

HURT CAN HELP

LEELA

My tribe has a saying: 'If you're bleeding,
look for a man with scars.'

The Robots of Death by Chris Boucher (1977)

• • • • • •

A huge, cumbersome 'sandminer' drives through raging sandstorms on a ravaged, desert planet. The effete, pampered crew have been on board for eight months, pursuing deposits of a mineral called lucanol which will make them all rich. The crew are served by robots – until the robots suddenly start murdering them, one by one.

As they struggle to keep control of the sandminer, one member of the crew – Toos – injures her wrist. The Doctor's friend Leela quickly comes to her aid, knowing instantly how to tie a bandage in order to ease Toos's pain. Despite the apparent sophistication of the sandminer crew, Leela has more practical experience from her life as a member of a 'primitive' tribe.

While some of our life experiences can be very painful and difficult to live through, we can use them to positive effect when others face their own difficult moments.

3 APRIL

TRY BEFORE YOU DECIDE

RIVER SONG
What book?

THE DOCTOR
Your book. Which you haven't
written yet, so we can't read.

RIVER SONG
I see. I don't like the cover much.

The Angels Take Manhattan by Steven Moffat (2012)

• • • • • •

Rory Williams vanishes from 21st century New York on a picnic trip to New York, and the Doctor traces him back to the Big Apple on 3 April 1938. All the clues are in a pulp detective paperback he found in his jacket, written by Melody Malone.

The author is really River Song. Helpfully, she is relating the entire adventure as it happened. Unhelpfully, once the Doctor realises the book describes their current events as they are experiencing them, he refuses to read on because it is too dangerous. He reluctantly decides to get handy hints from reading the chapter titles in its table of contents.

We can't truly know our future, so why do we leap to firm conclusions on the flimsiest of evidence? You can't judge a book by its cover – you need to sample it to decide for certain. Don't let your preconceptions stifle your enthusiasm. Give new things a chance.

4 APRIL

I'VE GOT A FEELING

THE DOCTOR
There's something alien about that tower. ... I've got that
pricking sensation again, the same just as I had
when I saw those Daleks were near.

The War Machines by Ian Stuart Black (1966)

• • • • • •

Arriving on Earth in the summer of 1966, the Doctor is immediately troubled by the new Post Office Tower, standing tall over London. As he tells his friend Dodo, the pricking sensation he gets in his hands is exactly like what happens when he's in the proximity of Daleks.

It soon becomes apparent that there's a sinister presence in the tower – a human-made computer WOTAN which possesses a powerful and ruthless intelligence. And yet it later turns out that the Doctor's senses were very acute. Because in *The Evil of the Daleks* (1967) we learn that that same summer there's also a Dalek in London, involved in a particularly diabolical trap to ensnare the Doctor. If only he listened to those instincts, he wouldn't walk straight into the trap...

Sometimes logic only gets us so far and when we're faced with difficult choices we need to trust our feelings and instincts instead.

5 APRIL

PROJECT MANAGEMENT TRIANGLE

THE DOCTOR
What's your plan, Zygella?

BONNIE
I don't have a plan.

THE DOCTOR
Come on, you don't invade planets without having kind of plan.
That's why they're called planets, to remind you to plan it?

The Zygon Inversion by Peter Harness and Steven Moffat (2015)

• • • • • •

Shapeshifting Zygon Bonnie has taken on the appearance of Clara Oswald. To maintain the illusion, she has incarcerated Clara in a pod. Bonnie says that Clara is dead, but the Doctor notices the Zygon has an involuntary wink when he asks her certain questions – Clara is communicating to him from her imprisonment via a telepathic connection with her impersonator.

The Doctor's plan is to locate where Clara is being held. He has a pressing deadline for this, he will use whatever he has immediately to hand and he doesn't care what it costs.

The fundamentals of planning a project are quality (how well must it be done), schedule (how soon do you need it done) and cost (what resources, like people or money, do you need to get it done). When the pressure is on, you may trade off one of those things against the others. Good, fast, cheap – choose two of three.

6 APRIL

WHEN I SAY RUN...

THE DOCTOR
Run!

The Faceless Ones by David Ellis and Malcolm Hulke (1967)
The Three Doctors by Bob Baker and Dave Martin (1972–73)
Image of the Fendahl by Chris Boucher (1977)
Four to Doomsday by Terence Dudley (1982)
Vengeance on Varos by Philip Martin (1985)
Paradise Towers by Stephen Wyatt (1987)
Doctor Who by Matthew Jacobs (1996)
Rose by Russell T Davies (2005)
New Earth by Russell T Davies (2006)
The Eleventh Hour by Steven Moffat (2010)
Robot of Sherwood by Mark Gatiss (2014)
Rosa by Malorie Blackman and Chris Chibnall (2018)

• • • • • •

Here's a useful fact for you. The First Doctor never tells anyone to run in any of his TV adventures – he's more likely to tell them to wait so he can catch up. But every other Doctor has yelled this instruction, and so saved someone's life.

There's an awful lot of running in *Doctor Who*. After all, there's a whole universe of deadly creatures and robots to escape from.

But look again and that's not always what's happening. Sometimes the Doctor runs headlong *into* danger, eager to help those who need it. We could all be a bit more courageous and active in helping. So imagine the Doctor taking hold of your hand – and run.

7 APRIL

REVEAL YOUR EMOTIONS

THE DOCTOR
Letting it get to you. You know what
that's called? Being alive. Best thing there is.
Being alive right now, that's all that counts.

The Doctor's Wife by Neil Gaiman (2011)

● ● ● ● ● ●

Rory Williams has been through the wringer. A malign entity pursues and plagues him in the TARDIS and torments his wife Amy Pond with a vision of his death from old age.

Rory receives a telepathic memory from Idris, a woman into whose body the malign entity placed the consciousness of the TARDIS. She helps him and Amy reach the TARDIS control room, where Rory finally meets Idris. But her body is failing. She passes one final message to him before dying in his arms.

Because he's a nurse and trained for such situations, Rory thinks he should not let it get to him. The Doctor reassures him that there's no shame in that.

Don't be afraid to reveal your emotions, particularly when you are with people you know and trust. Accepting that you're sad and letting it show is a healthy part of being alive. Without sadness, we wouldn't recognise what it's like to be happy. Giving and receiving comfort are marks of love and friendship.

8 APRIL

REFLECTED JOY

THE DOCTOR
Thank you, Sir Keith. By the way,
how's Sutton and Miss Williams?

SIR KEITH GOLD
Oh, they've left already. I believe he
is driving her to London in his car.

THE DOCTOR
Nothing like a nice happy ending, is there?

Inferno by Don Houghton (1970)

· · · · · ·

A huge mining operation drills through the Earth's crust — and unleashes primordial forces that transform anyone who touches the lethal green slime into monsters. If that's not bad enough, the Doctor is transported to a parallel universe much like our own but with more vicious versions of his friends. There, the mining operation is at a more advanced stage and it ends up destroying the whole world...

The Doctor narrowly escapes back to his own Earth, just in time to stop the disaster being repeated. But he's shaken by the experience — even a year later, he still speaks of the 'terrible catastrophe' he witnessed when 'a whole world just disappeared in flames.'

Yet when he's told that two members of the mining operation have fallen in love, he immediately brightens. Whatever our struggles and torments, we can still delight in other people's good news. Be glad for other people's happiness and you'll share in that joy.

9 APRIL

MAKE IT EASY

NIKOLA TESLA
That instrument detects energy? Is it your own design?

THE DOCTOR
I made it! Mainly out of spoons.

NIKOLA TESLA
You're an inventor!

THE DOCTOR
I have my moments.

Nikola Tesla's Night of Terror by Nina Métivier (2020)

• • • • • •

Opening a door. Using cutlery. Reading a book. When things just work, and using them seems natural, the design has become invisible and you take it for granted.

Tesla's lab is full of his work in progress for transforming power and communications systems. It also contains one of the Orbs of Thassor. When the Doctor examines it, Tesla is fascinated and thrilled by her sonic screwdriver, which she built herself from Sheffield steel.

It's a moment when two designers recognise the skill they have, the value of their ability and their joy in creating things.

Good design is something you don't always notice. We don't struggle with how to use something – we just get on with the task in hand. Behind every straightforward activity there's a designer who loved the buzz of having an idea and bringing it to life. Follow their example and do your best to make your suggestions easy to understand and follow.

10 APRIL

ACCUSE THE ACCUSER

THE DOCTOR
Lies. There's something else going on here.
The High Council has no right to order
Peri's or anyone else's death.

The Trial of a Time Lords Parts Five to Eight (aka 'Mindwarp')
by Philip Martin (1986)

· · · · · ·

Put on trial for his life by his own people, the Doctor is shown recorded evidence that he has put his friend Peri in danger. The Doctor can't deny that his curiosity sometimes lands both himself and his friends in trouble, but refutes the allegation. Besides, he was rushing to save Peri when he was taken out of time to stand trial.

But the Doctor then discovers that this meant he couldn't save Peri from a fate engineered by the Time Lords. They're the ones who endangered her, and that's apparently led to her death!

The Doctor is devastated by this, and rightly furious. Until now, he dismissed the claims made against him. Now he is fiercely determined to fight the charges and expose the truth.

Some people try to avoid blame or distract attention by accusing other people of the things they themselves have done. You're so busy defending yourself you can miss what's really happened.

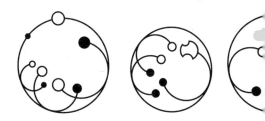

11 APRIL

SELF-PROJECTION

THE DOCTOR
Yes, I shall miss them, silly old fusspots.

The Chase by Terry Nation (1965)

• • • • • •

When a fierce battle ensues between a squad of Daleks and the robot Mechonoids, the Doctor's friends Barbara and Ian realise that they can use the Daleks' time machine to get home to London, 1965. The Doctor is appalled, convinced that they have only a 50:50 chance of surviving the journey – let alone of reaching the right destination. Of course, what he doesn't say in all his protests is that he's also upset at having to say goodbye to such dear, trusted friends.

Barbara and Ian do get home safely, and the Doctor acknowledges quietly afterwards that he'll miss them. Then he calls them 'fusspots' – but he was the one who was making a fuss!

When we're worried or upset, we sometimes try to defend ourselves and control our anxiety by projecting it onto other people. But this only prevents us seeing what the issue really is, and can lead to self-victimisation where we try to make out that it's others who are at fault, not us. Just being aware of this kind of behaviour can help us stop doing it – and of course can help prevent us being subject to other people's projections!

12 APRIL

EVIDENCE-BASED DECISIONS

THE DOCTOR
Never guess. Unless you have to.
There's enough uncertainty in the universe as it is.

Logopolis by Christopher H Bidmead (1981)

· · · · · ·

A pale figure on a bridge gestures towards the TARDIS on the river-bank far below. The Doctor goes to talk with the stranger, and Adric observes their conversation from a distance.

Adric knows that they arrived by the River Thames to flush out the Doctor's old enemy, the Master. The Doctor won't tell him the identity of the mystery figure on the bridge, so mathematical genius Adric puts two and two together and makes five: it must be the Master.

The Doctor admonishes Adric without correcting him about the stranger's true identify. He's spotting connections in a chain of circumstances that fragments the law that holds the universe together – and so guessing most certainly won't help.

Expectation inspires us with possibilities in a way that dry facts do not. But random conjecture is no substitute for informed deduction, whatever the situation. Equip yourself with facts before decisions are made.

13 APRIL

SAVE THE WORLD

THE DOCTOR
You want me to tell you that Earth's going to be OK?
Cos I can't. Unless people face facts and change,
catastrophe is coming. But it's not decided.

Orphan 55 by Ed Hime (2020)

• • • • • •

It's hard not to feel pessimistic about the fate of our planet. Almost every day another record is broken – the worst storms, heaviest rainfall, strongest winds and hottest heatwaves. The natural world faces astounding loss: in Britain, half of the natural biodiversity has been lost since the Industrial Revolution.

Can individuals make a difference through more considered consumption? Well, up to a point. A behavioural shift is what's really needed – for manufacturers, suppliers and those who regulate them in law.

Are there reasons for optimism? Yes. The wind and the sun come free. Truly renewable energy is not just cheaper than fossil fuels; it could save trillions. What's more, millions of people across the globe now demand action. This immense and powerful citizens' movement has the potential to compel action and persuade politicians to take real steps. A peaceful revolution that secures genuine change for the better. The Doctor would approve.

14 APRIL

LANGUAGE EVOLVES

THE DOCTOR
People never put the word 'space' in front of something just because everything's all sort of hi-tech and future-y. It's never 'space restaurant' or 'space champagne' or 'space...' you know... 'hat'. It's just 'restaurant', 'champagne' or 'hat'.

CLARA OSWALD
What about 'spacesuit'?

THE DOCTOR
Pedant.

Sleep No More by Mark Gatiss (2015)

· · · · · ·

The Doctor and Clara Oswald arrive in the darkened Le Verrier lab in orbit around Neptune. In the gloom, Clara is pretty sure that they're in a Japanese restaurant. It's in the future so that makes it a space restaurant, right? When the Doctor lectures her about word usage, Clara finds a counter example.

Language is always changing, evolving and adapting to accommodate fresh ideas, inventions and technologies. New words are borrowed or invented, the meaning of old words drifts. It's not fixed like a rock, so there's no point trying to police how people use it when they speak. The tighter you try to squeeze language to control it, the more it slips through your fingers like sand.

15 APRIL

COMFORT FOOD

THE DOCTOR
Who wants fish and chips?

The Rebel Flesh by Matthew Graham (2011)

· · · · · ·

What's a better comfort food than chips? The Doctor drops off Amy and Rory to grab some while he sorts out other stuff. On this occasion, his plans are thwarted by a solar tsunami, which is at least a better excuse than finding that the chippy is closed.

The Doctor and Rose buy chips when she returns home from the end of the world. Jack Harkness longs for them when incarcerated on the *Valiant*. Clara Oswald remembers them as a reassuring memory of her mum after getting lost on Blackpool beach. Sarah Jane Smith thinks they are as familiar as pussycats and Liverpool Docks. Bill Potts has a short-lived career frying them.

It certainly beats kronkburgers on Satellite 5, washed down with a zaffic drink. (Think beef flavoured Slush Puppy – or perhaps don't.)

Cooking doesn't have to be complicated. Simple tasty bakes, casseroles, soups and stews are perfect for cold evenings or for a filling meal to see you through a wet weekend. But there are occasions when you just want a takeaway, and that's all right too. Food we fancy can give us a real boost, and we can always eat more healthily the next day. What are you having for dinner tonight?

16 APRIL

THE GILDED CAGE

STEVENS
Freedom from fear, freedom from pain...

THE DOCTOR
Freedom from freedom?

The Green Death by Robert Sloman (1973)

* * * * * *

Mr Stevens, director of Global Chemicals, announces that the company's new oil refinery in Llanfairfach, Wales, can produce 25 per cent more petrol and diesel fuel from a given quantity of crude oil. He also claims that the process will produce only minimal pollution. This all seems very impressive and, as it turns out, far too good to be true.

Stevens and the company are actually in thrall to BOSS, a brilliant but immoral computer with designs on the whole world. Stevens tries to assure the Doctor that mind control by BOSS would be beneficial: people would be much happier as they wouldn't be allowed to know any different.

Beware the smooth words of corporations who often like to promise, or at least suggest, that everything can be simple, easy and safe. Of course, we want to believe such reassuring words, which is what helps companies be so effective in selling us things we might not otherwise buy.

Real life isn't always so simple or painless. Freedom isn't always easy. But it can be easily lost.

17 APRIL

SAVOUR OTHER CULTURES

THE DOCTOR

Time travel's like visiting Paris. You can't just read the guide
book, you've got to throw yourself in. Eat the food, use the
wrong verbs, get charged double and end up kissing complete
strangers. Or is that just me? Stop asking questions, go and do it!

The Long Game by Russell T Davies (2005)

• • • • • •

Adam Mitchell is overwhelmed by his first trip in the TARDIS. In
the Fourth Great and Bountiful Human Empire, planet Earth is at its
height. It's covered with mega-cities, has five moons, a population of 96
billion, and is the hub of a galactic domain stretching across a million
planets and a million species.

On closer examination, the space station they're on doesn't
exhibit the culture, art, politics, fine food and good manners Adam's
been promised. But the Doctor gives him a credit card for pocket
money, tells him to stop asking nagging questions, and sends him off
to explore for himself.

When you visit a foreign country, don't just head for familiar
burger and chips in the nearest themed pub. Make it your opportunity
to understand a culture, language, architecture and cuisine different
to your own. Who knows how your own tastes will be changed by
the experience.

18 APRIL

FEAR AND UNDERSTANDING

THE DOCTOR
Victorian showmen used to draw the crowds by taking
the skull of a cat, gluing it to a fish and calling it a
mermaid. Now someone's taken a pig, opened up its
brain, stuck bits on, then they've strapped it in that ship
and made it dive bomb. It must've been terrified.

Aliens of London by Russell T Davies (2005)

• • • • • •

A spaceship thunders over London then plummets into the Thames, captured live on TV news. A body is recovered from the ship and taken to Albion Hospital. But the 'alien' pilot turns out to be a pig in a space-suit – and it's still alive.

The Doctor greets it with a cherry 'Hello!', but the space pig suddenly takes fright and runs off down a corridor where it is sadly shot dead by an overzealous soldier.

Someone constructed the pilot to distract everyone from a more subtle alien invasion. The Doctor's compassion for the poor creature and his feelings of horror at what has been done to it help him to discover the truth.

The Doctor learns, and solves problems, through empathy and compassion.

19 APRIL

KNOW YOUR LIMITS

THE DOCTOR
We have only six minutes. That's as long
as I can stand sub-zero temperatures.

Four to Doomsday by Terence Dudley (1982)

• • • • • •

Fearing for her life on an Urbankan spaceship, the Doctor's friend Tegan Jovanka hopes to escape back to Earth in the TARDIS. Since she can't understand the flight manual, she resorts to operating various controls at random. As a result, the TARDIS only travels a short distance, stranded in space within sight of the Urbankan craft.

The Doctor and Adric set out to recover the TARDIS but have limited resources. Adric dons the one full spacesuit available while the Doctor puts on a space helmet which will at least allow him to breathe. Then he launches himself through the void in the direction of his ship.

It's a perilous journey, but the Doctor can survive in environments that would be fatal to us, and he pushes himself to take risks. Importantly though, he also knows what his body is capable of – and its limits.

Whatever the good reasons behind it, reckless action can put other people in danger. Yet, with calm consideration, we can often achieve extraordinary things in responding to a crisis.

20 APRIL

UNDERSTAND YOUR OPPONENT

MITCH

How can you be so sure?

THE DOCTOR

I learned how to think like a Dalek long ago.

Resolution by Chris Chibnall (2019)

• • • • • •

Archaeologist Mitch discovers the remains of the third Dalek Custodian from the 9th century. He and his colleague Lin have no idea what they found, no understanding of how dangerous it is. The Doctor has plenty of experience, of course. She knows that a Dalek mutant is cruelly controlling Lin to allow it to travel around without its casing.

When the Ninth Doctor savagely told a previous sole survivor it should just die, the creature shocked him by saying he would make a good Dalek. The Tenth Doctor acknowledges that a Dalek looked inside him and it saw hatred.

Thinking like your enemy doesn't make you the same as your enemy. There is a line you do not have to cross, when you can still understand without sympathising. Don't just automatically reject your opponent's beliefs out of hand. When you comprehend them, even if you do not agree with them, you have the means to anticipate them – and the ability to move beyond their influence.

21 APRIL

HOLIDAY BEHAVIOUR

THE DOCTOR
The second most beautiful garden in all of time
and space, and we can never come back here.

Face the Raven by Sarah Dollard (2015)

• • • • • •

The Doctor loves to visit interesting holiday destinations. The Eye of Orion. The Phosphorous Carousel of the Great Magellan Gestalt. The Planet Barcelona where dogs have no noses.

He's taken Clara Oswald around the universe to see its many wonders, though she's become a bit more reckless of late after the death of her boyfriend, Danny Pink. Honestly, one of these days she's going to get herself killed.

The Doctor's disappointed that he'll have to cross this latest venue off his list because of Clara's behaviour. She put her own life in danger again and almost got eaten by a creature in her efforts to prevent the Doctor having to marry a giant sentient plant.

Keep your perspective when you're visiting a new place so that you don't disgrace yourself and your travelling companions by acting out of character. You don't want to be one of those people who can go to a place twice only because the second visit is to apologise for the first time.

22 APRIL

SHARED EXPERIENCE WHEN APART

THE DOCTOR
Ah, the Moon. Look at it. Of course, you lot did a
lot more than look, didn't you? Big silvery thing in
the sky. You couldn't resist it. Quite right.

The Impossible Astronaut by Steven Moffat (2011)

· · · · · ·

The Doctor has a habit of leaving large gaps between his visits. Well, he has things to do, like visiting King Charles II, and escaping from a prison camp in World War II. When he turns up to take Rory Williams and Amy Pond to Lake Silencio in 1969, they work out that he's nearly two hundred years older than their previous meeting.

He avoids the couple's questions by saying they've been looking at the Moon. (He also discusses Jim the Fish with River Song. Let's talk about him another time.)

Our Moon has synchronous rotation; it completes one full rotation over exactly the same period that it orbits the planet. So wherever we are on Earth, we always see the Moon's nearside.

Even a few days can feel like two centuries when you're separated from a loved one. Wherever you are in the world, look up into the sky on a clear night and know you are both seeing the same Moon.

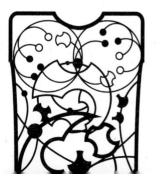

23 APRIL

TAKE A BREAK

THE DOCTOR
You know what I need more than
anything else in the universe?

TREMAS
No, Doctor.

THE DOCTOR
Breakfast.

The Keeper of Traken by Johnny Byrne (1981)

• • • • • •

Arriving on the idyllic planetary system of Traken, the Doctor and his friend Adric are accused of being evil invaders attacking the planet's wizened ruler. Kassia, a consul with some psychic ability, thinks such evil-doers should be killed. Her kindly husband Tremas, however, is prepared to hear the Doctor's defence.

This is a brave gesture on the part of Tremas because if the Doctor and Adric are found guilty, his life will also be forfeited. Together, they undertake scientific tests to prove the innocence of the Doctor and Adric – and reveal the real culprit.

As the sun comes up, the Doctor suggests breakfast. This means going back to Tremas's home, a safe place away from those who want the Doctor and Adric dead. This gives the three of them – and Tremas's daughter Nyssa – a chance to regroup and make plans.

It's said that breakfast is the most important meal of the day, and more generally, when you're under serious pressure it always helps to take a break and get something to eat!

24 APRIL

EVERYONE NEEDS HELP SOMETIMES

THE DOCTOR
Ordinary people lost their jobs. Couldn't pay the rent and
they lost everything. There are places like this all over
America. No one's helping them. You only come to
Hooverville when there's nowhere else to go.

Daleks in Manhattan by Helen Raynor (2007)

• • • • • •

There were hundreds of Hoovervilles across the United States in the
1930s – shanty towns set up around soup kitchens by the dispossessed
and destitute during the depression. In New York, many homeless
families pitched camp in Central Park.

Former soldier Solomon leads the informal community the best
he can. He asks the despairing residents not to steal or fight, because
the way to survive is to stick together and act like human beings, now
that's all they have. He explains to the new arrival that the desperate
people in Hooverville include stockbrokers and a lawyer, but that he
is their first doctor.

Calamity can befall anyone, no matter how rich or poor. What
people take for granted today can be suddenly gone because of economic
trouble, war, disease or natural disaster. When catastrophe strikes
anywhere in our world, try to help and support the victims as best you
can. Together we're stronger, and one day you might be the one in need.

25 APRIL

MIRROR, MIRROR

THE DOCTOR
What is the one thing evil cannot face – not ever?

TEGAN JOVANKA
What?

THE DOCTOR
Itself.

Kinda by Christopher Bailey (1982)

• • • • • •

The verdant planet Deva Loka, also known as S14, is home to the peaceful, enigmatic Kinda who turn out to be far more sophisticated than they first appear. A group of would-be colonisers from another world dismiss the Kinda as 'primitive' because they recoil from the sight of a mirror, fearful that it might somehow capture their soul.

But there's another lifeform on Deva Loka: the evil Mara. It usually inhabits 'the dark places of the inside' but succeeds in making a telepathic connection with Tegan using her dreams as a conduit.

The Doctor realises that the Kinda's fear of mirrors is a clue to their power. To defeat the huge, snake-like manifestation of the Mara and free the people it has possessed, he traps the creature within a circle of polished solar generator panels. The Mara is faced with infinite reflections of itself and can only escape by withdrawing to the dark place from which it came.

Most of us like to think that we're basically good people. However, we might occasionally behave badly and not necessarily be aware how we're affecting others. Every now and again it's a good idea to hold up a mirror to our own actions and see ourselves as others do.

26 APRIL

TALK IT OUT

THE DOCTOR
Are you thinking what I'm thinking?

THE DOCTOR
Inevitably.

THE DOCTOR
Hah! I'm glad we're on the same...

THE DOCTOR
...wavelength. You see? Great minds.

The Almost People by Matthew Graham (2011)

• • • • • •

A factory crew handle hazardous environments with doppelgängers created from self-replicating fluid called the Flesh. After a solar tsunami strikes the factory, it's hard to tell the sentient duplicates from the originals.

The Eleventh Doctor tends to chatter away with his constant internal dialogue as ideas spill from him in times of excitement or crisis. So, he's delighted he can now do it in person with his own newly created avatar.

It's liberating to say things out loud. You clarify what you're thinking or admit how you're feeling when you express it. Test your assumptions and share your worries with someone. If there's no one around, speaking it aloud still means you need to articulate it. Have a word with yourself.

27 APRIL

PUT OTHERS FORWARD

RALPH CORNISH
Doctor, I'll need your help to communicate
with the ambassadors.

THE DOCTOR
Here's Miss Shaw. She's much more
practical than I am. Goodbye, Brigadier.

The Ambassadors of Death by David Whitaker (1970)

• • • • • •

At the headquarters of Britain's Space Control, three Martian ambassadors extend the hand of friendship to humanity. The humans learn that the touch of a Martian is deadly, but eventually come to appreciate the gesture. So begins a new age of interplanetary peace and diplomacy, the historic moment televised live to homes around the whole world.

The Doctor has been instrumental in this extraordinary moment, ensuring that, despite the efforts of one disgruntled former astronaut, the Martians are made welcome. But then the Doctor makes his own noble gesture: he steps back into the shadows. Of course, the Doctor has a greater wealth of experience in dealing with aliens, yet instead he ushers forward his friend Liz Shaw to take the lead role – and all the glory.

Encourage other people and help them to take opportunities to learn and grow. Even when you know best, it's sometimes preferable to shut up and keep out of the way.

28 APRIL

LEARN FROM EXPERIENCE

THE DOCTOR

Something seems impossible. We try – it doesn't work,
we try again. We learn, we improve. We fail again, but
better. We make friends, we learn to trust, we help each
other. We get it wrong again. We improve together,
then ultimately succeed. Because this is what being alive
is. And it's better than the alternative. So come on, you
brilliant humans. We go again. And we win.

Eve of the Daleks by Chris Chibnall (2022)

• • • • • •

It's déjà vu all over again. The Daleks track the TARDIS to execute the
Doctor as punishment for destroying their war fleet.

They succeed immediately, exterminating the Doctor and her
friends in a storage facility. The End.

Well, not quite. The TARDIS traps them inside a time loop. The
relentless Daleks learn the Doctor's tactics each time the loop repeats.

But it shortens on each reset, so they only have so many chances.
The Doctor uses the penultimate loop to plan tactics that make the
most of time available to each of them. Six previous failures are acceptable if it makes a final seventh attempt successful.

If at first you don't succeed, try again. Don't just repeat your
actions. Learn from your mistakes, work out whose help you need,
picture a successful outcome and go for it.

29 APRIL

TIDY UP

THE DOCTOR
It's my cot. I slept in there.

AMY POND
Oh, my God. It's the Doctor's first stars.

A Good Man Goes to War by Steven Moffat (2011)

• • • • • •

The attacking army has been routed and fled the military base on Demon's Run. The Doctor's allies gather with him in the hangar room. Amy Pond has brought her tired newborn baby, Melody.

The Doctor collects an old-fashioned wooden cot from the TARDIS. It has planet mobiles above it and Gallifreyan script on the side. He's giving it to Melody, after keeping it since he was a baby.

The Doctor's not one to throw things away: at times, he produces so many things from his pockets that you'd think they were dimensionally transcendental. And the many rooms in his TARDIS are cluttered with clothes and equipment and junk. The boot cupboard alone is so huge that it's furnished.

You'll never use all that stuff you've got all over the place. Declutter things in three ways:

- Throw away rubbish.
- Donate things to others.
- Keep important or sentimental items in specific places.

If something is neither useful nor brings joy or happy memories, you can get rid of it.

30 APRIL

SERIOUSLY CHEEKY

THE DOCTOR
Just some old friends of mine.

LOBOS
But these are amphibious creatures.
You are not an amphibian.

THE DOCTOR
Oh, I'm not, am I?

The Space Museum by Glyn Jones (1965)

• • • • • •

Taken prisoner on the planet Xeros, the Doctor is interrogated by authoritarian Governor Lobos, who uses a thought-selection machine to present the Doctor's mental pictures on a screen. This should mean the Doctor can't lie – but he soon turns the tables. First, he thinks of walruses swimming, then he pictures himself wearing a bathing suit!

This is the Doctor standing up to authority even while sitting down. He's polite, he's charming, and yet he declines to give Governor Lobos the one thing he wants: his surrender. This makes Lobos cross and he sends the Doctor away to be made a permanent exhibit in a museum. But why has the Doctor's mild-mannered protest so effectively annoyed the governor?

Often, people with authority expect to be taken seriously. But this means they depend on us to acknowledge their power – and if we don't, that position is threatened. What strength there is, just in a joke.

MAY

1 MAY

MAGIC DANCE

THE DOCTOR

You're right, Jo: there is magic in the world after all.

The Dæmons by Guy Leopold (1971)

• • • • • •

Many thousands of years ago, an alien Dæmon, Azal, visited Earth and influenced the early development of humans. The image of Azal – a cloven-hooved, horned figure – has been immortalised in our mythology ever since. And Azal himself remained on Earth, held in suspended animation on his ship.

Azal's technology is so advanced that, to modern humans, it is largely indistinguishable from magic. Indeed, specific words and rituals are used to awaken the Dæmon from his millennia-long sleep. But the Doctor is keen to point out to his friend Jo that there's a scientific explanation for all strange phenomena. By way of demonstration, his car, Bessie, seems to magically drive off by itself, although the Doctor soon reveals he's been operating it in secret using a clever remote control.

In the end, with Azal prevented from destroying humanity, the Doctor and his friend Jo join a merry village May Day dance to celebrate new life. The Doctor delights in the festivities. For all he's a rationalist, he throws himself into this enjoyable magical tradition.

Sometimes it's enough to enjoy things without having to explain or analyse them, or worry about looking silly. Today, go and do something daft and fun.

2 MAY

VALUE OF SCHOOL

THE DOCTOR

Any number that reduces to one when you take the sum
of the square of its digits and you continue iterating until it
yields one is a happy number. Any number that doesn't, isn't.
A happy prime is a number that is both happy and prime.
Now type it in! I don't know, talk about dumbing down!
Don't they teach recreational mathematics any more?

42 by Chris Chibnall (2007)

• • • • • •

Forty-two is a pronic number (product of two consecutive numbers),
an abundant number (smaller than the sum of its proper divisors), and
a sphenic number (product of three distinct prime numbers). Amongst
other things, it's also a primary pseudoperfect number.

It's also the number of minutes left before the SS *Pentallian* plunges
into the sun. To save the crew (7) the Doctor must go through pass-
word-sealed doors (29) with a single chance (1) for each. He spots that
the next solution is a sequence of happy primes: 313, 334, 367 ... 379.

You may wonder whether you'll ever need all that maths you
learned at school. Mostly, it taught you numeracy and how to understand calculations in your working life. Subjects you didn't enjoy can
still be enlightening – even if your only recreational use for a happy
prime is as an answer in a quiz.

3 MAY

CRUEL OR BE KIND

THE DOCTOR
I can understand your military purposes
but why murder a hatful of harmless humans?

Horror of Fang Rock by Terrance Dicks (1977)

· · · · · ·

In a remote lighthouse in the first decade of the 20th century, the Doctor battles a shape-changing Rutan stranded on Earth. The creature thinks the planet could play a strategic role as a base from which the Rutans will launch their final assault against the Sontarans – a species they have been at war with for millennia.

The Rutan dismisses the human population of Earth as 'primitive bipeds of no value', and murders them one by one to keep its presence secret. Its victims include the innocent young lighthouse-keeper Vince Hawkins, as well as other people who aren't quite so nice – but who still don't deserve to die.

The Doctor isn't convinced by the Rutan's argument that it *had* to kill these people; in fact, the deaths seem to convince the Doctor that it is necessary to destroy the Rutan.

How you behave often influences how others respond to you. Treat them with kindness, and it will be reflected back – like the beam of a lighthouse. But meanness and cruelty will be reflected back too.

4 MAY

THE POWER OF PAUSING

THE DOCTOR

No, of course I had to jump! Rule one of being interrogated –
you're the only irreplaceable person in the torture chamber.
The room is yours. So work it. If they're threatening you
with death, show them who's boss – die faster!

Heaven Sent by Steven Moffat (2015)

• • • • • •

The Doctor is falling. Confronted by a deadly threat in the highest
room of a locked castle, he's thrown a stool through a leaded window
before throwing himself out into the mist without looking. Is he
plunging to his death? Because rule one of dying is: don't.

Now he's thinking things through about what will happen. He
imagines himself in the TARDIS. Concentrating. Focusing. Assuming
he's going to survive.

You are the only person who is in every scene of your life. Every
place you go has you in it. You're always thinking about what you're
doing there. Sometimes, whether you like it or not, you're the centre
of attention: getting married, accepting an award, giving a speech. No
need to rush. Take a deep breath and take your time. Assume the best
outcome. Everyone else there wants you to succeed and is prepared to
wait for you to be ready.

5 MAY

DON'T JUDGE BY APPEARANCES

THE DOCTOR
The pig and the showgirl.

MARTHA JONES
It just proves it, I suppose: there's someone for everyone.

Evolution of the Daleks by Helen Raynor (2007)

• • • • • •

Facial traits that make a man conventionally attractive include a winning smile, a square jaw and prominent cheekbones. How about floppy ears, an upturned nose, and piggy eyes?

Angelic blonde revue singer Tallulah loves Laszlo, the handsome stagehand at New York's Laurenzi Theatre. Unhappily, her sweetheart is captured for conversion into one of the Daleks' mutant human-pig hybrid slaves. Laszlo escapes full conditioning, but his face is transformed into that of a real swine.

Laszlo shows his continued devotion by delivering flowers secretly to his girlfriend even though he can't bear to reveal himself to her. Then his selfless support fighting the Daleks reveals his true bravery.

Tallulah knows he is the smartest guy she ever dated. So it's no surprise to the Doctor that she settles down with Laszlo in the Manhattan shanty town of Hooverville. Acceptance is what New York is good at.

What makes someone different enough to be someone worth loving? It's not their appearance, it's their character. Judge people by what they do, not what they look like.

6 MAY

PEOPLE LEARN FOR THEMSELVES

THE DOCTOR
Oh dear, I suppose I'd better follow them.
See that they don't get into any harm.

The Smugglers by Brian Hayles (1966)

• • • • • •

Ben Jackson and Polly from 1960s London can accept that the wicked computer WOTAN takes over people's minds, and that the TARDIS is bigger on the inside and moves about. But they draw the line at the Doctor's suggestion that it also travels in time.

So when their first trip on board the TARDIS deposits them in Cornwall, they think it's a bit of a holiday. Ignoring the Doctor's warning that they're in the 17th century, they head off to explore – and soon get caught up with a bunch of murderous pirates who are searching for the late Captain Avery's treasure.

No matter your experience or expertise, some people won't be told and need to learn things the hard way, for themselves – even if they get hurt in the process. Sometimes all you can do is keep an eye on them, and offer support when things go wrong.

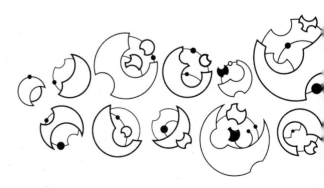

7 MAY

TIME MOVES ON

AMY POND
Doctor, she's River, and she's our daughter.

THE DOCTOR
Amy, I know. But we have to let her make her
own way now. We have too much foreknowledge.
Dangerous thing, foreknowledge.

Let's Kill Hitler by Steven Moffat (2011)

• • • • • •

Amy Pond and Rory Williams finally track down their missing baby, River Song. Turns out she grew up hiding as their childhood friend Mels, who hijacks the TARDIS, is accidentally shot dead by Hitler and regenerates. Then she kills the Doctor, discovers her real identity and saves him by surrendering all her remaining regenerations – all on the first occasion that she ever meets him. It's been quite a day.

The Doctor delivers the recovering adult River to the care of a hospital in the far future. In the TARDIS, he explains to her parents why they must leave her behind.

Most of us know someone who is a parent, and understand the 'firsts' that are important to them: first nappy, first smile, first words, first steps. They won't recognise the lasts as they happen: last time they carry them on their shoulders, last time they hold their hand. Accept that the children in your life will move on at some point – university, job, marriage – and become their own person. They're always somewhere in the world and will find you when they need you.

8 MAY

FAIR BUT FIRM

THE DOCTOR
I can take you anywhere you want. A billion light years
from your home planet. You'd never be found.

TERILEPTIL LEADER
No, Doctor, a barren rock in space is not an
acceptable alternative – especially when you are
my prisoner and your ship is for the taking.

THE DOCTOR
I can't let you do that.

The Visitation by Eric Saward (1982)

• • • • • •

A group of Terileptils imprisoned for life in the tinclavic mines on
Raaga stage an audacious escape and blast off in a spaceship. But the
vessel is badly damaged in an asteroid storm and burns up in Earth's
atmosphere in the year 1666. An escape pod reaches the planet's
surface, but only four prisoners survive.

Wounded, outnumbered and fearful of discovery by their own
people, the Terileptils use their technological skills to enslave the
local villagers. Despite their actions, the Doctor offers to take the
prisoners to a new world that they can make their own, but the aliens
refuse, determined instead to kill everyone on Earth and steal the
Doctor's TARDIS.

You can be generous and kind and forgiving of people's actions.
But if people persist in bad behaviour, there's comes a point where you
must stand up to it and say 'no'.

9 MAY

ORDINARY EXTRAORDINARY

THE DOCTOR
An army's nothing. Because those ordinary people, they're the
key. The most ordinary person could change the world.

The Age of Steel by Tom MacRae (2006)

. . . . . .

The Cybermen have conquered a parallel version of Earth and begin
'upgrading' their human prisoners – turning them into new Cybermen.

The Cyber Controller can't understand why anyone would object
to this transformation, because in his view, becoming an emotionless
Cyberman makes humans more powerful, freeing them from grief,
rage and pain. Besides, says the Cyber Controller, the Doctor has no
means of stopping a whole army of Cybermen.

But the Doctor's response is aimed not at the Cyber Controller
but at his gang of human friends who he knows are listening in. The
Doctor's words encourage these ordinary, imperfect people to seek out
and share the hidden cancellation code that will unlock the Cybermen's
emotional inhibitors – and effectively drive the creatures mad.

Mickey Smith isn't a genius – some people call him an idiot. Yet he
persists in trying to crack the code because he'd do anything to save
his friends. His determination saves them and the world.

We don't have to be special or powerful to make a difference. The
first step is that determination. What do you want to change?

10 MAY

DISAGREE RESPECTFULLY

THE DOCTOR
Ryan, I've lived for thousands of years.
So long I've lost count. I've had so many faces.
How long have you been here? You don't
know me. Not even a little bit.

YASMIN KHAN
Don't talk to him like that.

RYAN SINCLAIR
Yeah, I'm not having that.

Fugitive of the Judoon by Vinay Patel and Chris Chibnall (2020)

• • • • • •

The Doctor wants her fam to be involved without her having to be in charge of everything. It's a very flat team structure.

It's been a day of unwelcome discoveries for the Doctor. She's dug up a whole past life that she cannot recollect. The Master and Jack Harkness, people she does remember, have returned unexpectedly. So Ryan Sinclair's supportive words do not immediately reassure her.

Yasmin Khan firmly rejects the Doctor's despairing reply. So does Ryan – and, more importantly, he calmly explains why. They know she brought the fam together, and together they've saved others. She's given them the strength to tell her when she is wrong.

The fam's reaction show us that disagreements don't have to be a slanging match. Express your opposition to someone respectfully and calmly, no matter who they are, and they are more likely to be grateful that you spoke up.

11 MAY

TAKE THE SCENIC ROUTE

THE DOCTOR
Brigadier, a straight line may be the shortest distance between
two points but it is by no means the most interesting.

The Time Warrior by Robert Holmes (1973–74)

• • • • • •

Top scientists keep disappearing, even when they're under lock and
key in a secure facility run by UNIT. The Doctor discovers that the
scientists are being transported back in time to the 13th century and
made to work for an aggressive Sontaran called Linx.

The Doctor is all set to pursue the missing scientists but his friend
the Brigadier is sceptical that the TARDIS will get him to the right
place and time as the ship often makes unexpected detours

As the Doctor says, these detours often land the TARDIS somewhere more strange and exciting than he might have expected. And
that's true of the Doctor's attitude to life: wandering about with
curiosity, following paths that look intriguing, soaking up knowledge
and experience wherever he goes. Try it for yourself. Wherever you're
going today, take a different, less direct route with an open mind.

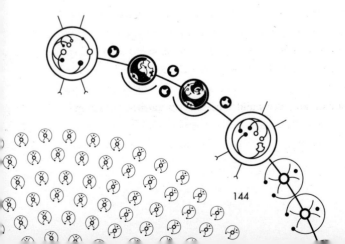

12 MAY

SHARE YOUR DREAMS

JOHN SMITH

I have written down some of these dreams in the form
of fiction. Not that it would be of any interest.

JOAN REDFERN

I'd be very interested.

JOHN SMITH

Well, I've never shown it to anyone before.

JOAN REDFERN

'A Journal of Impossible Things.' Look at these creatures.
Such imagination!

Human Nature by Paul Cornell (2007)

• • • • • •

John Smith dreams he is an adventurer, a daredevil, a madman. But how can he be this 'Doctor' who travels in a funny little blue box when he's really teaching at Farringham School for Boys in 1913?

The Doctor has transformed himself into a human so he can escape aliens who are on his scent. His displaced memories leak out when he sleeps, and he sets them down in an illustrated journal.

School Matron Joan Redfern is John's confidante, and the first person he tentatively shows his book. When he does, she is complimentary and encouraging.

Sharing your dreams can build trust and strengthen your bond with someone you love. It's a way of discussing your passion and enthusiasm. Their encouragement gives you motivation and security when things seem uncertain.

13 MAY

"I WILL NOT SHUT OUT THE LESSONS THAT THEY TEACH"*

CHARLES DICKENS
Can it be that I have the world entirely wrong?

THE DOCTOR
Not wrong. There's just more to learn.

The Unquiet Dead by Mark Gatiss (2005)

• • • • • •

The novels of author Charles Dickens (1812–70) remain hugely popular more than 150 years after his death. Dickens was also a tireless campaigner to improve society for everyone. He exposed the horrors of poverty in Victorian Britain, fought to end the death penalty, and used his celebrity to support all manner of causes.

In 1869 in Cardiff, Dickens tells the Doctor that he has rallied against fantasists. As a master storyteller, the author revels in a well-performed illusion – but he knows they're not real.

However, when alien gas-creatures called Gelth start possessing and animating dead bodies, Dickens begins to wonder if he's got things very wrong. But the Doctor reassures him. New knowledge, however strange and unexpected, doesn't take anything away from our experience – it adds to it. Dickens previously thought he knew everything about the world but is now inspired and reinvigorated by the incredible events he's witnessed.

Be like Dickens and share in the delight of gaining new knowledge, and having your eyes opened to new experiences.

* Dickens, *A Christmas Carol* (1843)

14 MAY

CELEBRATE YOUR ENTHUSIASMS

THE DOCTOR
Science geek? What does that mean?

MARTHA JONES
That you're obsessively enthusiastic about it.

THE DOCTOR
Oh, nice!

The Lazarus Experiment by Stephen Greenhorn (2007)

• • • • • •

Martha Jones smuggles the Doctor into a black-tie event. Her sister Tish has organised it as Head of PR for Professor Richard Lazarus.

The Doctor wants to find out what Lazarus meant when he said he'll demonstrate a device that will change what it means to be human. Tish wants to find out how the Doctor got into the event without being on her invitation list.

The Doctor questions Tish about the Professor's plans. When he mentions a sonic microfield manipulator, Tish teases her medically trained sister that she should have known Martha would bring a 'science geek' to the gathering as her plus-one. The Doctor is pleased when Martha explains what Tish's words mean.

If you are mocked for being knowledgeable or interested about the details of subject, especially if it's technical or specialist or niche, be like the Doctor and celebrate that instead.

15 MAY

SAY IT WHILE YOU CAN

CLARA OSWALD
I have something I need to say –

THE DOCTOR
We do not have time!

CLARA OSWALD
No, my time is up, Doctor. Between one heartbeat and the last is all the time I have. People like me and you, we should say things to one other. And I'm going to say them now.

Hell Bent by Steven Moffat (2015)

• • • • • •

The Time Lords trapped the Doctor in a Confession Dial, but the Doctor refused to give them what they needed because he wanted to save Clara Oswald. He returns to Gallifrey and tricks them into rescuing Clara from the moment of her death. He'll save her but remove all her memories of him.

The revived Clara is appalled to learn the Doctor's refusal meant he endured four and a half billion years inside the Confession Dial.

This is the first time Clara tells the Doctor how she feels. We don't hear her words – it is a private moment between them (and they're planning an escape at the same time).

Don't delay saying what's important to the people in your life. No point holding on until your final moments – or theirs. Don't wait years (or millennia). If you care for them, tell them now.

16 MAY

EQUALLY NO

LEELA
I thought you didn't like killing.

THE DOCTOR
I don't. The virus has a perfect right to exist as a virus,
not as a giant swarm threatening the entire Solar System.
Everything has its place – otherwise the delicate
balance of the whole cosmos is destroyed.

The Invisible Enemy by Bob Baker and Dave Martin (1977)

. . . . . .

On a moon of Saturn around the year 5000, the crew of Titan Base succumb to a sentient virus. The virus doesn't just make them sick, it controls them... and makes them sprout strange, silvery whiskers!

The Doctor also succumbs to this illness, but fortunately for him, a miniature clone version of himself and his friend Leela are injected into his body where they battle the nucleus of the disease – a prawn-like creature with articulate views on its moral right to exist.

Accepting these cogently expressed arguments, the Doctor counters that he has an equal right to fight for his own life, and the nucleus agrees. The Doctor also argues that the virus can't simply spread out of hand across the universe.

Some people can argue very persuasively that they should be allowed to do whatever they like. It's up to the rest of us to push back in the name of fairness.

17 MAY

THE STENCH OF HISTORY

MARTHA JONES
I don't know how to tell you this, oh great genius,
but your breath doesn't half stink.

The Shakespeare Code by Gareth Roberts (2007)

• • • • • •

The Doctor takes his new friend Martha Jones back in time to London, 1599, where at the Globe Theatre they watch a play by William Shakespeare. To Martha's excitement, they then get to meet the famous writer – who starts composing some of his most famous poems about her!

Shakespeare is brilliant, funny and charming, and in battling the evil Carrionites he is also brave. Martha is in awe of him, and flattered by his interest. But in an age long before fluoride toothpaste and good dental hygiene, she is never going to snog him.

There's a serious point behind Martha's instinctive reaction. Depictions of history in TV and other media can add to a belief that life was much better in the past. It can seem simpler, more natural, more real. But these depictions don't often show people's teeth as they really would have been at the time. And then there's the higher mortality rates, the squalor – and the smell. Don't look to return to the past; look to improving the future.

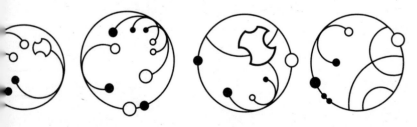

18 MAY

ARE WE THE BADDIES?

THE DOCTOR
Liz, these creatures aren't just animals.
They're an alien life form, as intelligent as we are.

Doctor Who and the Silurians by Malcolm Hulke (1970)

· · · · · ·

Daleks, Cybermen, Ice Warriors, Zygons ... The Doctor has thwarted numerous invasions of Earth by marauding aliens. But what happens when *we* are the invaders?

The Silurians had an advanced technological civilisation at the time of the dinosaurs, and were able to predict an impending global catastrophe. As a result, they built a hibernation facility where they would sleep safely until the danger had passed. But when they finally awake in the 20th century, they discover 'their' planet overrun by apes, who then try to kill them. Scared, confused and angry, the Silurians feel they have no choice but to fight back.

The Doctor tries valiantly to mediate between Silurians and humans, but both sides see each other as the monsters, and cannot countenance the idea that they themselves might be in the wrong.

It's all too easy to see the faults of others while ignoring our own, especially when we feel threatened. But even the best of us can be mistaken. Admit that possibility and you might spare yourself and others a lot of conflict.

19 MAY

SHARED READING

THE DOCTOR

Reading's great. You like stories, George? Yeah? Me, too.
When I was your age, about, oooh, a thousand years ago,
I loved a good bedtime story. *The Three Little Sontarans.*
*The Emperor Dalek's New Clothes. Snow White and the
Seven Keys To Doomsday*, eh? All the classics.

Night Terrors by Mark Gatiss (2011)

• • • • • •

Eight year old George Thompson is frightened. Unknown to his mother
and father, he is not their human child but an empathic Tenza who has
established himself in their loving home. He fears that his parents are
rejecting him when they seek professional help for George's irrational
childhood fears, and his psychic distress call reaches the Doctor across
time and space.

His father worries that George is frightened by things on the telly
or in books. The Doctor comforts the boy about the value of stories.

Whether you're a parent, relative, babysitter or family friend,
reading to a child comforts them, improves their language skills,
develops their creativity, encourages them to read more themselves
and builds your relationship. It's something they won't want you to do
forever, so relish it while you can. Don't miss the opportunity – and
don't miss out pages, either.

20 MAY

HONESTY IS THE BEST POLICY

THE DOCTOR
There's something I'd like to show you.

Black Orchid by Terence Dudley (1982)

• • • • • •

At Lady Cranleigh's fancy dress party in 1925, the Doctor is accused of attacking Ann Talbot, a young woman who looks just like the Doctor's friend Nyssa. This isn't the only duplication: the Doctor deduces that the real culprit must be someone else who was wearing the same masked costume as he was. But the police aren't having any of it.

The Doctor tries to explain that he was in the company of Lady Cranleigh at the time of the attack, yet she refuses to confirm his story. The more the Doctor tries to explain the strange events he's become involved in, the less people believe him!

Lady Cranleigh is clearly lying for her own reasons. So the Doctor simply decides to reveal his real identity – which is of course stranger than anything he's told the police so far. He tells them he is a time-traveller, and as vital evidence in support of his case, he shows the police the interior of his TARDIS. Amazed at the revelation, they finally accept his story.

If you want someone to trust you, be honest with them about who you are.

21 MAY

JUSTIFY YOUR TITLE

THE MASTER
Kneel. Kneel, or they all die.
Call me by my name.

THE DOCTOR
Master.

THE MASTER
Beg your pardon?

THE DOCTOR
Master.

THE MASTER
Can't hear you, love.

THE DOCTOR
Master.

Spyfall Part Two by Chris Chibnall (2020)

· · · · · ·

Using a title is supposed to convey respect and courtesy for that person's position. The Adjudicator. The Portreeve. The Prime Minister. The Master.

He likes to make people to call him 'Master', through hypnosis or coercion. Although he frequently calls his old adversary 'Doctor', the Doctor very rarely returns the compliment: the Fourth calls him 'Master' in the Pharos project; the Fifth on Castrovalva; the Eighth in his Cloister Room; the Tenth when facing him as prime minister.

By making the Thirteenth Doctor kneel before him and say his name repeatedly, the Master wants to humiliate her in front of everyone in the Royal Gallery of Practical Science. Whereas she knows that's no hurt to her self-esteem if it will save innocent lives.

Whether he's masquerading as a vicar, a mystic, a soldier or the PM, the Master can only establish his authority through deception or by force. Your title is an honorific. You're given them as recognition of your achievements, then you justify them by how you continue to behave.

22 MAY

ALL KNOWLEDGE IS PROVISIONAL

THE DOCTOR
Never throw anything away, Harry. Where's my 500-year
diary? I remember jotting some notes on the Sontarans.
It's a mistake to clutter one's pockets, Harry.

The Sontaran Experiment by Bob Baker and Dave Martin (1975)

• • • • • •

Some 10,000 years in the future, on the barren moors that were once the city of London, Sontaran Field Major Styre conducts horrific experiments on captured humans as part of his military assessment survey.

But just as Styre concludes that humanity can be easily dismissed, his whole data set is rendered worthless by new information. The Doctor strides boldly up to Styre and claims (falsely, but Styre never learns the truth) that the experiments have all been conducted on a lesser order of humans. The Doctor says he himself represents humanity's true warrior class – and challenges Styre to a duel!

Styre loses because, while he's distracted, Harry – a genuine human – sneaks onto the Sontaran spaceship and sabotages some vital equipment so all Styre's energy is drained away leaving little behind but his skin! The rest of the Sontarans decide to use this knowledge… and leave Earth well alone.

Things can change quickly. Be adaptable. Allow new evidence or ideas to change your mind.

23 MAY

MAKE A GOOD EXIT

THE DOCTOR
Ah, yes, thank you. It's good. Keep warm.

The Tenth Planet by Kit Pedler and Gerry Davis (1966)

• • • • • •

The First Doctor's final words to companions Ben and Polly come just after the defeat of the Cybermen at the South Pole in 1986. Ben helps him on with his cloak before they brave the snow to get back to the TARDIS, and even though the weary Doctor seems to be dying, he still shows concern for his young friends.

We now know that out in the snow the First Doctor meets the Twelfth Doctor. The First Doctor's last words in *Twice Upon a Time* (2017) are, 'Here we go: the long way round.' He's responding to something said by his future self: a sign that he's listened and understood.

Then there's *The Three Doctors* (1972–3) and actor William Hartnell's last words as the First Doctor: 'I shudder to think what you'll do without me.' He's brilliant, he knows it – and so do his other selves.

Be like the First Doctor: show concern for others; listen attentively; and make a really good exit.

24 MAY

FEAR DOESN'T HAVE TO BE A WEAKNESS

THE DOCTOR
Courage isn't just a matter of not being frightened, you know.
It's being afraid and doing what you have to do anyway.

Planet of the Daleks by Terry Nation (1973)

• • • • • •

Codal is part of a task force confronting the Daleks. He is captured in the Spiridon jungle while drawing pursuers away from his fellow Thals.

The Doctor finds Codal in a Dalek cell and commends his bravery. Codal dismisses it, saying he didn't think about his actions. He's been terrified ever since landing on the planet. Unlike the others, he's a scientist and not a soldier. He didn't have the courage to be the only one in hundreds not to volunteer for service – even though the Thals have only recently developed space flight for a voyage of this length.

The Doctor's little tutorial on bravery reassures Codal that what he's described, and what he did in the jungle, are certainly examples of courage.

Being afraid of danger and uncertainty is natural, not a failing. Fear isn't a weakness; failing to act because of it is. In any situation, true bravery appears when you're understandably frightened but still choose to do the right thing.

25 MAY

IT'S OK TO BE VULNERABLE

MARTHA JONES

People are dying out there. They need him and I need him.
Because you've got no idea of what he's like. I've only just
met him. It wasn't even that long ago. But he is everything.
He's just everything to me, and he doesn't even look at me
but I don't care, because I love him to bits. And I hope
to God he won't remember me saying this.

The Family of Blood by Paul Cornell (2007)

· · · · · ·

Hiding in human form, the Doctor believes he is John Smith, a school-teacher in 1913. Martha Jones has stayed close to monitor events. Neither of them anticipated that John would fall in love with school matron Joan Redfern.

When his alien pursuers catch up with him, they start to destroy the village to flush him out. He doesn't want to become the Doctor again, because that will be like executing John and abandoning the woman he loves. Martha explains his duty by confessing her own feelings for the Doctor.

Love can be unexpected. You can keep it to yourself, or wear your heart on your sleeve. By exposing your true emotions, you make yourself vulnerable, but it can lead to more profound conversations, deeper love and commitment.

26 MAY

WORK WITH WHAT YOU'VE GOT

THE DOCTOR

I understand your ideals – in many ways I sympathise with them.
But this is not the way to go about it, you know? You've got no
right to take away the existence of generations of people.

CAPTAIN YATES

There's no alternative.

THE DOCTOR

Yes, there is. Take the world that you've got and try
and make something of it. It's not too late.

Invasion of the Dinosaurs by Malcolm Hulke (1974)

• • • • • •

Captain Mike Yates is a brave and loyal officer in UNIT, and a long-
time friend of the Doctor's. So when Yates gets involved in a plot to
create a better world by rewriting history and obliterating most of
humanity, it's a particularly shocking betrayal.

Yet the Doctor tries to reason with his friend. He is sympathetic
to Yates's aims if not the means by which he hopes to achieve them.

Often, the most effective, lasting solution to a problem is not
to try to sweep the whole issue away in a big, dramatic gesture, but
to build on what's there with cooperation and mutual agreement –
perhaps in small increments. Take people with you, rather than leaving
them out completely.

27 MAY

WHO TO TRUST

THE DOCTOR
May I ask why, of all people here, you've come to me?

PRINCESS JOANNA
There's something new in you yet something older
than the sky itself. I sense that I can trust you.

The Crusade by David Whitaker (1965)

• • • • • •

When the TARDIS lands in Palestine in the 1190s, the Doctor and his friends walk straight into the Third Crusade! The Doctor and Vicki befriend King Richard the Lionheart but make enemies amid the intrigues of the English court.

The king's sister, Joanna, must also tread carefully. Although she is Richard's favourite, she feels he's excluding her and suspects it's because he's planning something involving her that she's not going to like. Joanna has only just met the Doctor, and she knows he lied to Richard and the court about Vicki's true identity. But Joanna sees he did this for Vicki's protection, and that he can be trusted. She's right – but that doesn't mean he'll betray the king to help her.

Sometimes we must think carefully before deciding who we can trust. A true friend might not tell us what we want to hear, and they might also have conflicting responsibilities to other people.

28 MAY

SHARING OPINIONS

RIVER SONG

When you love the Doctor, it's like loving the stars themselves.
You don't expect a sunset to admire you back. And if I happen
to find myself in danger, let me tell you, the Doctor is not stupid
enough, or sentimental enough, and he is certainly not in love
enough to find himself standing in it with me!

THE DOCTOR

Hello, sweetie.

The Husbands of River Song by Steven Moffat (2015)

• • • • • •

The staff of the space cruise ship *Harmony and Redemption* are required
to have a verifiable history of indiscriminate slaughter, so it's no
surprise that head waiter Flemming is in league with a tyrannical
cyborg. He's promised the robot the Doctor's head. Flemming has
stolen River Song's diary and knows her history with people like Jim
the Fish (no room to explain here) and her love for the Doctor.

River denies that the Doctor would turn up to rescue her.
Unfortunately, she's overlooked the fact that the stranger assisting on
her current mission is the Doctor himself.

Be careful how you express your opinions about people. They may
hear from others what you said about them. Or they may be in the
room and overhear you.

29 MAY

BEGINNING AT HOME

THE DOCTOR

In all my travellings throughout the universe I have battled against
evil, against power-mad conspirators. I should have stayed here.
The oldest civilisation, decadent, degenerate and rotten to the
core. Power-mad conspirators – Daleks, Sontarans, Cybermen?
They're still in the nursery compared to us. Ten million years of
absolute power, that's what it takes to be really corrupt!

The Trial of a Time Lord Parts Thirteen and Fourteen (aka 'The Ultimate Foe')
by Robert Holmes and Pip and Jane Baker (1986)

• • • • • •

Put on trial by his own people, the Doctor discovers that he's really
an unwitting victim in a much larger criminal conspiracy. A group of
Time Lords are guilty of massively abusing their great powers.

The Doctor long ago ran away from his home planet to battle
evil and fight monsters. But, as he says, he might have done better to
engage with the corruption of his own people. It's often easier to see
from afar the wrongs that others do, while failing to acknowledge or
deal with shortcomings closer to home. You don't have to travel the
universe to make a meaningful difference; you can start where you
are right now.

30 MAY

DUTY TO THE WORLD

THE DOCTOR
My dear Mister Chinn, if I could leave, I would – if only to
get away from people like you ... and your petty obsessions!
'England for the English'? Good heavens, man!

MR CHINN
I have a duty to my country!

THE DOCTOR
Not to the world?

The Claws of Axos by Bob Baker and Dave Martin (1971)

• • • • • •

The Nuton Power Complex in the south-east of England supplies power for the whole of Britain. An alien spaceship landing nearby is a threat to national security but the softly spoken Axons offer humanity the gift of Axonite, a chameleon-like molecule that can provide unlimited food and power.

Greedy Mr Chinn from the Ministry of Defence sees the huge potential of Axonite, but he only cares about how he and his country will benefit, with little thought for the rest of the world. His greed prevents him from heeding the Doctor's warnings...

Much of our identity is shaped by where we're from – our family, home town, country. The Doctor, not being from Earth at all, reminds us that this can be a narrow, parochial view. We're all part of humanity, sharing one, fragile world.

31 MAY

INDIRECT CURES

THE DOCTOR

Throw in the apple cores very hard, put the lot in a shallow tin and bake in a high oven for two weeks. What is it?

MARTHA TYLER

That bain't no way to make a fruitcake!

Image of the Fendahl by Chris Boucher (1977)

* * * * * *

Martha Tyler has lived all her life in a cottage close to a time fissure. The fissure is a weakness in the fabric of space and time, and prolonged exposure to it has given Martha some powers of telepathy and precognition.

When scientists based in the former Fetch Priory conduct experiments on an ancient skull, Martha experiences terrifying visions of giant, slug-like aliens called Fendahleen. The psychic shock is so powerful that neither Martha's grandson John nor the Doctor's friend Leela can get through to her.

But when the Doctor shares a recipe for fruitcake involving peanuts mixed with treacle, it's so nonsensical that Martha suddenly snaps out of her trance-like state and objects! The Doctor's clever, left-field approach is far more effective than trying to force her to speak.

Sometimes the best cure for our woes is to be distracted from them by something daft and fun.

JUNE

1 JUNE

USE THE DOCUMENTATION

SALLY SPARROW
He can hear us. Oh, my God, you can really hear us?

LARRY NIGHTINGALE
Of course he can't hear us. Look...
I've got a transcript, see? Everything he says.
'Yup, that's me.' 'Yes, I do.' 'Yup, and this.' Next it's...

LARRY NIGHTINGALE/THE DOCTOR
'Are you going to read out the whole thing?'

LARRY NIGHTINGALE
Sorry.

Blink by Steven Moffat (2007)

· · · · · ·

Sally Sparrow plays back an Easter Egg video of a man speaking on one of her DVDs. She wants to understand what he means in his half-conversation. Movie buff friend Larry brings a transcript of what the man says that he found online.

It dawns on them that the man's recorded conversation fits what they are now saying. Video man also has a completed transcript. Unwittingly, Larry completes the transcript by writing on his down-loaded copy what he and Sally are saying. It's a breakthrough that ultimately defeats a bunch of Weeping Angels and frees the Doctor and Martha from imprisonment in the past.

You should always rely on the available documentation when you can get it. And make sure it's kept up to date.

2 JUNE

BETTER LATE THAN NEVER

THE DOCTOR
It's never too late, as a wise person once said. Kylie, I think.

The Idiot's Lantern by Mark Gatiss (2006)

• • • • • •

On the morning of Tuesday, 2 June 1953, an alien entity reaches through TV screens to consume the electrical activity of the brains of 27 million people in the UK. They have all tuned in to watch the coronation of Queen Elizabeth II, broadcast live from Westminster Abbey. Now they are food for an alien entity called the Wire.

The Wire was executed by her own people but managed to escaped in the form of electricity and fled across the stars to Earth. She now hopes to create a new physical body for herself by feasting on the combined energy of this huge TV audience.

With so many people already consumed by the Wire, Londoner Tommy Connolly worries that it's too late to stop the creature. But in reply, the Doctor quotes the 1989 song 'Never Too Late' by the famous Australian singer Kylie Minogue. According to the lyrics, it's never too late to change your mind or to admit a mistake.

It's possible the Doctor's being a bit flippant quoting Kylie in a high-stakes situation, but as he's proven time and time again – it's never too late to do the right thing and try to help someone.

3 JUNE

TELL SOMEONE

THE DOCTOR
I'm a Time Lord. I'm the last of the Time Lords.
They're all gone. I'm the only survivor. I'm left
travelling on my own cos there's no one else.

ROSE TYLER
There's me.

The End of the World by Russell T Davies (2005)

• • • • • •

Five billion years in the future, the Doctor and his new friend Rose
Tyler arrive on the Platform One space station to witness the destruction of planet Earth. It's a bit of an overwhelming experience for Rose
– but the Doctor is also brought to tears when friendly tree-person
Jabe from the Forest of Cheam expresses sorrow for his loss after
learning where he comes from.

When Platform One is sabotaged, Jabe sacrifices her life to help the
Doctor save everyone else. He returns Rose to Earth in her own time,
worried that adventures in time and space might be too dangerous
for her. But he also shares with Rose the truth about himself that Jabe
recognised. He is the last of his people, and travelling all by himself.
Except now he has a new friend who takes his arm and, smiling, they
go off together to buy some chips.

Whatever you're suffering, don't bottle it up, tell someone you
trust. (And maybe have chips too!)

4 JUNE

THE RIGHTS STUFF

THE DOCTOR
Aliens Act, 1730. You are a gentlemen of the law?
Then you are doubtless familiar with Article 17.
You cannot hang a citizen of a foreign power,
without first informing his ambassador.

The Highlanders by Elwyn Jones and Gerry Davis (1966–67)

* * * * * *

In Scotland in 1746, Solicitor Grey decides that the Doctor and his friends are in league with Highland rebels and so should be put to death. Thinking quickly, the Doctor claims to be a German physician – Doctor von Wer – and cites a law that should protect him.

In fact, the Doctor is bluffing. There is no Aliens Act 1730, while the British Nationality Act 1730 comprises three rather than seventeen sections (not articles). Though the later Aliens Act 1793 has a Section 17, it's about the issuing of warrants to conduct foreign nationals out of the country.

But Grey doesn't know the law – which is odd for a solicitor. Even odder, he decides to execute the Doctor and his friends anyway, even though that might be breaking the law. It's all evidence that he's rather dodgy…

Don't take it as read that figures in authority know either your rights in law or their responsibilities to you. Make sure you know your rights, and always stand up for them.

5 JUNE

HOLD ON TO SUNSHINE
FOR THE RAINY DAYS

THE DOCTOR
What's the point in them being happy now if they're
going to be sad later? The answer is, of course,
because they are going to be sad later.

The Doctor, the Widow and the Wardrobe by Steven Moffat (2011)

• • • • • •

The Doctor says this to Madge Arwell, who is desperate for her
children Lily and Cyril to have the best Christmas ever – before they
learn the terrible news that their father has died. All Madge wants is for
her children to be happy but she finds herself shouting at them instead.
The Doctor gently explains the turbulent brew of emotions we call grief.

In time, we all lose people dear to us. Sometimes we simply drift
apart or move away; sometimes people die. Grief can smother everything for a while, leaving us upset and angry and numb all at once. It's
awful and exhausting. If you don't understand that already, sadly you
will someday...

But that's all the more reason to cherish what we have. Recognise
the good times as you're having them. Tell the people you love that you
love them. None of us know how long we've got together, so make the
most of it while you can.

6 JUNE

DON'T PUT IT OFF

THE DOCTOR
Things to do, people to see. There's always more.

DORIUM MOLDOVAR
Time catches up with all of us, Doctor.

The Wedding of River Song by Steven Moffat (2011)

* * * * * *

The Doctor will die at a fixed point at Lake Silencio, Utah at 5:02 pm on 22 April 2011. He's in no rush to get there so he spends two centuries avoiding it.

He boasts to Dorium Moldovar of the things he could do: invent a new colour, save the dodo, join the Beatles, help Rose Tyler with her homework, go on all of Jack Harkness's stag parties in one night. Dorium is a wiser head on this occasion, and admonishes him.

The Doctor acknowledges that it's time to end his farewell tour when he learns he cannot visit his old friend the Brigadier, who died peacefully a few months previously.

In theory, the Doctor can go back into the past and visit him in happier times, but the rest of us have no such option. But even he will eventually run out of excuses to put off the inevitable. Big decisions and important actions may be daunting or scary, but don't just avoid them. It may prevent you from making a better-informed, more timely decision.

7 JUNE

KNOWLEDGE IS POWER

THE DOCTOR
If I tell them everything, our usefulness will be ended.

The Web Planet by Bill Strutton (1965)

• • • • • •

The planet Vortis is home to an abundance of different, giant-sized insects. But ant-like Zarbi take the Doctor and Vicki prisoner, demanding information about the moth-like Menoptra. The ongoing conflict between Zarbi and Menoptra is none of the Doctor's business but he's guarded in his answers because he knows his knowledge is of value.

What's more, the Doctor constantly asks questions to increase his sum of knowledge. For example, why did Ian's gold pen fly out of his hand? Is this connected to the mysterious force that dragged the TARDIS off course and now traps it on the planet? And is that force some natural phenomenon or an intelligent, deliberate power? The unexpected answers he receives and the deductions he makes change his sense of what's happening on Vortis. This knowledge helps the Doctor and his friends to survive, and to end the conflict.

We often like to share our knowledge – especially when we think we know best. Try being more guarded, and question what you know. Life is rarely as simple or straightforward as we like to make out...

8 JUNE

COUNSEL OF PERFECTION

RYAN

Here's your present from Peru.

THE DOCTOR

Ryan, will you dissect it for me? You must have
done it at school. Doesn't need to be elegant.

RYAN

Good, cos it won't be.

Praxeus by Pete McTighe and Chris Chibnall (2020)

• • • • • •

The Doctor has assigned all her mates errands. She's checking tide
patterns for survivors of a US submarine disaster near Madagascar. She
sends Yasmin Khan and Graham O'Brien to explore unusual energy
patterns from active alien tech in Hong Kong. And Ryan Sinclair
returns from investigating why birds have gone haywire near a rubbish
dump in Peru.

Ryan meets the Doctor in a bio-lab. When he hands over a dead
bird from his backpack, the Doctor tells him to dissect it. She knows
Ryan's dyspraxia makes it difficult to perform coordinated movements.
But she doesn't say she's worried about that; she just assigns him the
task and reassures him that his efforts will be worth it.

You don't have to be perfect with everything. Sometimes good
enough will do. That's true whether you're trying something yourself,
or asking someone else for help. If you avoid setting unnecessarily high
standards, you can achieve or exceed expectations.

9 JUNE

THE GOOD LIFE

THE DOCTOR
Emotions have their uses.

CYBER LEADER
They restrict and curtail the intellect and logic of the mind

THE DOCTOR
They also enhance life! When did you last have the
pleasure of smelling a flower, watching a sunset,
eating a well-prepared meal? For some people,
small, beautiful events is what life is all about!

Earthshock by Eric Saward (1982)

• • • • • •

On the bridge of a huge space freighter in the year 2526, the leader of
an army of Cybermen debates philosophy with the Doctor. The Cyber
Leader believes that the Doctor's emotions are a great weakness in
someone otherwise so powerful.

As evidence, the Cyber Leader threatens the life of the Doctor's
friend Tegan Jovanka. The Doctor protests, and the Cyber Leader
agrees to let Tegan go, satisfied he now has a way to force the Doctor
to obey him.

In fact, it's *because* the Doctor has friends that he's able to defeat
the Cybermen on this and many other occasions – even when it might
mean that his friends come to harm.

The Doctor believes that it's the emotional bonds between people
and pleasurable experiences in life that give meaning to human existence
– things that emotionless Cybermen could never begin to understand.

10 JUNE

COMBAT GASLIGHTING

BILL POTTS

Let me remember just for a week. Just a week. OK, well, just
for tonight. Just one night. Come on, let me have some good
dreams for once. OK. Do what you've got to do. But imagine,
just imagine how it would feel if someone did this to you.

THE DOCTOR

You can keep your memories.
Now get out before I change my mind!

The Pilot by Steven Moffat (2017)

• • • • • •

The Doctor is disguised as a lecturer, and no one at the university
can know who he really is. New student Bill Potts may be a problem.
She attends his lectures, even though she never enrolled as a student.
Impressed by her attitude, the Doctor offers to be her personal tutor.

Expecting theoretical lectures on quantum physics and poetry,
Bill unexpectedly gets practical lessons on time travel, alien planets,
Daleks and super-intelligent space oil. She persuades the Doctor not to
erase those memories, which she believes are the only exciting things
that have ever happened to her.

When someone tries to persuade you that your memories or
perceptions are wrong or not valid, that's gaslighting. They may not
realise they're doing it, or they may be tricking you. Don't allow
them to belittle or dismiss your personal experience. Your last resort
is to walk away.

11 JUNE

EXTERNAL PERSPECTIVE

OSWIN OSWALD
I'm human.

THE DOCTOR
Not any more. Because you're right – you're a genius.
And the Daleks need genius. They didn't just make
you a puppet. They did a full conversion.

Asylum of the Daleks by Steven Moffat (2012)

• • • • • •

Oswin Oswald, Junior Entertainment Manager of the Starship *Alaska*, has been shipwrecked somewhere. The rest of her crew have been missing for a year. She has provisions, but she's keen to move on.

The Doctor arrives on the same planet to destroy an army of battle-scarred Daleks. Oswin guides him through the labyrinthine complex they are in, using her technical skills and knowledge. She offers to deactivate the forcefield that protects the Daleks from destruction, but only if the Doctor rescues her.

When he locates her, the Doctor discovers that she has imagined her life here. Unknown to Oswin, her captors trapped her on arrival and converted her into a Dalek.

We don't see ourselves as other do. Even our voices sound different to us, and our reflections are reversed. To understand how you affect others, listen when they offer candid, constructive observations about your weaknesses – and your strengths.

12 JUNE

THINK WIN-WIN

BRIGADIER LETHBRIDGE-STEWART
I think You'll find the salary is quite adequate.

THE DOCTOR
Money? My dear chap, I don't want money.
I've got no use for the stuff.

Spearhead from Space by Robert Holmes (1970)

· · · · · ·

Stranded on Earth in the 20th century without the use of the TARDIS, the Doctor offers to work as scientific advisor to army offshoot UNIT. Together they thwart an invasion by the Nestene Consciousness and its terrifying Auton servants, after which the Doctor realises he and the Brigadier haven't even agreed terms.

The Doctor says he doesn't want money but if he's ever to regain control of the TARDIS he needs a laboratory, equipment and the help of Dr Elizabeth Shaw. Then there are the fancy clothes he's taken a shine to, and he'd also like his own car — all of which must be paid for.

The important thing is that the deal struck between the Doctor and the Brigadier is of benefit to them both — a win-win situation. Some people seem to think deal-making is a kind of battle that you try to 'win' against the other person, but aiming for mutual benefit means the deal will last. In the case of the Doctor and the Brigadier, it is the foundation of their long and deep friendship.

13 JUNE

BREAKDOWN COVER

THE DOCTOR
Normally this door is power operated. We'll have
to work it by hand. Where's that crank handle?

Death to the Daleks by Terry Nation (1974)

● ● ● ● ● ●

The gleaming, technologically sophisticated city of the Exxilons must be one of the 700 wonders of the universe. The way it is powered is particularly ingenious: a high beacon drains electrical energy from the very atmosphere itself.

Unfortunately, this also means it drains energy from any passing spacecraft and electrical equipment, including the TARDIS. The Doctor's ship is a living thing containing thousands of instruments. Its energy sources never stop – and yet on Exxilon, they suddenly fade to silence, the lights all going out. When the Doctor turns on a torch, even the energy from that is drained away too.

The more complex and advanced a machine or device, the more there is that can potentially go wrong. The Doctor keeps a crank handle ready for emergencies. You might not have a TARDIS but in your daily life you'll come across all sorts of electronic devices. What would you do if they suddenly stopped working? Have a think about how you could prepare for a breakdown.

14 JUNE

PROVIDE SPECIFIC PRAISE

THE DOCTOR

You've built this system out of food and string and staples?
Professor Yana, you're a genius.

PROFESSOR YANA

Says the man who made it work.

THE DOCTOR

Oh, it's easy coming in at the end, but you're stellar.
This is magnificent. And I don't often say that
because, well, because of me.

Utopia by Russell T Davies (2007)

• • • • • •

Malcassairo is the last outpost of humanity, one hundred trillion years in the future. Professor Yana has a plan to transport the surviving humans to Utopia.

Yana respects the Doctor's opinion and is excited to meet another scientist. But he's modest about his own achievements – even the affectation of his title when universities haven't existed for over a thousand years.

Nevertheless, the Doctor praises Yana's ingenious techniques in assembling the equipment. That's a big thing for this particular Doctor, who is more often ready to pat himself on the back.

Look for opportunities to praise people genuinely with specific examples. It shows you're attentive, boosts their confidence, and builds relationships. And it's really most unlikely that the person you're complimenting will turn out to be the Master in disguise.

15 JUNE

DON'T JUMP IN

THE DOCTOR
I'm still quite socially awkward, so I'm just going
to subtly walk towards the console and look at
something. And then, in a minute, I'll think of something
that I should've said that might've been helpful.

GRAHAM O'BRIEN
OK. Well, I'm glad we had this chat, eh?

Can You Hear Me? by Charlene James and Chris Chibnall (2020)

• • • • • •

The immortal Zellin provokes fear to extract nightmares from the scared and vulnerable. The Doctor tells him humans are stronger for facing down their fears, doubts and guilt.

The fam have different reactions to their induced nightmares. Ryan Sinclair persuades his best mate Tibo to get counselling for his anxiety. Yasmin Khan recognises that the advice she was unwilling to accept three years ago from police officer Anita is something that she now wants to acknowledge.

Since his wife's death, Graham O'Brien needs someone to talk to about his constant fear that his cancer will return. Despite teasing the Doctor that her motivational speech needs work, he still chooses to confide in her. The Doctor admits she finds it hard to reassure him, which Graham accepts.

People may want to talk when they're worried. You won't always have immediate solutions to offer them. Start by listening and thinking. It's never too late to find the right thing to say.

16 JUNE

STRENGTH IN NUMBERS

VEET
What will we do with two guns against all those guards?

THE DOCTOR
You can't do anything, but there are 50 million people in this city.
Think how the guards will react to that number!

The Sun Makers by Robert Holmes (1977)

• • • • • •

The citizens of Pluto have miserable lives. They're overtaxed, over-burdened by a ruthless bureaucracy and forced to breathe air laced with green, anxiety-inducing pentocyleinic-methyl-hydrane (PCM) gas.

When the Doctor and Leela encourage these poor people to rise up against their oppressors, a young woman called Veet quite reasonably asks how they can take on so many armed and deadly guards. But on a world governed by cold economics, the answer all comes down to the numbers. If the people are united, the guards can't withstand them all.

It's much easier to accomplish something if you can find people of like mind to join you in the endeavour. You can encourage and support one another. The more of you there are, the more chance you have to overcome obstacles in your way. And then, together you can enjoy the rewards that come from getting the job done.

17 JUNE

GOOD SAMARITAN

THE DOCTOR
Why are you here?

BILL POTTS
Because I figured out why you keep your box as a phone box.
'Advice and Assistance Obtainable Immediately.' You like that.
You don't call the helpline because you *are* the helpline.

Smile by Frank Cottrell-Boyce (2017)

· · · · · ·

The Doctor and Bill Potts escape the United Earth Colony Ship *Erehwon* around which microbot lifeform the Vardy built a city. The whole thing is a living death trap that awaits an unwitting colony ship en route to the planet. The Doctor plans to return and destroy the place – though he tells Bill to remain safely in the TARDIS.

So he is surprised when Bill reappears alongside him in the city. She's looked at the sign outside the TARDIS and realised what it really means. The Doctor may claim he's just mucking in because he was passing by, but Bill knows he's never passed by in his life – including when he found her at the university.

Compassionate and helpful people don't walk away when others are in need. So long as it's safe to do so, you can help them, even if you are not the official authorities.

18 JUNE

BETTER WITH FRIENDS

ROSE TYLER
You were useless in there.
You'd be dead if it wasn't for me.

THE DOCTOR
Yes, I would. Thank you.

Rose by Russell T Davies (2005)

* * * * * *

In 2005, the Nestene Consciousness invades Earth with living plastic creatures called Autons. To stop the Consciousness, the Doctor must track down the transmitter that it's relying on to boost its control signal. The Doctor knows the transmitter must be a huge, metal, dish-like structure – but where to start?

Luckily for him, he's just met Rose Tyler who points out the 135-metre-tall London Eye standing right behind him. Beneath this enormous Ferris wheel, they find the vicious, raging Consciousness. When the Doctor is captured by Autons, Rose helps by knocking the Doctor's phial of anti-plastic into the lair of the Nestene invader, bringing its terrifying invasion to an abrupt end.

The Doctor gratefully acknowledges that Rose saved him – and the whole world. No wonder he offers to take her with him in the TARDIS to see the universe.

Be like the Doctor: recognise other people's contributions to your achievements, always give them credit and reward them where you can. Besides, adventures are much better when they're shared with others.

19 JUNE

CHALLENGE CONVENTION

THE DOCTOR
Right, phase two sorted. Now for phase one.

AMY POND
Oh no, phase two comes after phase one.

THE DOCTOR
Humans, you are so linear.

Dinosaurs on a Spaceship by Chris Chibnall (2012)

• • • • • •

The Doctor does something different to solve the mystery of a Silurian Ark approaching the Earth in 2367 CE: he puts together a gang.

He casually scoops up Rory Williams and Amy Pond from home to accompany Egyptian Queen Nefertiti and big game hunter John Riddell, and kidnaps Rory's domesticated dad Brian in the process.

Steering the Ark away from approaching Earth missiles, the Doctor's unconventional method doesn't do things in order. His friends take this approach to heart. Brian decides to travels the world. And instead of returning to 1334 BCE, Nefertiti joins Riddell in the early 20th century.

The more often you do certain tasks, the more you get set in your ways. That's OK for some things – you don't want to work out how to pedal every time you cycle to the shops. But maybe there's a new shop down the street and you can walk to it instead. Challenge how you've always done things, and your experience may be better.

20 JUNE

PEOPLE ARE SURPRISING

VICKI

I realise you're a man of many talents, Doctor,
but I didn't know fighting was one of them.

THE DOCTOR

My dear, I am one of the best. Do you know it was I that
used to teach the Mountain Mauler of Montana?

The Romans by Dennis Spooner (1965)

• • • • • •

Appearances can be deceptive. The First Doctor looks elderly but is actually younger than any of the later, more youthful-looking incarnations. He seems forgetful and erratic yet has a brilliant mind for solving problems. Then there's his career as a wrestler.

Other incarnations are adept at Venusian aikido or grapple with enemies including Kraals and Cybermen. The First Doctor fights as well – knocking out the unpleasant man running a gang of road-builders in revolutionary France, or thrashing his walking stick at invisible Visians on the planet Mira. But the idea of him as wrestling and training wrestlers, presumably while wearing a leotard... It boggles the mind!

There are things you've done, things you know, that would surprise even people who know you well. That's true of other people. Life is richer for it. So, today, find out something new and surprising about somebody you know.

21 JUNE

TAKE THE CHANCE

THE DOCTOR
I can't fix myself, to anything. Anywhere. Or anyone.
I've never been able to. It's what my life is. Not because
I don't want to. Because I might. But if I do fix myself
to somebody, I know sooner or later it'll hurt.

Legend of the Sea Devils by Chris Chibnall (2022)

. . . . . .

Dan Lewis plucks up courage to leave a phone message for Diane, who he's growing closer to. She returns the call to ask if they can meet soon.

Yasmin Khan has confessed her love for the Doctor. The Doctor hesitantly says she cannot make a commitment to Yaz. She wishes things could last forever, but she learned recently that her time is heading to its end.

The Doctor asks if they can just live in the present, while they still have it. Yaz doesn't really want to do what's being asked of her, and wishes the Doctor had the courage to know that something will hurt, and do it anyway. But Yaz doesn't want to lose what they have already.

If you have feelings for someone, it's natural to worry about their reaction. Perhaps they will reciprocate, perhaps not. Overcome your embarrassment, because you'll never know if you don't ask.

22 JUNE

YOU CAN'T GO BACK

THE DOCTOR
Now listen to me, both of you. There are some rules
that cannot be broken, even with the TARDIS.

Time Flight by Peter Grimwade (1982)

• • • • • •

The Doctor and his companions are distraught when their close friend Adric is killed on board an exploding space freighter. Tegan crossly suggests that the Doctor could do more than grieve; he could use the TARDIS to go back in time and change what happened, enabling them to save their friend.

It's a tantalising idea. Who wouldn't want to save the life of a close friend? And why stop there – because *no one* need be lost. Every battle could be won, every moment finessed… You could keep amending and editing history until it was perfect.

But there would never be any freedom or choice. History would be *imposed* on the people who lived it.

On some occasions, the Doctor *can* change history. But there are good reasons why this is the exception rather than the rule. It would be a terrifying abuse of power.

What's more, as the Doctor tells his companions, their late friend's life wasn't wasted because he chose to try to help others. You can make the same choice.

23 JUNE

POWER AND RESPONSIBILITY

THE DOCTOR
True, I am guilty of interference – just as you are guilty of
failing to use your great powers to help those in need.

The War Games by Terrance Dicks and Malcolm Hulke (1969)

• • • • • •

The Doctor stands trial, accused of repeatedly breaking the most important law of the Time Lords: that of non-interference in the affairs of other planets. It's a fair cop, but instead of feeling guilty, the Doctor is *proud* of his meddling.

As evidence in his defence, he presents clips of Quarks, Yeti, Ice Warriors, Cybermen and Daleks, and says it would be wrong *not* to battle such evils – a criticism he levels at the Time Lords who are judging him.

It's a compelling idea: those with power and authority have a moral obligation to stand up for what's right and to fight against what's wrong. Even the Time Lords have to admit the persuasiveness of the Doctor's case and they duly dispatch him to Earth in time to deal with multiple crises.

You don't need to be powerful to fight for what's right. Sometimes, speaking up for what's right can persuade other people with more authority to take action.

24 JUNE

RESPECT PEOPLE'S CHOICES

THE PREACHER
He's called Joshua. It's from the Bible. It means the Deliverer.

THE DOCTOR
No, he isn't. I speak horse. He's called Susan,
and he wants you to respect his life choices.

A Town Called Mercy by Toby Whithouse (2012)

• • • • • •

The Doctor encounters different alien races across the universe and throughout time who speak a wide variety of languages. Fortunately for the Doctor (and for us) there's help at hand.

The Ninth Doctor tells Rose that there's a telepathic field that gets inside her brain as a gift of the TARDIS. The Fourth Doctor tells Sarah Jane it's a Time Lord's gift that he allows her to share.

The Eleventh Doctor has a particular talent with languages. He understands babies babbling, and how they choose to name themselves – such as Stormageddon, Dark Lord of All, rather than Alfie. And when cadging a ride in a town called Mercy, he can understand what the horse is saying.

We may have been assigned our names at birth, but we can also make our own choices when we know who we are. It's something that others should respect. If you're not sure how someone wants to be identified, ask them. Get it from the horse's mouth.

25 JUNE

CONTROL YOUR RESPONSE

THE MASTER
I like it when you use my name.

THE DOCTOR
You chose it. Psychiatrist's field day.

THE MASTER
As you chose yours. The man who makes people better.
How sanctimonious is that?

THE DOCTOR
So, Prime Minister, then.

The Sound of Drums by Russell T Davies (2007)

• • • • • •

It's natural to feel anxious or angry when people mock you, no matter whether they know you well or they are strangers. When they even ridicule your name, it's a very personal affront.

After tracking him from the end of the universe at Malcassairo all the way back to Earth, the Doctor phones the Master to ask how he became prime minister, Harold Saxon. The Master avoids answering the question by impugning the Doctor's personal motivations.

The Doctor overcomes the desire to argue, declines to take the bait and successfully returns to the purpose of his call. He avoids accepting the terms that the Master wants to debate on and moves onto a subject he will always talk about – himself!

You can't control haters; you can only control your response. Let them waste their time thinking about you, and don't waste your energy thinking about them.

26 JUNE

DIVIDED WE FAIL

MELANIE BUSH

She might think she's harnessed the brain of a Time Lord but she's reckoned without one thing... The Doctor's character!

Time and the Rani by Pip and Jane Baker (1987)

* * * * * *

The evil Rani is plotting to turn the planet Lakertya into a time manipulator, enabling her to rewrite the whole of creation. To achieve her aim, she needs to make some very complex calculations which are beyond the scope of any single genius.

So, the Rani kidnaps a dozen of the most brilliant and creative minds from history and wires them into a single, gestalt brain. These geniuses include Egyptian astronomer and mathematician Hypatia (c. 360–415 CE), French chemist and microbiologist Louis Pasteur (1822–95), German theoretical physicist Albert Einstein (1879–1955) and the Doctor, who can add to the mix a unique conceptual understanding of the properties of time.

Yet rather than adding to the overall gestalt intelligence, the Doctor instead causes chaos by talking nonsense. His puns and bad jokes cause so much confusion that the Rani is forced to disconnect him from the brain before he does permanent damage.

Don't just impose a task; make sure team members understand and buy into what you're trying to achieve.

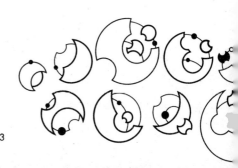

27 JUNE

ASK WHY

IDAS
It's forbidden.

THE DOCTOR
Why?

Underworld by Bob Baker and Dave Martin (1978)

· · · · · ·

Having travelled through a spiral nebula, a spaceship called the *P7E* found itself surrounded by countless small rocks which were attracted to its mass. The more rocks clustered round the ship, the more massive it became. Eventually, a new planet was formed, with the *P7E* at its core.

The descendants of the crew endured a difficult life in the dark honeycomb of tunnels within this strange planet. The majority, known as Trogs, had to dig away at the rock to gain food and sustenance. They were overseen by cruel guards who were in turn controlled by a callous computer called the Oracle.

Later, when the Doctor and Leela arrive, they are horrified by these conditions and want to confront the authorities. It has never occurred to a young Trog called Idas to question the way things are. But prompted by the Doctor he is soon leading a rebellion.

Things don't always have to be the way they are. Asking questions about the way we do things is the first step to doing them better.

194

28 JUNE

POSITIVE OUTLOOK

THE DOCTOR
I have a time machine. I can be back before we left.

BILL POTTS
But what if you get lost, or stuck, or something?

THE DOCTOR
I've thought about that.

BILL POTTS
And?

THE DOCTOR
Well, it would be a worry, so best not to dwell on it.
Look at this building. Look at it. You know what I like
about humanity? Its optimism. Do you know what
this building is made of? Pure, soaring optimism.

Smile by Frank Cottrell-Boyce (2017)

• • • • • •

The Doctor tells Bill Potts that a journey back to his office in the TARDIS for a cup of tea can encompass everything that ever happened or will happen – all before the kettle boils. Where would she like to go?

He dismisses Bill's worry that something could prevent them returning, instead pointing out the beauty and wonder of the futuristic colony city in which they have just arrived.

You'll enjoy life more by assuming a positive outlook. Take sensible precautions, but don't let fear of a worst-case scenario spoil your enjoyment of the moment.

29 JUNE

DON'T TEMPT FATE

PROFESSOR ZAROFF
Nothing in the world can stop me now!

The Underwater Menace by Geoffrey Orme (1967)

• • • • • •

Professor Hans Zaroff deserves a certain level of respect. He led the field in producing food from the sea before his apparent death sometime around the year 2050. In fact, he went into hiding in the underwater city of Atlantis where he pioneered extraordinary scientific projects: turning people into fish and plotting to blow up the world.

Extraordinary, yes. A good idea? Not really.

Zaroff was determined and ruthless. When the Doctor asked challenging questions, he faced being fed to Zaroff's pet octopus. But the Doctor was right to query the logic and practicalities of Zaroff's plan... If only the professor had listened, he might not have drowned.

Self belief is important in order to get things done, but don't let it blind you to your own faults. A bit of humility and openness to questions will lower the chances of you making mistakes.

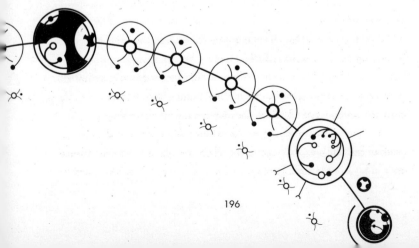

30 JUNE

FIND YOUR OWN VOICE

THE DOCTOR
It's called the TARDIS. It can travel anywhere
in time and space. And it's mine.

CLARA OSWALD
But it's... Look at it, it's...

THE DOCTOR
Go on, say it. Most people do.

CLARA OSWALD
...smaller on the outside!

THE DOCTOR
OK. That is a first.

The Snowmen by Steven Moffat (2012)

• • • • • •

Nothing seems to faze Victorian barmaid Clara Oswin Oswald. Telepathic snow. A potato-headed alien with a memory worm. A woman made of ice.

The Doctor and Clara flee Dr Simeon and his snowmen to the roof, pursued by the ice woman. At the top of a spiral staircase is a police box, floating on a cloud. Clara originally chased the Doctor down in his horse-drawn cab, and now she is seeing his real home. The Doctor expects a familiar response, but Clara has her own unique take on things.

We don't have to repeat received wisdom. There's a pleasure in avoiding the obvious, and enjoyment when you see and describe things anew in your own terms. Find your own unique way to express yourself.

JULY

1 JULY

WRONGS FOR RIGHT REASONS

THE DOCTOR
You know Barbara was frightened – frightened for
your safety. She thought you were going to be hurt.

The Rescue by David Whitaker (1965)

• • • • • •

Poor Vicki. Her mother died and her father decided to leave everything they knew on Earth for a new life on another world. Vicki was happy to go with him – but their space rocket crashed on the planet Dido. There, most of the survivors were killed in mysterious circumstances leaving only Vicki and a wounded man called Bennett still alive.

But Vicki made the best of things, befriending a gentle, vegetarian sand beast – until the Doctor's friend Barbara shot it dead! It was a terrible mistake and Vicki was distraught. But the Doctor took the time to talk to her gently. Barbara acknowledged what she did was wrong, but she'd done it for the right reasons.

Sometimes, a person who annoys or hurts us doesn't mean to – they might even think that they're helping! Understanding that might take away some of the sting of what they've done. (It also helps if they say sorry!)

2 JULY

BE A QUEEN

QUEEN THALIRA
It would be different if I was a man. But I'm only a girl.

SARAH JANE SMITH
Now just a minute. There's nothing 'only' about being a girl,
Your Majesty. Never mind why they made you a queen, the fact
is you *are* the queen, so just you jolly well let them know it.

The Monster of Peladon by Brian Hayles (1974)

• • • • • •

The young, new queen of planet Peladon is faced with multiple crises
– as well as a number of old men who won't listen to her counsel. The
Doctor tries to negotiate between the various factions, but it's plucky
reporter Sarah Jane Smith who gets Thalira to stand up for herself
and take charge.

It's striking that even a queen can feel herself to be powerless, but
Sarah Jane helps Thalira to be more assertive in how she speaks and
stands – and it works. Soon, the queen is using her privileged position
to help those of her subjects who truly lack power.

When it matters, make yourself heard. Follow Thalira's example
for extra self-confidence: try wearing something formal, stand up
when you're speaking, and speak calmly but directly.

3 JULY

TIME TO MOVE ON

MARTHA JONES
Spent all these years training to be a doctor. Now I've got
people to look after. They saw half the planet slaughtered
and they're devastated. I can't leave them.

THE DOCTOR
Of course not. Thank you. Martha Jones,
you saved the world.

Last of the Time Lords by Russell T Davies (2007)

• • • • • •

The Doctor is full of ideas for what he and Martha can go and do
next. Starfire over the coast of Meta Sigma Folio, perhaps, where
the sky is like oil on water. Maybe visit Charles II or Henry VIII or
Agatha Christie.

Martha has other plans. She's spent a lot of time with the Doctor
thinking she was second best. Now she realises she has abilities
and opportunities of her own. She leaves behind a mobile phone so
the Doctor can keep in touch. But he's going to have to visit those
luminaries with someone else.

Breaking ties doesn't have to mean abandoning things. There
is no need to regret what you might have had if you take a positive
step towards plans of your own. You'll know when it's time to move
on from a place, a job or a relationship. Listen to your feelings and
trust yourself.

4 JULY

SHOW YOUR INDEPENDENCE

THE DOCTOR
Don't despair, Kate. Your dad never did. Kate Stewart,
heading up UNIT, changing the way they work.
How could you not be? Why did you drop Lethbridge?

KATE STEWART
I didn't want any favours. Though he guided me,
even to the end. Science leads, he always told me.
Said he'd learned that from an old friend.

The Power of Three by Chris Chibnall (2012)

• • • • • •

A 'nepo baby' is someone who gets a career boost from their parents' fame. Does nepotism help would-be actors, journalists, politicians, writers... civil servants?

Kate Stewart is slightly surprised that the Doctor makes the connection after she ropes him in to investigate the slow invasion of Earth by Shakri cubes. Her father was Alistair Gordon Lethbridge-Stewart of UNIT, for whom the Doctor was once Scientific Advisor.

She's established her credentials as Chief Scientific Officer at the same organisation. Kate has been determined to earn it, though she benefited from her father's guidance even after his retirement.

You can't choose your parents. And it's not unusual to join a profession where your relatives are everyday role models. They shouldn't guarantee you a job, but don't be reluctant to seek their advice – so long as you demonstrate your independent credentials.

5 JULY

HOW NOT TO BE SEEN

THE DOCTOR

If you wanted to hide a tree, where would you hide it? In a forest.

The Invasion of Time by David Agnew (1978)

• • • • • •

On returning home to Gallifrey, the Doctor acts very oddly, seizing power as Lord President, being rude to his old teacher Cardinal Borusa and banishing his friend Leela to the austere wasteland outside the Capitol.

In fact, the Doctor is engaged in a brilliant, complicated plan to outwit an invasion of the planet by psychic beings called Vardans who can read his mind. But then there's a second set of invaders – old foes of the Doctor who have arrived in startling numbers.

To vanquish these enemies, the Doctor needs a special weapon which uses the Great Key of Rassilon as a component – an object imbued with fearsome power. Borusa denies having any such item, even though he has a huge assortment of keys in his office...

Just as the Doctor's erratic behaviour hides his true intentions from the Vardans, Borusa's collection of keys hides the genuine article.

Often, achieving a task or finding something hidden is just a matter of not letting yourself be distracted.

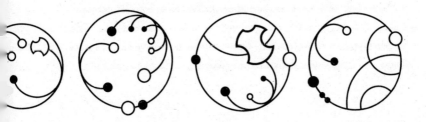

6 JULY

STAY SECURE ONLINE

THE DOCTOR
The security is absolute.

CLARA OSWALD
It's never about the security. It's about the people.

The Bells of Saint John by Steven Moffat (2013)

• • • • • •

Strong unique password. Two-step verification. Antivirus software. Firewall. Staying secure in an online world seems to be full of confusing terminology and technology.

Rescued by the Doctor from being uploaded to a database, Clara Oswald has computing stuff in her head she didn't know before. The Doctor may be from space and the future with two hearts, but her recent experience has endowed Clara with insane hacking skills.

People make it so easy for her to crack their online security because of the sloppy way they share their personal information online. They base their passwords and verification on pet names, hobbies, birthdays, holiday destinations – but then openly tell anyone what those are in what they post on Instagram and TikTok and Twitter.

Don't be the weak link in your own online security. Don't use *password123* or your car registration. Invent something for 'mother's maiden name'. Make your passwords and security questions unique and unguessable. And if that unsolicited offer in an email looks too good to be true, it probably is.

7 JULY

LEADERSHIP DECISIONS

THE DOCTOR
It's not just his life at stake, it's yours. You wanna sacrifice
yourself for this? You want me to sacrifice you? You wanna
call it, do it now! All of you. Yeah. Cos sometimes this
team structure isn't flat. It's mountainous. With me at the
summit, in the stratosphere. Alone. Left to choose.

The Haunting of Villa Diodati by Maxine Alderton (2020)

· · · · · ·

The Doctor likes to involve her team in decisions. She has high expectations and gets the best from them. But there are times when even
the Doctor can't win.

She detects the Cyberium, a super-computer, fused to the cerebral
cortex of poet Percy Bysshe Shelley. It's killing him, and only Ashad,
the lone Cyberman, can remove it to save him. The Doctor's friends
tell her not to surrender the Cyberium. It contains the knowledge and
future history of all Cybermen. Armies will rise and billions will die.

Save the poet or save the universe? The Doctor angrily points out
this isn't a debate: it must be her judgement.

Leaders take difficult actions when there is no perfect solution.
Decisions can't always be reached by consensus, and that may not make
them popular. Speak candidly, explain your choice and move boldly.

8 JULY

ONLY CONNECT

THE DOCTOR
You can't expect him to behave normally.
We don't know how long he's been down here.
Talk to him about the things that he might remember.

The Space Pirates by Robert Holmes (1969)

. . . . . .

The vast mining corporation on the planet Ta was founded by Dom Issigri, who disappeared in mysterious circumstances. Then the Doctor and his friends find the old man imprisoned in his own study, deep below the planet's surface.

Dom has been held prisoner for so long, and left in such a state of terror, that even his friend Milo Clancy can't get through to him. The Doctor advises Milo to speak of the good times the two men shared. Milo does so, at first talking about his own beloved spaceship, the *LIZ-79*, and the races he and Dom used to enjoy.

But only when Milo mentions Dom's daughter Madeleine does the old man respond. That emotional connection, that deep well of love, breaks through the many years of fear Dom has endured, and he at last recognises his friend.

You can make a connection, even with people you don't know, by asking them about what they love – their children (if they have them), their hopes and aspirations... even their favourite song.

9 JULY

DO THE LEGWORK

NYSSA
What now?

THE DOCTOR
No other choice: we must check every hostel on foot.

Arc of Infinity by Johnny Byrne (1983)

• • • • • •

The Doctor's friend Tegan Jovanka travels to Amsterdam to meet her cousin, Colin Frazer – only to discover he's disappeared. Tegan checks into one of the Jeugdherberg Central (JHC) youth hostels and then sets out to find him, but after a long search both she and Colin end up imprisoned in a crypt by Omega, a notorious stellar engineer from Time Lord history.

Omega lets the Doctor know that Tegan is his prisoner, but Tegan manages to tell the Doctor she is in Amsterdam and say 'JHC.'

Arriving in Amsterdam, the Doctor and his friend Nyssa learn there are several JHC hostels – but they can't use the TARDIS to narrow down the search for Tegan without revealing to Omega that they're on his trail. There's nothing else for it but to run around Amsterdam on foot, ticking off possible hostels as they go.

Sometimes, there's no clever shortcuts if you want a job done properly. You just have to take a deep breath and put in the time, effort – and legwork!

10 JULY

SECOND OPINIONS

MR COPPER
Human beings worship the great god Santa, a creature with
fearsome claws, and his wife Mary. And every Christmas Eve,
the people of UK go to war with the country of Turkey. They
then eat the Turkey people for Christmas dinner like savages.

THE DOCTOR
Excuse me. Sorry, sorry, but, er, where
did you get all this from?

Voyage of the Damned by Russell T Davies (2007)

* * * * * *

It's useful to have an expert on hand. Physicist Professor Brian Cox and businessman Lord Sugar have opinions on the Shakri cubes. Astronomer Sir Patrick Moore dials in to a conference call during the Prisoner Zero crisis. When the Doctor first meets Liz Shaw, he tells her he's a doctor of 'practically everything'.

Starship *Titanic* is on a cruise from the planet Sto in the Cassavalian Belt. Passengers want to experience primitive cultures. Unfortunately, their tour guide is historian Mr Copper, who plans a trip for them to old London town in the country of UK, ruled over by good King Wenceslas.

The Doctor learns that Mr Copper got his first-class degree in Earthonomics from Mrs Golightly's Happy Travelling University and Dry Cleaners. It's always worth considering whether people you rely on for important advice really do have the necessary credentials – and seek a second opinion if they do not.

11 JULY

UNITED WE STAND

THE DOCTOR

Oh, the Great Architect must be delighted. How are we going
to unite the people of Paradise Towers to defeat him?

Paradise Towers by Stephen Wyatt (1987)

• • • • • •

Paradise Towers is an architectural marvel of the 21st century: 304 floors of flats and apartments with a swimming pool right at the top. But its brilliant architect, Kroagnon, doesn't like people actually living in his buildings and, in his eyes, spoiling them. The residents rebel, and Kroagnon is trapped deep inside his own building.

A generation later, Paradise Towers is in a parlous state, with rival gangs of feral young girls called Kangs, aggressively officious Caretakers, plus the elderly carnivorous Rezzies who try to eat anyone they can catch. But so divided are the occupants of Paradise Towers, they hardly notice the robot cleaners are going round killing people.

The Doctor and Mel bring these disparate groups together and give them common purpose, building a new sense of community. Whatever our differences, if we stand united we have a better chance of confronting injustice and changing things for the better.

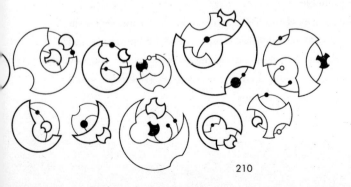

12 JULY

BE DECISIVE

BILL POTTS
Every choice I make in this moment,
here and now, could change the whole future.

THE DOCTOR
Exactly like every other day of your life.
The only thing to do is to stop worrying about it.

Thin Ice by Sarah Dollard (2017)

• • • • • •

What are the rules for time travel? Bill Potts is new to this kind of thing. She's chosen the right clothes for this trip to icy London in the early 19th century. But what are the right behaviours?

She's heard about the butterfly effect theory, where the movement of an insect's wing starts a sequence of air movements that build and grow and eventually create a typhoon. She worries whether some small change she makes in the past could have knock-on effects that means subsequently she is never born. The Doctor teases her that's what happened to Pete, who is no longer with them.

It's impossible to know how every tiny change affects large complex systems like atmospheric circulation. It's equally impossible to determine the likely outcome of every small thing you ever do. If you can't predict something in everyday life, there's no need to fret about it. Don't be frozen by indecision.

13 JULY

YOU'RE SWEET ENOUGH

THE DOCTOR
That's why the disease doesn't affect everyone.
It's the sugar. Not everyone takes it.

The Moonbase by Kit Pedler (1967)

. . . . . .

In the year 2070, the weather station on the Moon is in crisis. One by one, its crew are succumbing to an overwhelming, mystery disease – and then they disappear from the base. The Doctor applies himself to the problem and undertakes a series of careful, scientific tests. Baffled, he stops for coffee... and inspiration strikes.

It turns out that the Cybermen have poisoned the sugar to weaken the crew prior to a full-scale attack. They've then stolen off with the sick. This is a particularly cunning plot for the emotionless Cybermen, preying on a human weakness for sweetness that they can no longer enjoy themselves.

Of course we all need our comforts in life, but if the crew of the Moonbase had been a little more health conscious, this ploy would never have worked. Cutting down your intake of sugar is good for your health – and might even help to thwart the Cybermen, too!

14 JULY

GIVE IT A TRY

THE DOCTOR
A frequency-modulated acoustic lock. The key
changes ten million zillion squillion times a second.

CLARA OSWALD
Can you open it?

THE DOCTOR
Technically, no. In reality, also no.
But still, let's give it a stab.

The Rings of Akhaten by Neil Cross (2013)

• • • • • •

The Doctor and Clara Oswald face a door they cannot open. It's the way into the temple within the Pyramid of the Rings of Akhaten, a holy site for the Sun-singers of Akhet. Behind it is Merry Gejelh, Queen of Souls. The young girl was snatched from them and taken into the temple as a sacrifice and they're determined to save her.

The Doctor isn't sure they can reach the sacrifice. His attempt to shoulder-charge the door only hurts him. Eventually, his sonic screwdriver locks on to the acoustic tumblers and he is able, with great physical effort, to raise the immensely heavy door.

Even when the situation seems impossible, it's worth making an attempt. You may succeed against the odds. Whereas you have one hundred percent failure on every time you don't try. Even if we don't succeed at first, failure is how we learn.

15 JULY

COMMIT TO YOURSELF

DAN LEWIS
All this is amazing, and I've had the most incredible time. But it's not my life. And my life's far from perfect, but I need to get back to it. I need to attack it. And I can now. Cos I've been with you.

THE DOCTOR
I get it. Life's important. Home's important.

The Power of the Doctor by Chris Chibnall (2022)

. . . . . .

Instead of going out on the town with his girlfriend Diane, Dan Lewis is out in space. He helps the Doctor and Yasmin Khan defeat an attack on a Toraji Transport Network bullet train. In the struggle, his helmet visor is cracked and Yaz saves him.

The Doctor drops him off in Liverpool, and Dan reaches a decision: she doesn't have to come back for him. He has a life that he should be living here on Earth. He would have been gutted to float off into space and never get his second chance with Diane.

Doing things you enjoy brings you pleasure. Staying interested in what you do and who you're with keeps you engaged. Feeling that what you do matters ensures you have meaning in your life. So set out boldly on your own when the time feels right.

16 JULY

USE THE TIME YOU'VE GOT

THE DOCTOR
Four minutes? That's ages! What if I get bored. I need a
television, couple of books. Anyone for chess? Bring me knitting!

The Night of the Doctor by Steven Moffat (2013)

• • • • • •

The Doctor comes to the rescue of a young woman called Cass on a gunship racing out of control through space. Unfortunately, Cass wants nothing to do with any Time Lord – she thinks they're no different from Daleks now, in the midst of the raging Time War.

After the Doctor is unable to persuade her that he only wants to help, the ship smashes down on to the surface of the planet Karn. Cass is fatally injured in the crash. So is the Doctor.

Yet the infamous Sisterhood of Karn use their Elixir of Life to restore him for a brief time. Anyone else would surely be horrified to learn they have just four minutes to live. The Doctor, however, immediately thinks of all the fun things he can cram into that time.

In fact, this is a central idea in the philosophy of Stoicism, which flourished among the ancient Greeks and Romans. One Roman Emperor, Marcus Aurelius, put it like this in his famous book, *Meditations*:

'Don't act as if you were going to live ten thousand years. Death hangs over you. While you live, while it is in your power, be good.'

215

17 JULY

RESPECT AND MERCY

THE DOCTOR

Five thousand years ago Mars was the centre of a vast empire. The jewel of this solar system. The people of Earth had only just begun to leave their caves. Five thousand years isn't such a long time. They're still just frightened children, still primitive. Who are you to judge?

SKALDAK

I am Skaldak! This planet is forfeit under Martian law.

THE DOCTOR

Then teach them. Teach them, Grand Marshal. Show them another way. Show them there is honour in mercy.

Cold War by Mark Gatiss (2013)

• • • • • •

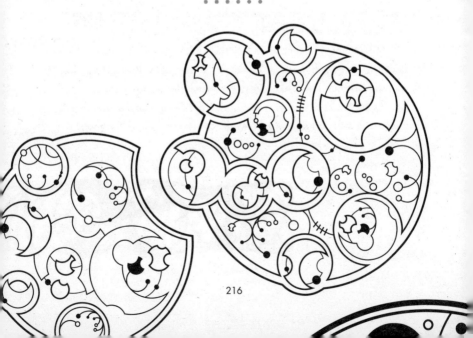

At the height of the 1980s Cold War, a Soviet submarine travelling near the North Pole unintentionally revives Grand Marshal Skaldak from five thousand years of captivity in the ice.

The crew's attack on him is a declaration of war, according to the Ice Warrior code. Skaldak understands the Earth superpowers' doctrine of mutually assured destruction and plans to use the submarine's nuclear missiles to provoke a global thermonuclear war that will destroy humanity.

In an age when apocalyptic modern weapons can wipe out civilisation, by accident or design, respect and mercy must be the watchwords of a MAD world – whether we are politicians or voters. But they are also traits that we all should embrace to teach fresh generations to curb future perils born of old prejudices.

18 JULY

SEEK THE TRUTH

UNSTOFFE
One day, even here, in the future men will turn to
each other and say, 'Binro was right.'

The Ribos Operation by Robert Holmes (1978)

• • • • • •

The planet Ribos has two long seasons – one of sun, one of ice – and was commonly thought to be a world fought over by Sun Gods and Ice Gods. Then, one night, a man called Binro dared to take careful measurements of the 'ice crystals' fixed in the sky.

From this close study, Binro claimed that Ribos was not in a fixed position but instead orbited its sun, travelling far away and then returning – the cause of the planet's long seasons. What's more, the so-called ice crystals were really other suns.

Such ideas shocked the people of Ribos. When Binro wouldn't apologise he was mocked, tortured and left to rot in a place called Shur's Concourse. Then he met a petty criminal called Unstoffe who came from another world – and confirmed that Binro was right.

Truth isn't always easy to find. It can take hard work to build up a firm base of evidence, just like Binro had to do with his astronomical measurements. Even then, people might not like what the evidence shows. Truth is hard won, and precious.

19 JULY

BE PREPARED

DONNA NOBLE

I've been ready for this. I packed ages ago, just in case.
Cos I thought, hot weather, cold weather, no weather,
he goes anywhere. I've gotta be prepared.

THE DOCTOR
You've got a hatbox.

DONNA NOBLE
Planet of the Hats, I'm ready!

Partners in Crime by Russell T Davies (2008)

• • • • • •

Donna Noble was once an unwilling passenger in the TARDIS. Since
that first encounter, she's been on the lookout for the Doctor. And
now that she's found him, she's dragging him off to find his space-
time machine.

They find her blue Peugeot in the same alleyway as the TARDIS.
The boot is full of luggage, prepared for the very moment she caught
up with the Time Lord. There's so much of it that you'd think her car
was bigger on the inside.

Forward planning is always helpful: it's handy to have a small bag
of essentials packed. Passport, driver's licence, overnight change of
clothes, little bag of toiletries. Then you're all set for a spontaneous
trip with a mate at a moment's notice. Although you can probably leave
the designer millinery at home.

20 JULY

TIME TO GO

THE DOCTOR
It's July – July the 20th, to be precise.

POLLY
What are you getting at?

BEN JACKSON
Don't you see, Duchess?
July the 20th, 1966, is when it all began!

The Faceless Ones by David Ellis and Malcolm Hulke (1967)

• • • • • •

Having negotiated peace with the alien Chameleons, the Doctor and his friends head back to Gatwick Airport where the TARDIS should be waiting for them. But then the Doctor reveals the date – and Polly and Ben realise they're back in England on the very day they left it to join the Doctor on his adventures.

Both of them are thrilled by the prospect of returning home, but don't want to leave the Doctor, either – especially if he still needs their help. The Doctor can see how much they want to return to their old lives, so (despite having lost the TARDIS!) he reassures them he'll be fine.

It can be hard to end things, especially if it's a relationship with someone who's been close to us. But sometimes we know in our hearts that it's time to walk away. Do it as quickly, cleanly and as kindly as you can, so that everyone can move on with their lives.

21 JULY

RECONNECT

THE DOCTOR
What's the point in surviving if you never see anyone, if you hide yourself away from the world? When did you last open the shutters? New friends, fireworks. That's what life should be.

Knock Knock by Mike Bartlett (2017)

. . . . . .

The Doctor confronts Bill Potts's strange new landlord, who has exploited insect-like creatures in an antiquated old house to preserve his terminally ill mother. Eliza has survived for more than seven decades at the expense of unfortunate residents.

Eliza is unaware of this human cost, until the Doctor tells her what has happened and shows her life beyond the confines of the house. The tragedy is that her son will not accept her request to leave so he can go and see the world, and they die in her room together.

Some of us feel more isolated since the pandemic lockdown, more nervous about getting out and about after getting used to staying at home. Consider what steps you can take to experience the outside world – on your own or with friends – or how you can encourage others to do so. Sun and fresh air in the summer is a great time to try this.

22 JULY

DEEDS NOT WORDS

THE DOCTOR
By midnight tonight, this planet will be pulled
inside out. There will be nothing left.

Doctor Who by Matthew Jacobs (1996)

• • • • • •

On 31 December 1999, the evil Master sneaks aboard the Doctor's
TARDIS and manages to open the Eye of Harmony, the almighty
power source at the very heart of the ship. This has instantaneous
effects – some way across San Francisco, the Doctor suddenly recovers
his memory – but it has a less positive impact on Earth.

Within minutes, the molecular structure of the planet is changing.
At first the effects are subtle but they will rapidly become more
catastrophic. Yet the brilliant surgeon Dr Grace Holloway finds the
Doctor's grave warnings hard to believe – and she calls an ambulance
to get psychiatric help for him.

Calmly and sincerely he persists. And then, to Grace's aston-
ishment, the Doctor demonstrates the phenomenon… by stepping
through a window without breaking any glass. It's an astounding
demonstration, and uncanny evidence that what he says is true.

Putting a good argument across is all very well, but if you really
want to convince someone that what you're saying is true, deeds can
be more effective than words.

23 JULY

KNOW YOUR VALUE

THE DOCTOR
Your leader will be angry if you kill me. I'm a genius!

The Seeds of Death by Brian Hayles (1969)

• • • • • •

Towards the end of the 21st century, Ice Warriors led by Commander Slaar take control of the 'T-Mat' relay station on the Moon as the first stage in their invasion of Earth. They brutally gun down most of the human staff on the Moonbase, except for one man who goes into hiding, and another who – in fear for his life – helps the invaders operate the T-Mat systems.

When the Doctor arrives on the Moonbase, Slaar commands the Ice Warriors to locate and destroy him. But when they corner him, the Doctor says that obeying this order will only anger Slaar – because the Doctor is, he implies, more valuable alive. The Ice Warriors comply and take the Doctor prisoner, which of course leads to their undoing.

We all have different talents, skills and experience which can be valuable to other people. But before we can get them to recognise our worth, we need to recognise it ourselves. Know your value, and be proud of your worth.

24 JULY

COMMIT TO THE TASK

ALEC PALMER
This is my house, Doctor, and it belongs to me.

CLARA OSWALD
This is actually your house? You went to the bank and said,
'You know that gigantic old haunted house on the moors?
The one the dossers are too scared to doss in? The one the
birds are too scared to fly over?' And then you said,
'I'd like to buy it, please, with my money.'

ALEC PALMER
Yes, I did, actually.

Hide by Neil Cross (2013)

• • • • • •

The Doctor is excited to meet Major Alec Palmer, VC. He's a member of the Baker Street Irregulars, and the Ministry of Ungentlemanly Warfare, who specialised in espionage, sabotage and reconnaissance behind enemy lines. He's a talented watercolourist, professor of psychology and now ghost hunter.

Major Palmer isn't excited to meet the Doctor. He thinks the Doctor has turned up from Military Intelligence at his investigation of the Caliburn Ghast in 1974 to steal the work and take credit for it. They've done it before, so Palmer now has bought the house to secure his rights.

Palmer's example is extreme, but if you're committed to something, do it wholeheartedly. If you want to convince people you're serious, put your money where your mouth is.

25 JULY

LIVING WITHOUT FEAR

THE DOCTOR
I had to face my fear. That was more
important than just going on living.

Planet of the Spiders by Robert Sloman (1974)

• • • • • •

We're all afraid of something. On Metebelis 3, the Third Doctor encounters giant, psychic spiders ruled by a particularly large and terrifying specimen known as the Great One. This enormous spider is powerful enough to control the Doctor's mind – he is utterly in her thrall.

The Doctor surely knows when he faces the Great One a second time that he is walking to his death. Bravely, nobly, he does so anyway, as it's the only way to defeat her and free her oppressed human subjects.

But afterwards, the Doctor's dying words to Sarah Jane Smith are very revealing. By facing his fear, the Doctor has also set himself free. The effect is profound: he becomes a new person. (Literally, in fact, because he also regenerates.)

You don't need to battle monsters to face your own fears. Today, try something challenging that takes you out of your comfort zone. The confidence you might gain could well prove transformative!

26 JULY

DO WHAT YOU LOVE

THE DOCTOR

I used to hotwire warp drives for fun on a weekend as a teenager
– not that we had weekends or teenagers – basically, I used to
do this a lot and people got mad. But now it's going to save our
lives, so who was right all along and is now the real winner?

Ascension of the Cybermen by Chris Chibnall (2020)

• • • • • •

In the immediate aftermath of the Great CyberWars, the remaining
Cybermen forces attack a battered settlement where they hunt
the remnants of humanity to extinction. As her friends watch, the
Doctor gets to grips with a warp-shuttle in a desperate bid to escape
the onslaught.

Teenager Ethan shoves her aside because he knows a faster way.
He's adept with technology. Ethan has done this kind of thing since he
was four, when his dad first taught him how to hijack Cyberships. He
knows how to take them apart and how to burn them to the ground.

If you love what you do, it can be your career, a job change, a
passion project, or a retirement role. Find what inspires you, and you'll
have fun, be productive, and inspire others.

27 JULY

ISOLATION OF THE ISOLUS

THE DOCTOR

Fear, loneliness – they're the big ones, Rose. Some of the most terrible acts ever committed have been inspired by them.

Fear Her by Matthew Graham (2006)

● ● ● ● ● ●

There's excitement in the air in Dame Kelly Holmes Close on the morning of 27 July 2012, ahead of the opening ceremony for the London Olympic Games. But there's fear and apprehension, too, because children are suddenly disappearing.

The Doctor and Rose Tyler investigate, and discover a frightened, lonely 12-year-old girl called Chloe Webber who has formed a powerful empathic link with the alien Isolus. The being is usually sustained by its intense emotional link to its mother or siblings in space, but now those feelings are all focused on Chloe.

The disappearing children are the result of Chloe's longing for a new family of friends: she and the Isolus transfer the children to a hand-drawn, make-believe world in which they can play.

Chloe is a scared and lonely child, but that doesn't justify her actions. 'Kids can't have it all their own way,' says Rose. 'That's part of being a family.'

Yet understanding what drives Chloe (and the Isolus) to behave in this way helps the Doctor and Rose tackle the root cause and return the missing children. Sometimes the most effective way to deal with problematic behaviour is through understanding.

28 JULY

SEE FOR YOURSELF

POLLY
But you saw them!

BEN JACKSON
There were no such creatures – there
are no such things as Macra!

THE DOCTOR
Don't blame him, Polly. Ben has come under control
of the evil forces at the heart of this colony.

The Macra Terror by Ian Stuart Black (1967)

. . . . . .

Pleasures abound on an unnamed planet where the Second Doctor and his friends find a human colony. There's music and dancing, steam baths, beauty treatments, moonlight treatment and effervescent sprays. The colonists even tidy up this scruffy incarnation of the Doctor – at least, for a few seconds.

Everything seems so lovely that it's hard to believe claims that the colony is being preyed upon by enormous, crab-like Macra. The people in charge, plus the Doctor's friend Ben, insist that there's no such thing, even though they've actually *seen* Macra!

Some people hold strong convictions, even despite evidence which might contradict their beliefs. Remember to ask for evidence and reliable sources, and try to see the truth for yourself. There's a famous saying that if someone insists that it's raining and someone else insists that it's dry, you don't need to *believe* either of them – you can go and look out the window.

29 JULY

SMALL CHANGES ADD UP

THE DOCTOR
Yes, that's it: we'll cause trouble.
Start a fire, my boy.

Planet of Giants by Louis Marks (1964)

• • • • • •

When the doors of the TARDIS open mid-flight, the Doctor and his friends are exposed to powerful space pressure and end up reduced to the size of an inch! Landing in an ordinary garden they face a whole series of enormous perils such as being stepped on by normal-sized people or attacked by a curious cat.

Then the Doctor discovers a murderous plot involving a new kind of insecticide so deadly it could threaten the world. Appalled at this prospect, he determines to act, even though he's still tiny. Yet he's too small to call for help, and when he and his friends manage to operate a phone, their voices can't be head by normal-sized people. But that doesn't stop the Doctor trying...

It doesn't matter how big you are – or feel. You can make a difference so long as you're determined. Small efforts soon add up: it's a combination of the Doctor's various different attempts to stop the villains that ultimately means he succeeds!

30 JULY

START SOMEWHERE

DONNA NOBLE
But your own planet. It burned.

THE DOCTOR
That's just it. Don't you see, Donna? Can't you understand?
If I could go back and save them, then I would. But I can't.
I can never go back. I can't. I just can't, I can't.

DONNA NOBLE
Just someone. Please. Not the whole town. Just save someone.

The Fires of Pompeii by James Moran (2008)

• • • • • •

Donna Noble knows the fate of the Doctor's home planet. So she can't understand why he will allow the population of Pompeii to perish.

The eruption of Vesuvius in 79 CE is a fixed point in history. Pompeii's destruction cannot be prevented. By defeating the alien Pyroviles, the Doctor ensures that time is unchanged – and that everyone dies.

The Doctor abandons Lobus Caecilius and family, even while they cower as the eruption destroys their home. He's prepared to leave them to their fate, until Donna begs him to show mercy. Not everyone in Pompeii: just them.

When faced with a project that's huge and daunting, you may feel powerless to act. Unable to complete everything at once, what can you possibly achieve? Rather than do nothing, choose something, no matter how small. Start somewhere, even if you're overwhelmed.

31 JULY

ABOVE THE TITLE

MARTHA JONES
What, people call you 'the Doctor'?

THE DOCTOR
Yeah.

MARTHA JONES
Well, I'm not. As far as I'm concerned,
you've got to earn that title.

Smith and Jones by Russell T Davies (2007)

• • • • • •

Royal Hope Hospital in central London, together with its staff and patients, has been suddenly transported to the surface of the Moon. While rhino-like Judoon stalk the building, medical student Martha Jones instinctively asks intelligent questions about what's going on, which impresses a strange patient called 'John Smith'.

When Mr Smith reveals that he's really known as 'the Doctor', Martha isn't having any of it. She's training to be a doctor herself and a medical degree can take between five and eight years of hard work and long hours. It's little wonder she won't accept the authority of this 'Doctor' solely on his say so. Only when he's proved himself does she finally call him by his name.

Just because someone has power or authority doesn't guarantee that they're right. We're all entitled to ask for the evidence behind any claim or idea. Martha is right to be wary of the Doctor until he demonstrates that he can be trusted.

AUGUST

1 AUGUST

SET DEADLINES

THE DOCTOR
I just activated the TARDIS self-destruct system. One hour until
this ship blows. Don't try to leave. The TARDIS is in lockdown.
I'll open those doors when Clara's by my side.

Journey to the Centre of the TARDIS by Steve Thompson (2013)

• • • • • •

Recovery experts the Van Baalen brothers think the TARDIS is the
salvage of a lifetime. The Doctor needs their help to find the missing
Clara Oswald. The brothers are in no hurry, but the Doctor isn't
prepared to hang about.

He thinks people perform better under pressure, so he traps the
brothers with him in the TARDIS and sets the self-destruct. When
they quibble, he halves the time. So much for gentle persuasion.

It turns out that there is no self-destruct. Mind you, it also turns
out he's overlooked monsters in the TARDIS as it reconfigures the
architecture every five minutes, so his plans may have to change.

What have you been putting off? Unless you have a time machine,
you should figure out the tasks you need to complete, schedule them,
determine what's a reasonable period for your project, and start your
timer. A deadline helps to focus the mind — even if it's not attached to
a self-destruct.

2 AUGUST

EXCITING TO KNOW, EXCITING NOT TO KNOW

KIMUS
But I don't understand.

THE DOCTOR
Exciting, isn't it?

The Pirate Planet by Douglas Adams (1978)

• • • • • •

The Doctor knows lots about all kinds of arcane subjects. He knows, without having to look it up, that Bandraginus 5 – a planet of a thousand million souls – vanished about a hundred years ago without trace. He knows that the planet Calufrax is cold, wet and icy with no indigenous life of any sort.

But he doesn't know that the huge pirate planet Zanak has materialised around both Bandraginus 5 and Calufrax, then mined away all their resources and precious stones. And he doesn't understand why the psychic Mentiads of Zanak have attacked him. But as he says to Kimus, another native of the planet, it's *exciting* not to know.

Of course, the Doctor isn't saying that because he's proud of his ignorance. Instead, he takes not knowing as a opportunity to learn something new. That's the Doctor all over: exploring, asking questions, revelling in the thrill of discovery.* If you don't know something, then go and find out.

(* In *Image of the Fendahl* (1977), Martha Tyler asks the Doctor how he knows so much. 'I read a lot,' he tells her. That's good advice, too!)

3 AUGUST

HUMAN WORTH

THE DOCTOR

Human progress isn't measured by industry, it's
measured by the value you place on a life. An
'unimportant' life. A life without privilege. The boy who
died on the river, that boy's value is *your* value. That's
what defines an age. That's what defines a species.

Thin Ice by Sarah Dollard (2017)

· · · · · ·

Visiting the last great Frost Fair on the Thames in London, 1814, the Doctor and Bill Potts witness the death of Spider, a street urchin. The boy is dragged below the ice by a monstrous creature chained on the bed of the river. They confront Lord Sutcliffe in his mansion, suspecting he is an alien who exploits both the creature and the unwitting locals.

Sutcliffe's lack of humanity is not alien. He is a racist sociopath, indifferent to the fates of others in his venture to use the aquatic creature to create fuel. Just another single solitary human, like the boy Spider whose death he does not mourn.

An accident of birth that makes someone rich and powerful does not make their life worth more than someone raised in poverty. The deaths of others, named or unnamed, are things to care about, not to profit from.

Consider how you treat different people. Is there someone you've been overlooking?

4 AUGUST

THE DOCTOR DANCES

THE DOCTOR
I was wondering, Ray, if –

RAY
Thank you, Doctor: I'd love to.

Delta and the Bannermen by Malcolm Kohll (1987)

• • • • • •

Navarino holidaymakers are heading to Disneyland in 1959 when their spaceship, disguised as an old bus, crashes into a Soviet satellite and lands at the Shangri-La holiday camp in Wales instead. They make the most of their unexpected destination while a local mechanic, Billy, helps the Doctor repair their ship.

Billy is assisted by Rachel – better known as Ray – who has known him since childhood and even learned all about motorbikes in the hope that Billy would notice her one day. But at the 'Get to Know You' Dance, Billy clearly only has eyes for Delta, queen of the alien Chimeron, who is travelling with the Navarinos.

The Doctor spots how upset Ray is by this and so does the one thing he can to help her: he asks her to dance. It's just what she needs, and though he's a bit awkward on the dance floor, dancing makes Ray feel better.

You don't need to save the universe to be a hero. It's enough to be observant and kind, and even the smallest of gestures can go a long way towards helping someone.

5 AUGUST

FUTURE POTENTIAL

FUGITIVE DOCTOR
Have you ever been limited by who you were before?

THE DOCTOR
Now that does sound like me talking.

The Timeless Children by Chris Chibnall (2020)

• • • • • •

The Doctor is trapped in a paralysis field within the Matrix on her home world, Gallifrey. She is tired and confused after her captor, the Master, revealed the planet's secret history, and the Doctor's own part in it – hitherto hidden from her memories.

She learns she's had many more regenerations than she ever knew. The Doctor finds it hard to accept that everything she previously remembered was only part of her life. What did the Time Lords do to her, and how many lives has she had?

Buried within her mind is Ruth, a fugitive Doctor – one of her unknown former selves who she recently encountered incognito on Earth. This past Doctor appears to her in the Matrix to challenge the Doctor's fear that she is no longer who she thought she was.

Your achievements and fears and relationships and triumphs and tragedies (whether you remember them or not) – everything in your life to date has contributed to who you are now. They do not have to limit what you can still become.

6 AUGUST

WHAT YOU GIVE FOR YOUR FRIENDS

THE DOCTOR
It's no good. I can't get clear of the ship
without hurting Nyssa and Tegan.

Mawdryn Undead by Peter Grimwade (1983)

• • • • • •

The alien Mawdryn and seven comrades steal a metamorphic symbiosis regenerator from Gallifrey hoping to gain the power to regenerate. They succeed in their aim, except that they end up *perpetually* regenerating. Unable to die, they exist in eternal torment.

They tell the Doctor that one thing can end their suffering: the energy of a real Time Lord. The Fifth Doctor believes that he has eight regenerations left, so freeing Mawdryn and his comrades will use up all his remaining lives.

On that basis, the Doctor initially refuses to help and tries to flee. But his friends Nyssa and Tegan have been infected by Mawdryn's illness, and any attempt to leave Mawdryn's spaceship in the TARDIS makes them suffer. So the Doctor surrenders himself, not to help Mawdryn or to end his pain, but for the sake of his friends.

Some people dismiss feelings and emotions. Yet we'll do things we'd never otherwise dare, and we'll sacrifice a great deal, for the sake of our loved ones. Love can make us strong.

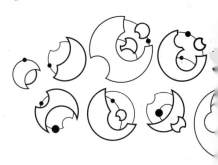

7 AUGUST

WHEN NO HELPS

TEGAN JOVANKA
Help me, Doctor! What's happening to me?
Please, look at me, Doctor. I need your help.

THE DOCTOR
No, I will not submit.

Snakedance by Christopher Bailey (1983)

• • • • • •

On the planet Manussa, the Doctor's friend Tegan Jovanka is once again possessed by the evil, snake-like Mara. The being then corrupts other people and aims to use a crystal called the Great Mind's Eye to allow it to return to the physical world once more.

The Doctor confronts the creature but refuses to look at it, or even acknowledge its presence. He knows that to submit would only help the evil creature grow stronger. With the help of a wise archaeologist called Dojjen, the Doctor resists the Mara's efforts to make him scared or angry. Even the pleas of the possessed Tegan do not succeed in breaking his focus. The Doctor ultimately frees Tegan from the Mara by *not* responding to her call for help.

Some people who behave badly feed off our emotive reactions so that responding angrily only makes them worse. It's not that we shouldn't react to bad behaviour, just consider how to react most effectively to make a difference.

8 AUGUST

MAKE YOUR MOVE

THE DOCTOR
I'm a scary, handsome genius from space
and I'm telling you no, she's not out of your league.

BILL POTTS
OK. Well, maybe I'll call her tomorrow.

THE DOCTOR
Call her tonight.

Extremis by Steven Moffat (2017)

. . . . . .

The Doctor telephones Bill Potts at her flat. She thinks he's nagging her about an essay she's writing. He's actually calling to send her on a date. Does she know a girl called Penny?

Bill doesn't think Penny would be interested. She's surprised that the Doctor even knows who she is. She'd be even more surprised to learn that she previously brought Penny back home and things went well, until the Pope frightened her off when he burst in shouting indignantly at them in Italian.

Helpfully, this abandoned date happened during an alien simulation that the Doctor has seen. He knows the simulation predicts Penny's potential interest in Bill – but also that Bill should seize her moment before the alien invasion it also foretells.

You won't know whether someone you fancy is interested unless you take a chance on asking them out. Don't wait for a friend to nudge you. And do it before things get too busy.

9 AUGUST

HOME IS WHERE YOU MAKE IT

THE DOCTOR
Where to now, Ace?

ACE
Home.

THE DOCTOR
Home?

ACE
The TARDIS!

Survival by Rona Munro (1989)

• • • • • •

When the Doctor's friend Ace wonders what her old mates are up to, the Doctor takes her back home to Perivale. But Ace considers the place to be the 'boredom capital of the universe', and they arrive on a day when there's not even anything decent on TV.

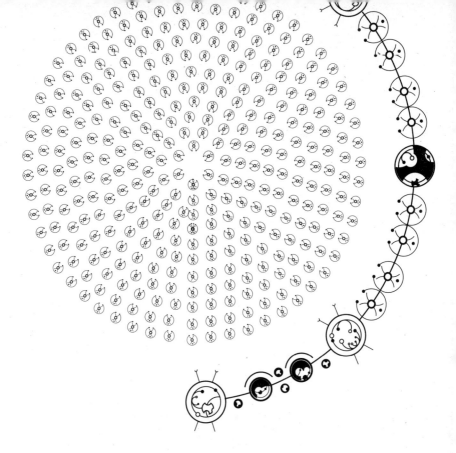

Soon they discover that a number of people – including Ace's friends – have mysteriously vanished from the area. Then Ace and the Doctor both vanish, too – and they find they've been transported to a savage alien planet. Feline vultures called 'kitlings' have selected them to become prey for the Cheetah People!

After battling the Cheetah people, Ace has become imbued with the power to lead the Doctor and other survivors back home. But tellingly, she lands them all outside the TARDIS – her new home. The place she grew up is somewhere to visit now.

Moving away from home is often a key step in growing up. The people you consider to be your family might not be the people you're actually related to. Find the place where you fit, and feel most comfortable. Make your own home.

10 AUGUST

ALL YOU NEED IS A SEED

THE DOCTOR
It's nothing. It's tiny. One of those insignificant little power cells
that no one ever bothers about and it's clinging onto life,
with one little ounce of reality tucked away inside.

Rise of the Cybermen by Tom MacRae (2006)

• • • • • •

The TARDIS suddenly falls out of the vortex of space and time into another dimension. The Doctor and his friends find themselves on a parallel Earth – very like the world they know except for subtle differences, such as Rose Tyler's dad still being alive.

While it's tempting to go off and explore, the Doctor is more concerned about his damaged ship. The TARDIS draws its power from our universe, and a parallel universe essentially offers the wrong kind of fuel. This means that the Doctor's ship is powerless and effectively dead.

Yet, on examining his ship more closely, the Doctor spots a faint, glimmering light – a tiny single power cell, somehow still surviving. But this tiny seed has the potential for extraordinary growth, so long as it's provided with energy from our universe. The Doctor gives it ten years of his own life and prompts a recharging cycle that revives the whole ship.

What's true of that small power cell is true of us, as well. It's easy to think that a big challenge can only be solved by some big intervention. In fact, meaningful change can be wrought by the tiniest seed, so long as it's encouraged to flourish and grow.

11 AUGUST

OTHER PEOPLE'S COMPANY

THE DOCTOR
Millions of planets, millions of galaxies, and we're on this one.
Molto bene. Bellissimo, says Donna, born in Chiswick. All you've
got is a life of work and sleep, and telly and rent and tax and
takeaway dinners, all birthdays and Christmases and two weeks
holiday a year, and then you end up here. Donna Noble,
citizen of the Earth, standing on a different planet.

Planet of the Ood by Keith Temple (2008)

* * * * * *

Donna Noble spent a lot of time looking for the Doctor, because she
thought it was so wonderful out in the universe. The Doctor sets the
TARDIS controls to random so they could end up anywhere, anywhen.

He wants her to experience the fear, joy and wonder that keeps
him travelling. On the frozen surface of the Ood Sphere, he contrasts
it with the life she once led. Not that Donna's listening properly – she's
wrapping up warm and more excited about spotting a rocket ship.

It's doubtful we'll ever visit a distant planet. But we can celebrate
the highlights in our lives beyond the everyday mundane, whether it's
a package holiday or a night in. It's who you're with that matters most.

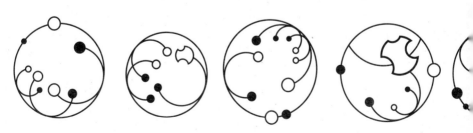

12 AUGUST

SIMPLE BUT EFFECTIVE

THE DOCTOR
Hang on, hang on! I've got a sonic screwdriver!

CLARA OSWALD
Yeah? I've got a chair.

The Crimson Horror by Mark Gatiss (2013)

• • • • • •

There's trouble at t'mill. The Doctor and Clara Oswald confront Mrs Gillyflower in her parlour. The Great Work of this 19th-century chemist and engineer is a eugenicist plot to launch a rocket filled with poison into the atmosphere.

They can see the rocket controls in Gillyflower's parlour. The Doctor's ready to use his sonic screwdriver to destroy them, but Clara has a better idea — she picks up a chair and smashes it into the controls.

She got the idea from the Doctor, who earlier freed her from captivity under a large bell jar by smashing it with a chair. A furious Mrs Gillyflower escapes but locks them in the room. The Doctor wrenches the chair from the shattered controls and hurls it through the parlour window — because yes, chairs are useful.

You can make best use of the tools at your disposal. Don't let technology get in the way when there's a simpler way of doing things just as efficiently.

13 AUGUST

RULES RULE, OK?

THE DOCTOR
You're wrong, your Honour.
There's one other witness I can call.

MEGARA
Who?

THE DOCTOR
You!

The Stones of Blood by David Fisher (1978)

• • • • • •

There's something odd about the Nine Travellers stone circle in Gloucestershire, which comprises more than nine stones. The Doctor and Romana investigate, then find themselves on board a spaceship in hyperspace where they encounter the Megara. These petty justice machines accuse the Doctor of removing the Great Seals of their cell without authorisation and put him on trial for his life.

The Doctor calls witnesses as part of his defence, but just when it seems that he's run out of options, he cannily calls one of the Megara as a witness to whom he can put questions.

At first, the Megara protest that this is unorthodox behaviour but they have to admit that it's not against their own law. As a result the Doctor gets the answers he needs to make sense of what's really going on and can then lead the Megara to the villain they're searching for on Earth.

It's sometimes not enough to just follow the rules, and the best outcome is the result of some unconventional thinking.

14 AUGUST

KNOW WHAT THEY WANT

THE DOCTOR
Check your readings. We die, your precious station dies!
The whole thing will blow. The company will make the
biggest loss in its history. A moment ago, we were too
expensive to live. Now we're more expensive dead.

Oxygen by Jamie Mathieson (2017)

• • • • • •

In the Power Core of *Chasm Forge*, the Doctor tries to save the crew and his friends from asphyxiation. Employees must purchase oxygen from the company to survive in their spacesuits. If the occupants can't afford it and die, the suits carry on operating with their corpses. The company algorithm calculates that it's more cost-effective to have the spacesuits kill and replace inefficient organic components – the remaining crew.

The Doctor rewires the human life signs to the coolant system: if they die, the nuclear core will blow and destroy *Chasm Forge* and all future profits from it. Their deaths will be brave and brilliant and unafraid but, more importantly, their deaths will be prohibitively expensive for the company.

In a negotiation, knowing what motivates the other side is the basis for getting what you want. You don't have to like it, but you can exploit it to your advantage.

15 AUGUST

TAG, YOU'RE IT

THE DOCTOR
Oh, the blossomiest blossom. That's the only sad thing.
I wanna know what happens next. Right, then,
Doctor Whoever-I'm-about-to-be. Tag, you're it.

The Power of the Doctor by Chris Chibnall (2022)

• • • • • •

A fatal confrontation with the Master has injured the Doctor's body beyond repair. She's returned her travelling companions back to Earth, and now faces her future alone.

She steps from the TARDIS into the evening air as her body begins to regenerate. She breathes in, her senses heightened in the focus of that moment. There's the perfume of the flowers around her on the clifftop, and the orange illumination of the rising sun suffuses the golden light that already builds around her.

The Doctor knows that she will regenerate. She doesn't know who she will become, only that she has loved being the Doctor-she-is, and that things are going to change. The Doctor-yet-to-come will take it from here, and she will let them.

When you change jobs, and someone else takes over, let them do it their own way. Hand over to them freely so they can get on with it. And trust that they'll be brilliant.

16 AUGUST

CHANGE THE RULES

THE DOCTOR

I'm just as angry as you are. As a matter of fact, I had a great deal to do with the banning of these miniscopes. I managed to persuade the High Council of the Time Lords they were an offence against the dignity of sentient lifeforms.

Carnival of Monsters by Robert Holmes (1973)

• • • • • •

The TARDIS lands on the SS *Bernice*, a ship in the Indian Ocean in 1926 – which is then attacked by a plesiosaur. Oddly, the passengers lose all memory of the terrifying attack, which then happens all over again, exactly as before.

Soon, the Doctor discovers that the ship, its passengers and the ancient marine reptile are all trapped inside a machine – a miniscope. They've been miniaturised and made to live the same repeated scenarios for the entertainment of alien observers.

Even though the human passengers of the SS *Bernice* are completely unaware of their predicament, the Doctor's friend Jo is utterly appalled by what's been done to them. The Doctor sets out to free them – along with the other creatures trapped inside the machine – and he reveals he has done this before.

If rules don't protect people from cruel and undignified behaviour, change the rules.

17 AUGUST

PUBLIC PROMISE

THE DOCTOR
Love, in all its forms, is the most powerful weapon we have.
Because love is a form of hope and, like hope, love abides in
the face of everything. You both found love with each other. You
believed in it, you fought for it, and you waited for it. And now,
you're committing to it. Which makes you, right now, the two
strongest people on this planet. Maybe in this universe.

Demons of the Punjab by Vinay Patel (2018)

• • • • • •

Umbreen and Prem are brought together just as India is separating
into two nations in 1947. Millions of people are leaving their homes in
the largest-ever forced migration that wasn't a result of war or famine.
Fifteen million people displaced and over a million deaths.

Politics parts people, but what will bring them together is love.
Umbreen has chosen a wedding location: the new partition fence
between India and Pakistan. The Doctor officiates, and speaks from
her hearts about their commitment.

A wedding need not be a lavish, expensive, overwhelming affair
involving hundreds of people. It can be a simple ceremony with a
handful of attendees. That's enough to celebrate a relationship, in front
of witnesses, family and friends. It's a public declaration of promises,
vows and aspirations. A formal affirmation of your love.

18 AUGUST

PRIORITISE

THE DOCTOR
Don't panic. Not the end of the world. Well, it could be
the end of the world but one thing at a time.

The Woman Who Fell to Earth by Chris Chibnall (2018)

• • • • • •

It's easy to get stuck on the negative. Things can seem very bad – especially when they really are. But imagine if the Doctor panicked every time the Earth was under threat. It would be constant panic!

No, even if the planet is in imminent danger and there's an alien creature all covered in teeth who wants to destroy the Doctor and her friends, she tries to keep calm, take a deep breath and think her way out of the problem. Whatever the problem, what is there at hand to help her and what can she actually do?

Yes, all right, easier said than done. You can't help how you feel when things are all going wrong. But you can also *use* that feeling. A little bit of panic – plus some adrenaline and a dash of righteous outrage – was exactly what the Doctor needed to kickstart her newly regenerated brain, and soon enough she'd outfoxed Tzim-Sha and saved Earth (yet again).

19 AUGUST

MAKE A POSITIVE IMPRESSION

CYBER PLANNER
The game has just started. Doctor, why is there no record of you anywhere in the databanks of the Cyberiad? Oh, you're good. Oh, you've been eliminating yourself from history. You know you could be reconstructed by the hole you've left.

THE DOCTOR
Good point. I'll do something about that.

Nightmare in Silver by Neil Gaiman (2013)

• • • • • •

Infected with Cybermites, the Doctor struggles to prevent them converting his body. He challenges the nascent Cyber Planner to a game of chess to decide who will take charge of his mind. If the Doctor loses, the Cyber Planner will have access to all his memories, along with knowledge of time travel.

When the Doctor tempts the Cyber Planner into accepting, he reveals snippets of information about himself – information not available to the Cybermen since the Doctor has been erasing records of himself.

When you leave this world, what will remain is the hole you leave: the people whose lives you improved, the opinions you influenced, the things you made, the hearts you touched. Your legacy outlasts you long after you are gone. It's a comforting thought when pondering your mortality – and the impression you wish to make while you're able.

20 AUGUST

DRESS TO IMPRESS

THE DOCTOR

I'm hardly dressed in the proper clothes to go
skulking after people, now am I?

The Reign of Terror by Dennis Spooner (1964)

• • • • • •

The Doctor's favourite period in Earth history is apparently post-revolutionary France. But it's one thing to read about the Reign of Terror and quite another to live through it. Arriving in 1794, the Doctor's friends are taken prisoner and carted off to Paris – to face execution by guillotine!

The city is on edge, full of spies and informers. The Doctor must be especially ingenious and brave to stand any chance of rescuing his friends. Yet, despite the dangers, he doesn't sneak in quietly and try to pass unobserved. No, he heads for a tailor's shop and picks out the most outlandish costume: a big cape, bright sash and hat adorned with enormous feathers – a get-up that demands to be seen! Then, in the outfit and insignia of a regional deputy from France's southern province, he strolls bold as brass into the Conciergerie prison. And it works.

When facing a challenge or feeling apprehensive, try dressing up a bit. Others will respond to your confident appearance, and assume you're a confident person too.

21 AUGUST

STEP AWAY FROM DANGER

THE DOCTOR

What a stupid place to land. You can tell that the
captain is not at the helm, can't you?

The Krotons by Robert Holmes (1968–69)

• • • • • •

On a planet with twin suns and a smell in the air like rotten eggs, the
timid Gonds live in fear of the crystalline Krotons. When the Doctor
intervenes, the Krotons set out to destroy the TARDIS, which they
engulf in a gas that dissolves anything it touches. Sure enough, when
the gas clears the TARDIS is no longer there!

Except that once the Krotons have lumbered away, the TARDIS
rematerialises in another spot nearby. It turns out that the Doctor
has, just this once, remembered to set the 'hostile action displacement
system', which makes the ship automatically dematerialise if it comes
under attack.

The irony is that the supposedly indestructible TARDIS often
lands the Doctor in the midst of hazardous situations. But no matter
how indestructible *you* think you might be, or however many times
you've faced a particular situation, if you don't feel safe or comfortable
you can always step away – even if it's just to give you time to think.

22 AUGUST

STAY FOCUSED

THE DOCTOR
The trick with misdirection: don't look where the arrow is
pointing, look where it's pointing away from. So, what's
already on our radar that we should be worried about right
now? Forget about war. What else could end the world?

The Pyramid at the End of the World
by Peter Harness and Steven Moffat (2017)

• • • • • •

A 5,000-year-old pyramid impossibly appears at the strategic inter-
section of Earth's three most powerful armies. It's way beyond human
technology. The Doctor recognises it is a challenge and a distraction.
Alien Monks created it to focus attention there, while they monitor an
unnoticed global catastrophe unfolding elsewhere.

The nations of the world worry about a potential World War III.
Meanwhile, unknown to all of them, the real threat to humanity is an
imminent accident in a Yorkshire biological research lab.

Misdirection is a deliberate distraction. We can spot simple
distractions from things around us such as using a phone when driving.
Watch out for subtler distractions: impossible promises, regret for
things past that prevent you acting now, or being told that if you
cannot fix everything you shouldn't try anything. The most dangerous
distractions are those you don't think could be happening.

23 AUGUST

STRENGTH OF MERCY

THE DOCTOR
It took courage to fight Maxtible's Turkish wrestler.

DALEK
The Daleks are afraid of nothing and no one.

THE DOCTOR
But Jamie saved the Turk's life.

DALEK
Human weakness.

THE DOCTOR
If he hadn't, he would have died in that room of yours. If you
want the human factor, a part of it must include mercy.

The Evil of the Daleks by David Whitaker (1967)

. . . . . .

The Doctor is forced by the Daleks to conduct an experiment on what
it means to be human – and why humanity keeps defeating the Daleks.
As the Doctor's friend Jamie is put through a series of dangerous
challenges, the Doctor and a Dalek discuss what his actions mean.

The Daleks think strength and dominance are all important. But
the Doctor shows them the better part of humanity: courage, pity,
chivalry, friendship and compassion. Then he uses these qualities to
confound the Daleks and cause them to destroy one another!

Such virtues aren't a weakness, they're a sign of strength –
and can often be more effective in achieving what you want than a
show of force.

24 AUGUST

NOW YOU SEE ME

REINETTE
You are in my memories. You walk among them.

THE DOCTOR
If there's anything you don't want me to see,
just imagine a door and close it.

The Girl in the Fireplace by Steven Moffat (2006)

• • • • • •

The Doctor discovers that a spaceship in the Diagmar Cluster in the 51st century, two and half galaxies from Earth, is somehow connected to 18th century France. Clockwork robots from the ship are using 'time windows' into the past in order to stalk a young woman at various points in her life.

Reinette Poisson (1721–64) is an actress, artist, musician, dancer, courtesan, fantastic gardener and uncrowned Queen of France. But what can the robots possibly want with her?

In an effort to find out, the Doctor reads the mind of this remarkable woman. But making the psychic link means that she in turn can walk among *his* memories. It's an intimate, exposing moment: Reinette sees not a great, powerful Time Lord, but a small and lonely boy.

Any deep connection we make with someone else opens up a bit of ourselves at the same time, allowing the other person to see and understand us more clearly. Sharing really is caring.

25 AUGUST

TAKE TIME TO MOURN

THE DOCTOR
You are always here to me.
And I always listen, and I can always see you.

RIVER SONG
Then why didn't you speak to me?

THE DOCTOR
Because I thought it would hurt too much.

The Name of the Doctor by Steven Moffat (2013)

• • • • • •

River Song has been dead for a very long time, the Doctor explains to Clara Oswald. River perished saving him in the biggest library in the universe, and in return he saved her consciousness to its digital database. Which is handy when River later wants to contact the Doctor's friends via a conference call mentally linked with Clara.

There is a time to live and a time to sleep. River knows that people cannot perceive her presence when she manifests herself as an echo in the tomb on Trenzalore. So it is a huge surprise to her when she finds out the Doctor is the only person in the room who can actually see her.

It's natural to feel pain when recalling someone we've lost. There isn't a timeline for grief. Take each and every day as it comes and try to make them count.

26 AUGUST

BE CHILDISH

SARAH JANE SMITH
Doctor, you're being childish.

THE DOCTOR
Well, of course I am! There's no point in being
grown-up if you can't be childish sometimes.

Robot by Terrance Dicks (1974–75)

• • • • • •

Regeneration doesn't just change a Time Lord's physical appearance: it shakes up the brain cells too so that their behaviour becomes erratic, at least to begin with. The Fourth Doctor, for example, starts off doing lots of odd things: getting a colleague at UNIT to skip on the spot with him, building a tower out of circuit boards – even dressing up as a clown and a Viking!

Now, some of this Doctor's childish behaviour serves a serious, practical purpose. In his second adventure, he plays with a yo-yo, but does so to make a simple assessment of gravity. From this he concludes, correctly, that the TARDIS has landed inside a space station.

But when Sarah protests that the Doctor's behaviour is childish, he agrees – proudly. He happily embraces silliness, mischief and joyous wonder at new experiences.

Today, follow the Doctor's example and do something daft. Award yourself bonus points if someone calls you out for being childish!

27 AUGUST

THINK IT THROUGH

THE DOCTOR
Should be a switch by the side.

DONNA NOBLE
Yeah, there is. But it's Sontaran-shaped.
You need three fingers.

THE DOCTOR
You've got three fingers.

The Poison Sky by Helen Raynor (2008)

• • • • • •

The first time you do something can be daunting. Though for most of us, that won't be working out how to evade alien guards and navigate their spaceship. And yet, even then, the answer may be right there in front of you.

Donna isn't convinced about being the Doctor's secret weapon aboard a Sontaran vessel. He reassures her over the phone that she can do it; for instance, she has more than enough fingers to operate the door control. The observation, and the reassurance, gives her the poise to continue her dangerous mission.

In strange surroundings, or when faced with a new problem, take a calming breath and see whether you recognise anything familiar. It may require lateral thinking. Or you may find that you already know the solution like the back of your hand.

28 AUGUST

SEA DOG DATABASE

K-9
I am familiar with boats, master.

THE DOCTOR
You old sea dog, you.

The Androids of Tara by David Fisher (1978)

• • • • • •

The Doctor's faithful robot dog K-9 was built by Professor Marius some time around the year 5000, though later on the Doctor constructed further models with additional modifications. As well as a nose laser, scanning and analytical tools, all versions of K-9 have extensive computerised databanks from which he can access useful information quickly.

On the planet Tara, this included knowledge about the correct way to handle a boat. When the Doctor needed to row across the moat of Castle Gracht, where his friend Romana was held hostage by the fiendish Count Grendel, K-9 seemed keen to put this knowledge to use.

But having defeated Count Grendel, the Doctor found K-9 calling for help in the boat, which was now adrift in the moat. Poor K-9! He had the theory in principle, but couldn't enact what he knew.

True knowledge is more than a collection of facts. What's needed is experience in the practical application of such learning. It's not what you know but what you can put into action.

29 AUGUST

DECISIONS IN THE MOMENT

THE DOCTOR
Go through, Nyssa. It's your only chance!

TEGAN JOVANKA
Where are you sending her?

THE DOCTOR
I don't know but if she stays in the room, she'll die.

Terminus by Stephen Gallagher (1983)

• • • • • •

When Turlough surreptitiously removes the space-time element from beneath the TARDIS console, it causes instability in the ship and the universe outside starts to break through. The Doctor's friend Nyssa, working alone in her bedroom, finds herself directly exposed to the danger.

But the TARDIS has a fail-safe protocol: on impending break-up, it seeks and locks onto the nearest spacecraft, and suddenly, an unfamiliar doorway appears in the wall of Nyssa's bedroom. The Doctor doesn't know what's on the far side but tells Nyssa to go through.

The doorway leads to a space liner where passengers are infected with deadly Lazar's disease. But the Doctor is right to send Nyssa through the door – in that moment, he saves her life.

We can't always know what the consequences of our actions will be. But don't let that stop you from taking action at all. Sometimes, all you can deal with is the immediate problem, and then the *next* immediate problem.

30 AUGUST

TIMEKEEPING

THE DOCTOR
How long's it been? A week? Two weeks?

RYAN SINCLAIR
Ten months.

THE DOCTOR
No, it can't be. I set identical temporal
coordinates to when I sent you back.

GRAHAM O'BRIEN
Yeah, but your time machine ain't the
best at running to time, is it, Doc?

Revolution of the Daleks by Chris Chibnall (2021)

• • • • • •

Arriving fashionably late means not so early that you're the first knock on the door, but not so long that the host wonders if you're lost.

But ten months is pushing your luck. The Doctor's friends don't hang around. They investigate Dalek sightings without her.

On the one hand, the Doctor's been incarcerated in space jail for decades. On the other hand, she did plan to return on time. But on the third (Alpha Centauran) hand, she relied too heavily on the TARDIS, and forgot to allow for space-time traffic on her journey. At least she has the grace to apologise when she eventually arrives.

Missing the start of a meeting wastes other attendees' time. Arriving late for a party is rude to your hosts. The way you respect timekeeping is the way you show friends, family and colleagues how much you respect *them*.

31 AUGUST

POSITIVE PERSPECTIVE

THE DOCTOR
That was the daisiest daisy I'd ever seen.

The Time Monster by Robert Sloman (1972)

• • • • • •

Jo Grant despairs when she's locked in an Atlantean dungeon, so the Doctor reassures her by telling a story from his own childhood when things had seemed pointless to him.

At his lowest ebb, too unhappy even for tears, the Doctor travelled halfway up the mountain behind his house to visit a monk. People said this old man had sat beneath a tree for half his lifetime, and knew the secret of life.

The landscape was bleak, cold, and so very grey. A few bare rocks had weeds sprouting from them between pathetic little patches of sludgy snow. The tree the monk sat under was as ancient and twisted as the old man himself. He was as brittle and dry as an autumn leaf.

The monk listened silently, expressionless as the Doctor poured out his troubles to him. Once the Doctor had finished, the old man lifted a skeletal hand and pointed at a flower; a little weed, just like a daisy. And the Doctor suddenly saw the beauty of it through the monk's eyes; it glowed with life like a perfectly cut jewel.

When he ran back down the mountain, the Doctor found the rocks weren't grey at all, but red, brown, purple and gold. And those pathetic little patches of sludgy snow were shining white in the sunlight.

Despair leaves you without hope, so the world can seem unremittingly bleak and grey. Ask for help and you may see exactly the same things from a positive perspective, unencumbered by your fears and preconceptions.

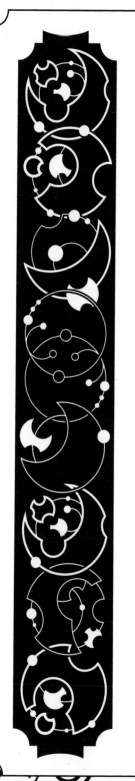

SEPTEMBER

1 SEPTEMBER

ABSENT FRIENDS

VICTORIA WATERFIELD
You probably can't remember your family.

THE DOCTOR
Oh yes, I can when I want to. And that's the point, really:
I have to really want to, to bring them back in front
of my eyes. The rest of the time they sleep in
my mind and I forget. And so will you.

The Tomb of the Cybermen by Kit Pedler and Gerry Davis (1967)

• • • • • •

The Doctor and his friends have to spend a night in the spooky cryogenic facility used by the Cybermen, who for now are dormant in the frozen chamber below. While the other humans sleep, the Doctor and his friend Victoria have a quiet moment to themselves, and address the recent death of Victoria's father.

It's a rare chance to hear the Doctor speak of his own long-lost family. He says to Victoria that she'll find lots of other things to think about on their adventures in time and space — and one way he stops himself dwelling on his own losses is by keeping busy. But it's still good to stop every now and again and remember.

Take a moment today to remember someone you've lost. What's one way you're better off for having known them?

2 SEPTEMBER

FAKE NEWS

THE DOCTOR
The Monks must have some kind of a machine that creates
and broadcasts the myths of their history. The ones that
are powered by, carried by, fed by your brainwaves.

The Lie of the Land by Toby Whithouse (2017)

• • • • • •

The Monks shepherded humanity through our formative years, instrumental in all advances of culture and technology: the Mona Lisa, the electric light bulb, the Moon landing. They defeated the Daleks, the Cybermen, the Weeping Angels. They have been with us since the very beginning. Two species, sharing a history as happily as we share a planet.

Don't believe me? Then you're in contravention of the Memory Crimes Act of 1975.

Except you're not. The Monks arrived only months ago, and control humanity by broadcasting a false history to a subjugated population, enabled by a psychic link established through Bill Potts.

Fake news and conspiracy theories propagate when people or organisations are selective or untruthful about important matters. Social media makes it easy to share and boost it – especially when it conveniently seems to support our own beliefs and prejudices. It's good to have an open mind – but not so wide open that your brain falls out.

3 SEPTEMBER

CHECKMATE ON WAR

ACE
A brilliant move. The black and white pawns
don't fight each other, they join forces.

The Curse of Fenric by Ian Briggs (1989)

• • • • • •

Long ago, the Doctor battled an evil force from the dawn of time. Pulling bones from the desert sands, the Doctor carved chess pieces and set them up in a 'game of traps'. He challenged his opponent to find the single, winning move. Failing to do so, the malevolent force was bottled up in a flask – like a genie in bottle – for 1,700 years.

This evil entity can influence events – even create a time storm – but it can't break free; that is until the flask is rediscovered in an army base near Maiden's Point, Northumbria, in 1943.

Once more, the Doctor sets up chess pieces in the 'game of traps'. And once more, the evil force – now known as Fenric – is confounded. But Ace, having seen soldiers of rival armies work together, solves the riddle that this ancient, powerful entity cannot.

It's not strictly within the rules of chess, but what's needed is exactly what Fenric lacks: an imaginative leap to change the very nature of this age-long conflict. In fact, the answer is to stop the chess game being a conflict at all. You can end a battle by *not* fighting.

4 SEPTEMBER

PAY IT FORWARD

THE DOCTOR
Why would you do this for me?

OHILA
You have helped us in the past.

THE DOCTOR
You were never big on gratitude.

The Night of the Doctor by Steven Moffat (2013)

• • • • • •

In a futile attempt to save the life of a spaceship pilot who had no reason to trust him, the Doctor has crash-landed on the planet Karn. The pilot is dead, the Doctor mortally wounded. The Sisterhood of Karn, Keepers of the Flame and Elixir of Eternal Life, offer to help him regenerate, but the Doctor is suspicious.

In contrast to his selfless sacrifice, High Priestess Ohila concedes that they want to save him because they need him in the war between the Daleks and the Time Lords. Her reminder that the Doctor helped the Sisterhood in the past recalls the sacrifice that her predecessor, Maren, made to save the Doctor's life during their struggle with Morbius.

The Doctor recognises that this is a time to pay it forward. You don't always need to do something to get something, and it doesn't always have to be in a crisis. Self-respect can be gained from helping others because it's the right thing to do, whether they are grateful or not.

5 SEPTEMBER

OUT OF THE SILOS

HARRY SULLIVAN
Strange how they've given us the run of the ship.
Why doesn't Vira try and stop us?

THE DOCTOR
Not her function, Harry. By the 30th century, human
society was highly compartmentalised. Vira is a medtech
and I suspect we're an executive problem.

The Ark in Space by Robert Holmes (1975)

• • • • • •

On a space station in the distant future, carefully selected specimens of humanity lie waiting in suspended animation. While Earth was ravaged by solar flares, these people quietly slept.

Those chosen to survive the global catastrophe were cross-matched and 'compat-evaluated' so that, as a group, they'd stand the best chance of ensuring humanity's long-term survival. They all had technical skills of the highest standard – even the Earth's High Minister didn't manage to make the grade.

But the strict selection process made these people arrogant. They considered everyone else 'regressive', forgetting that every life has value. Selected for specific tasks, they tended to overlook anything not within their remit, which made them vulnerable when an alien Wirrn invaded their ship!

Even brilliant people can learn from those outside their immediate bubble. Reach out to someone who isn't part of your everyday life – and listen to what they can tell you.

6 SEPTEMBER

ON NOT BEING THE LAST

THE FACE OF BOE
You are not alone.

Gridlock by Russell T Davies (2007)

• • • • • •

On the planet New Earth in the year 5,000,000,053, the Doctor has a final conversation with the dying Face of Boe. This enigmatic creature is thought to be millions of years old, and has lived a full and fascinating life. Now he is ready to die. But the Doctor is sorry to lose someone who is, like him, the very last of his kind.

The Doctor believes himself to be the last of the Time Lords, and now there is one fewer individual who can understand what that's like. We know the Doctor is weighed down by his solitary status, that he grieves for his people and feels terrible guilt for having survived. Yet the Face of Boe's last words to his old friend reveal that there's another Time Lord out there.

If we suffer a bad experience or loss, we can feel as if we're entirely alone – just like the Doctor. Family and friends can help to support us, but what often makes a difference is knowing someone who has been through something similar.

7 SEPTEMBER

LOVE AND NURTURE

THE DOCTOR
They stole a tissue sample at gunpoint and processed it.
It's not what I call natural parenting.

DONNA NOBLE
Rubbish. My friend Nerys fathered twins
with a turkey baster. Don't bother her.

The Doctor's Daughter by Stephen Greenhorn (2008)

• • • • • •

A machine splits a single set of the Doctor's chromosomes and recombines them in a new arrangement as Jenny. The Doctor says that means she is only technically his daughter. Well, technically, it makes the Doctor both biological father and mother.

The Eighth Doctor thought he was half-human on his mother's side, but the Thirteenth Doctor subsequently remembered she was found as a child and raised by her adoptive mother, Tecteun. The Doctor married River Song – though they have no children. Yet we know that the Doctor has a granddaughter, Susan.

Donna isn't bothered about the mechanics. She recognises dad-shock when she sees it – sudden unexpected fatherhood. And she knows from her friend Nerys about non-traditional ways to become a mum.

There are many different families: two parent, or single-parent; married, unmarried, and separated; mother and father or single-sex parents; adoptive parents, foster parents, step-parents, and more. Being a father or a mother is about more than just conception. It's about providing a loving and nurturing home.

8 SEPTEMBER

THE REAL PRIZE

THE DOCTOR

You're missing the point. Enlightenment was not
the diamond; enlightenment was the choice.

Enlightenment by Barbara Clegg (1983)

• • • • • •

An unlikely fleet of old-fashioned sailing ships from different periods
of Earth history sail through space. Powerful beings called Eternals
and their unwitting human crews are competing in a race across the
solar system, each hoping to win a remarkable prize.

The huge diamond referred to as Enlightenment is big enough to
buy a whole galaxy. With it, the Eternals would have power to invade
time itself.

Meanwhile, a sinister being known as the Black Guardian offers
this extraordinary prize to the Doctor's companion Turlough – in
exchange for the Doctor's life.

When the Doctor wins the race, he declines to claim the prize,
saying he isn't ready to possess such power (and that the Eternals
aren't either). Turlough seems tempted but then also declines. In this
moment, he chooses – finally, after several adventures – to side with
the Doctor against the Black Guardian.

As the Doctor says, true enlightenment is the choice we make
to treat other people well. You can make that choice and win this
extraordinary prize.

9 SEPTEMBER

LOOK ROUND THE BACK

ROMANA
How did you know?

THE DOCTOR
Well, he probably looked more convincing from the front.

The Power of Kroll by Robert Holmes (1978–79)

• • • • • •

The Doctor and Romana wade through the swamps of the third moon of Delta Magna in search of a segment of the all-powerful Key to Time. But Romana is captured by the native Swampies, who want to offer her in blood sacrifice to the giant squid-like creature they worship – a vast, tentacled being called Kroll.

The Swampies think Kroll is their protector and that such sacrifice will help them be victorious in battle over the humans exploiting their world. Romana is sceptical about the Swampies' beliefs – but then, as the ceremony continues, she finds herself menaced by a creature with claws.

But just as it looks as if she might be eaten, the Doctor arrives in the nick of time and knocks the creature's head off. It's only a mask, and the creature is actually a meek, embarrassed Swampie wearing an elaborate costume.

It's easy to overestimate a challenge, and making it more scary or daunting than it really is. Follow the Doctor's example and be sure of what you're facing. Often, that better understanding of what needs to be tackled can make it all more manageable.

10 SEPTEMBER

A TIME AND A PLACE

THE DOCTOR
I must admit, Yaz, I can't help feeling
that some of this is my fault.

YASMIN KHAN
Some? All of this is your fault.

Flux: The Halloween Apocalypse by Chris Chibnall (2021)

• • • • • •

There are plenty of occasions when the Doctor loves to hang around with her mates. This is not one of those times.

The Doctor has upset Karvanista, a Lupari warrior and self-proclaimed Vanquisher of the Thousand Civilisations. In response, he's slapped her and Yasmin Khan in handcuffs and locked them upside down to a gravity bar that hovers over a boiling acid ocean spouting acid geysers on a planet about to be engulfed by a giant red star, and guarded by KillDisks.

Despite these apparently overwhelming odds, the Doctor is already planning their escape through a combination of voice-activated commands, high-gravity circus skills and synchronised diving. Her grudging admission of blame provokes a confrontational attitude from Yaz, who spends the rest of the rescue complaining instead of helping.

If you're going to have an argument, pick your moment. You may have more pressing things that need your energy and attention.

11 SEPTEMBER

RISE TO THE CHALLENGE

THE MOMENT
You're the Doctor, too.

THE WAR DOCTOR
No. Great men are forged in fire. It is the privilege of
lesser men to light the flame, whatever the cost.

The Day of the Doctor by Steven Moffat (2013)

• • • • • •

'Doctor no more.' When he accepted the help of the Sisterhood of
Karn, the Eighth Doctor asked to be a warrior. It's what he thought he
needed to fight the Time War.

His subsequent experience convinced him he was unworthy of the
title 'Doctor'. Now he faces a crucial moment. He's witnessed how his
successors achieved peace between humans and Zygons, and agonises
over his own decision about ending the war between Time Lords and
Daleks: destroy his own people or to let the universe burn? Will those
future Doctors be who they are because of his choice, or in spite of it?

The strongest steel is forged in the hottest fire. It's during the
most testing of times that people's true bravery is seen – in the heart
of conflict or adversity or loss. Do you choose to rise to the challenge
and forge ahead, or to yield to the pressure?

12 SEPTEMBER

TIME FLOWS BY

THE DOCTOR
Funny old business, time. It delights in frustrating your plans.
All Kane's bitterness and hatred thwarted by a quirk of time.

Dragonfire by Ian Briggs (1987)

• • • • • •

The vicious criminal Kane was captured by his people on Proamon and exiled to the frozen, dark side of the planet Svartos.

For 3,000 years Kane plotted revenge against his own people – without knowing that he was wasting his time. A thousand years after he was exiled from his home world, its local, cold red star turned supernova and all the planets were engulfed in the explosion. Kane finally realizes that for two-thirds of his imprisonment, there has been no one to avenge himself on. All his efforts and diabolical schemes have been for nothing.

The Doctor is also long-lived and has suffered all kinds of loss and injustice. Yet his behaviour on Svartos is completely different to Kane's. The Doctor explores, makes new friends and even goes on a treasure hunt.

Humans don't live as long as the Doctor or Kane. We don't know how long our lives – or those of others – will be. Don't waste time in bitterness. Move on and make the most of what you have.

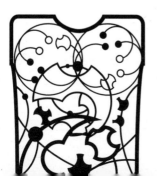

13 SEPTEMBER

MEETING YOUR HEROES

THE DOCTOR

Agatha Christie! I was just talking about you the other day. I said, 'I bet she's brilliant.' I'm the Doctor, this is Donna. Oh, I love your stuff. What a mind. You fool me every time. Well, almost every time. Well, once or twice. Well, once. But it was a good once.

The Unicorn and the Wasp by Gareth Roberts (2008)

• • • • • •

It's easy to get tongue-tied or make social gaffes when you meet people you admire. The Doctor and Donna have a similar experience when they are overjoyed to meet mystery writer Agatha Christie at a 1926 cocktail party. Eager to make an impression, the Doctor's conflicting instincts between social nicety and strict accuracy means he stumbles through his praise for her work.

Should you be lucky enough to have a brief encounter with one of your heroes, don't worry about the detail. Say something nice – even if it's just politely asking for an autograph. If you say something unkind, even without meaning to, a moment that could have been innocent fun will live unhappily in the memory.

14 SEPTEMBER

THE WONDER OF IT ALL

THE DOCTOR

The slightest accident in this stage of the proceedings and we'd all reverse instantly into antimatter, blasted out to the other side of the universe as a flash of electromagnetic radiation. We'll all become unpeople, undoing unthings untogether. Fascinating.

The Mutants by Bob Baker and Dave Martin (1972)

• • • • • •

The Time Lords send the Doctor and Jo Grant on a mission to the planet Solos in the 30th century. They give the Doctor a box containing evidence that the mutations of humanoid Solonians into monstrous-looking Mutts is not a disease but all part of their natural life cycle.

In fact, there's a third stage of development in which the Solonians become beautiful, flying beings with extraordinary powers. It's truly a wonder to behold – if only the ruling Overlords (humans from Earth) could see it that way.

Sadly, many people from Earth are interested only in continuing to rule and exploit the Solonians. They try to alter the planet's atmosphere to make it more like that of Earth, and the Doctor cautions them about the technology they're using.

But look – even the thought of his own total obliteration is a wonder to the Doctor. All life is rich and strange and fascinating, even at the end.

15 SEPTEMBER

EMAIL ETIQUETTE

THE DOCTOR

I've sent out a sort of round-robin email. All being well, the first intelligent, space-going system will be in touch fairly soon.

Empress of Mars by Mark Gatiss (2017)

• • • • • •

Victorian soldiers make an expedition to Mars in an interplanetary vessel they found in the South African veldt. They are assisted by a stranded, injured Ice Warrior who wants to return to his home planet. Unknown to the soldiers, his intention is to resurrect Iraxxa, his Ice Queen, who has been in hibernation on the now-barren planet for five thousand years.

The Doctor brokers a truce between the humans and Ice Warriors. He broadcasts a message out around the local galaxy to ask civilisations in the vicinity to come to the rescue of the resurrected Ice Warriors. Alpha Centauri responds first, offering to send a fleet to their aid at once.

Think about the best way to ask for assistance. Email, social media notifications, text messages, phone calls, mail-outs... Strike a balance about how and when you identify and contact interested parties. A thing that's urgent for you may be an unwelcome interruption for some. Target your audience. It's counter-productive if you spam and annoy everyone else.

16 SEPTEMBER

GIVE IT BACK

THE DOCTOR
Come along, help me find the Ghanta. Down there,
it's going to guarantee us the welcome of a lifetime.

The Abominable Snowmen by Mervyn Haisman and Henry Lincoln (1967)

• • • • • •

When the TARDIS lands in Tibet in 1935, the Doctor sees a chance to return something precious to the monastery at Detsen. When he visited once before, in 1630, the monastery came under attack – and the Doctor ending up leaving with the prized Ghanta.

The Ghanta is a small Tibetan bell with a dragon on it, a holy relic with an interesting history of its own. The Doctor is right in his belief that the monks will welcome its return, but he's a bit surprised to discover one of the monks remembers him from his previous trip, some 300 years earlier. There's something very odd and sinister going on...

We all borrow things and then forget to return them. Today, have a look around and see if you have something that belongs to someone else, get in touch with them and arrange to give it back. They might have forgotten they ever lent it to you, but they'll appreciate the gesture.

17 SEPTEMBER

TEAM DYNAMICS

MISS QUILL
I can't fire weapons!
I can't use swords and knives and screwdrivers!

THE DOCTOR
Your brain, Miss Quill. Best weapon there is.
Look at you! What an amazing team!
You'll be able to handle anything
that Time throws at you.

Class: For Tonight We Might Die by Patrick Ness (2016)

• • • • • •

Coal Hill is no ordinary school. It's a beacon across all of space-time to any being who might make mischief. Pupil 'Charlie Smith' is really an alien prince rescued by the Doctor. His new friends include a girl forced to share her heart with an extra-terrestrial and a boy with an alien prosthetic limb – not the second leg he expected when signing up for the football team.

The Doctor also transports an alien warrior to the school as Charlie's reluctant protector. Disguised physics teacher 'Miss Quill' despairs that she's prevented from lying or using weapons because of her violent history. The Doctor reassures her that she's not alone — she will help these amazing humans, and they'll help her.

The strength of a team is each member in it, and the strength of each member is the team. We reach our goals with the help of others. Teamwork without the team is just work.

18 SEPTEMBER

WHAT DO YOU GET?

THE DOCTOR
Everything's of interest to me and Cybermen
possess nothing that a human might want.

Revenge of the Cybermen by Gerry Davis (1975)

• • • • • •

Sometime around the 30th century, Professor Kellman, an exographer conducting a planetary survey of a new moon of Jupiter, is discovered to be in league with the Cybermen. His actions involve helping them to infect and kill the crew of a space station.

While Kellman's colleagues are shocked at his treachery, the Doctor is fascinated to know what exactly Kellman might gain from this alliance. Others don't think this is important but the Doctor persists – and so succeeds in exposing the truth. Kellman is in fact a double-agent on a long-term assignment to work *against* the Cybermen and lead them into a trap.

Whatever the ethics of Kellman's mission, motivation is often key to understanding people's behaviour, especially when they act oddly. For example, someone might act aggressively – apparently for no reason – if they're anxious and want to feel safe. This means that responding aggressively towards them would probably only make matters worse.

Kellman knows what he wants and acts ruthlessly to get it, but not everyone recognises the motive behind their behaviour.

19 SEPTEMBER

A GOOD QUESTION

THE DOCTOR
Just one question – do you happen
to know how to fly this thing?

The Time of the Doctor by Steven Moffat (2013)

• • • • • •

Sometimes you just need to ask the obvious question, loudly and directly. That's especially true when you don't think some things are right.

This brand-new incarnation of the Doctor clearly gets straight to the point. That may be something he's learned from the various friends and companions who've travelled in the TARDIS over the years. 'What is it, Doctor?' they'll ask, or 'What's happening?' and, 'What does that mean?'

Don't be afraid to admit you don't know something. Asking questions is how we empower ourselves. It can also help the person you're asking, because answering makes them clarify their own thoughts. And implicit in asking 'Why are things like this?' is another question: 'Is there another way?' That's why the Doctor being asked what's happening often leads to some new idea or connection.

There are no foolish questions. But be wary of easy and safe answers. As the Doctor could tell you, life is often strange and a bit scary. We make sense of it, we make things better, with questions.

20 SEPTEMBER

DON'T SPOIL THE FUN

THE DOCTOR
These books are from your future. You don't want to read
ahead. Spoil all the surprises. Like peeking at the end.

Silence in the Library by Steven Moffat (2008)

• • • • • •

Having a secret is exciting. The anticipation of what delight or surprise
it will provoke when you divulge it. The privilege of being entrusted
with information that's not to be shared. Or the superiority of being
in control of what and when you reveal.

Donna's curious about the 51st century books in the universe's
biggest library. The Doctor knows reading about past events means it
risks making subsequent choices to change them – or at the very least,
ruins the enjoyment of experiencing them for the first time.

In our 21st century, people share news, gossip, and enthusiasm
on social media, knowingly or by accident. We enjoy stories in books,
cinema and television at different times, and hope it won't be ruined
by someone blurting out the best bits before we've discovered them
for ourselves.

There's joy in celebrating when you've both already seen a movie
or read a book. Think about how, when and where you share story
secrets. They're called spoilers for a reason.

21 SEPTEMBER

ACCEPT YOUR PAST

THE DOCTOR

We all change, when you think about it. We're all different
people all through our lives. And that's OK, that's good. You've
got to keep moving, so long as you remember all the people that
you used to be. I will not forget one line of this. Not one day.
I swear. I will always remember when the Doctor was me.

The Time of the Doctor by Steven Moffat (2013)

• • • • • •

Times change, and so must the Doctor. Clara Oswald begged his
people to help him at the end of his lives, and they granted him a whole
regeneration cycle.

Clara doesn't want him to change. She's travelled with him across
time and space. Seen him grow old over centuries on Trenzalore. But
now, in the TARDIS, the process has begun. Any moment now, he's
coming – the next Doctor.

The person you are is the product of who you were. Choices made:
jobs, friends, partners, houses. Passions held: music, books, politics,
food. Events survived: school, illness, conflict. You don't have to let the
successes or mistakes of your past trap you there. You have choices and
enthusiasms and events still to come. You're the same, but different.

22 SEPTEMBER

POSITIVELY NOT

SENSORITE WARRIOR
He could have destroyed the entire Sensorite nation.

THE DOCTOR
Yes, but the fact is you didn't kill him.
Shows great promise for the future of your people.

The Sensorites by Peter R Newman (1964)

• • • • • •

In the 28th century, human soldiers land on a planet called the Sense Sphere and are attacked telepathically by Sensorites. Of course the soldiers fight back. Massively outnumbered, they retreat into caverns but wage war for a decade – as best they can. They poison the water supply to the Sensorites' city, and each year more and more Sensorites die.

The soldiers think they're good people, taking righteous action against monsters. But the Doctor reveals that the Sensorites didn't attack the humans; they were just trying to communicate. Given all those who've suffered and died, the Sensorites have every right to be angry. The humans should be punished! Something should be done! Yet these quiet, empathetic creatures do something extraordinary and respond with kindness, allowing the ragged, exhausted soldiers to return home to Earth.

We shouldn't put up with bad or aggressive behaviour, but showing mercy isn't a weakness – and it can help us to move on.

23 SEPTEMBER

NO MORE MR NICE GUY

JAMIE McCRIMMON
I don't think you could annoy that man even
if you want to. He's being as nice as pie.

THE DOCTOR
He's too nice.

The Invasion by Derrick Sherwin (1968)

• • • • • •

Tobias Vaughn, managing director of leading manufacturer International Electromatics, is a most obliging man. When the Doctor and his friends repeatedly break into IE buildings, Vaughn seems quite amused. Even when his expensive computerised receptionist is blown up by Zoe Heriot confusing it with logic, Vaughn just laughs.

Of course, this isn't how an ordinary person would respond to such provocation, and it leads the Doctor to suspect that Vaughn is no ordinary man. In fact, Vaughn is in league with the Cybermen, aiming to control Earth on their behalf. His body has already been made partially cybernetic – but despite his placid smile, he still retains his emotions.

We soon see Vaughn's quick and fiery temper when he doesn't get his own way. He's greedy and self-serving right to the end.

Beware the smiles and smooth words of people who are used to getting whatever they want; it's when their desires are frustrated that you really get to know who they are.

24 SEPTEMBER

LOOK BEYOND THE HEADLINES

CRAIG OWENS
Why's none of this on the front page?

THE DOCTOR
Oh, page one has an exclusive on Nina, a local girl
who got kicked off *Britain's Got Talent.*

Closing Time by Gareth Roberts (2011)

• • • • • •

We get news from the TV, newspapers and websites. Online social media tells us what's trending. The more we talk and tweet, the wider the stories spread.

Craig Owens doesn't know why the Doctor has turned up again to disturb his sleeping baby. The Doctor claims it's a social call, but Craig suspects something dangerous and alien – and he doesn't mean the Doctor.

Sheila Clark, Atif Ghosh and Tom Luker have all gone missing this week. Craig can't understand why that's not more widely known, and the Doctor says that he found those reports on pages 7, 19, and 22 – whereas other readers were more interested in celebrity gossip.

Headlines are what an editor decided was newsworthy. Trending messages on social networking are what many others picked up and posted. Don't let those be the only things that get your attention, raise a smile, or make you angry. You can find Sheila and Atif and Tom if you look more closely.

25 SEPTEMBER

GIVE IT A TRY

THE DOCTOR
Thing about me, I'm stupid. I talk too much. Always babbling on. This gob doesn't stop for anything. Want to know the only reason I'm still alive? Always stay near the door.

Forest of the Dead by Steven Moffat (2008)

• • • • • •

The Doctor and his party flee through the linked skyscrapers of the biggest library in the universe. He sends the others ahead of him while he tries to talk to the creature hot on their heels.

River Song isn't convinced the Doctor can reason with a carnivorous swarm in a suit. Nevertheless, the Vashta Nerada tell him new information about their origins – but not before they consume another victim and close in. The Doctor distracts them by chatting as he prepares to open a trapdoor beneath him and escape.

Don't be afraid to try something novel, go to a place you've not visited before or meet different people at a party or an event. You'll learn new things, make fresh connections and maybe change your perspective. And if things don't go too well, you can always prepare an excuse that allows you to pop out at a moment's notice.

26 SEPTEMBER

PUTTING PEOPLE FIRST

THE DOCTOR
As you know, sir, the sixth segment was in fact a human
being. If the pieces are maintained in their present
pattern it means that she'll be imprisoned forever.

The Armageddon Factor by Bob Baker and Dave Martin (1979)

· · · · · ·

The Key to Time is a crystalline cube that maintains the equilibrium of
time itself. It gives absolute power over every particle in the universe:
everything that has ever existed or ever will exist. Since this is too
dangerous for any being to possess, the Key to Time is usually broken
up into six segments and scattered throughout the cosmos with each
segment disguised in a different form.

The Doctor and Romana are assigned by the White Guardian
to collect the six segments from different worlds. But one segment
is disguised as a person – Princess Astra of Atrios – who has a
life of her own. The Guardian thinks this regrettable but isn't too
concerned, and the Doctor realises that this cannot be the White
Guardian, who would not be so callous, but instead is his antithesis,
the Black Guardian.

Humans often make decisions based on economics: what will it cost,
how much time will it take, and so on. More important is how economic
decisions will affect people and whether they will do any harm.

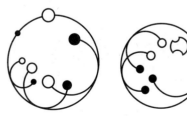

293

27 SEPTEMBER

WHAT'S YOUR ARGUMENT?

THE DOCTOR
Friend or enemy, it's a distinction that's lost on
the Silurians, I assure you. To them you're all
the same: ape-descended primitives.

Warriors of the Deep by Johnny Byrne (1984)

• • • • • •

In the year 2084, Earth is divided between two warring power blocs. On secret bases around the world, proton missiles are primed and ready for use – each bloc poised to annihilate the another.

Sea Base Four is one such military colony, based deep underwater near an oceanic fault. When the TARDIS arrives on the sea base, Commander Vorshak naturally concludes its crew are enemy agents from the other bloc. But the Doctor, Tegan and Turlough arrived quite by accident!

They're not the only ones to know little about the political situation. A combined force of Silurians and Sea Devils are planning to conquer the base and use its missiles to annihilate *all* of humanity, without making any distinction between the two sides.

Sometimes, we can get so caught up in an argument that it can become all-consuming and we lose perspective. We forget that other people aren't involved. And we might even miss other, more pressing concerns.

28 SEPTEMBER

TAKE THE FIRST STEP

THE DOCTOR
There's a new war now. I think these creatures are light-eating locusts, looking for rents and cracks between worlds to let themselves into dimensions of light. Once they break through, they eat. They will eat the sun, and then they will eat the stars. And they will keep eating until there are no stars left. So, whose side are you on now? Because as far as I can see, there's only one side left.

The Eaters of Light by Rona Munro (2017)

• • • • • •

Only a small cohort from the Roman Ninth Legion survived their stay in 2nd century Scotland. They were wiped out by an alien that breached a dimensional portal. As Keeper of the Gate, local Pict Kar was dedicated to halting the creature, until invading Romans attacked her community and she saw it as a way to defeat them.

The Doctor brings Romans and Picts together. They are angry because they are scared. If they continue slaughtering each other, they'll overlook the greater danger of the alien menace.

The enemy of your enemy is your friend. We must set aside past political, military and economic conflicts to confront future dangers to our planet: species extinction, global pandemics, asteroid strikes and climate change. Make your personal choice and act on it. Until you stop saying 'someone should', no one will.

29 SEPTEMBER

ALL GOOD THINGS COME TO AN END

SARAH JANE SMITH

The universe has to move forward. Pain and loss, they define us as much as happiness or love. Whether it's a world or a relationship, everything has its time. And everything ends.

School Reunion by Toby Whithouse (2006)

• • • • • •

Mr Finch, the head teacher of Deffry Vale School, is really an alien Krillitane who has been feasting on some unfortunate pupils. The rest have been fed with chips cooked in a special oil to make them more intelligent. By harnessing this brain power, Finch aims to crack the Skasis Paradigm – the equation that will explain the whole universe. This momentous discovery would give the Krillitane control over all space and time.

When the Doctor confronts Finch, the head teacher suggests that such power should be used for good – by the Doctor. Civilisations could be rescued, the Time Lords reborn, and all those that the Doctor has lost could be saved.

It's easy to see why the Doctor is tempted. But his great friend Sarah Jane Smith intercedes. Pain and loss are difficult, but without them life would have no meaning. Nothing lasts forever, which is what gives things – and more importantly people – true value. Understanding this lesson is what frees the Doctor from temptation.

30 SEPTEMBER

FILL YOUR POCKETS

THE DOCTOR
Where did you get those jelly babies?

ROMANA
Same place you get them. Your pocket.

The Pirate Planet by Douglas Adams (1978)

• • • • • •

Romana questions the locals on Zanak for useful information, and makes an excellent trade. They offer her gemstones that they just pick up from the street. Romana offers them jelly babies, pick-pocketed from the Doctor.

Somehow, the Fourth Doctor's pockets always seem to have exactly what he needs: a yo-yo to test gravity; an egg-timer and a football rattle to make distracting noises; an extending pointer to trigger a booby trap; a barrister's wig for a court appearance; a paperback to read while waiting; a radio, a magnifying glass, cutters, an eye-piece, ginger beer, his sonic screwdriver, an etheric beam locator, and bags of sweets.

His contradictory advice to his friend Harry Sullivan is never to throw anything away, but not to clutter your pockets. To ensure you pack wisely for your next trip, mentally work from your head to your toes: hat, comb, sunglasses, make-up, razor, via handbag and belt, right down to flip-flops and shoe polish.

Mentally pat each pocket or purse, asking what you'd expect them to hold: passport, tickets, money, cards, phone? Visualising things is a powerful prompt when preparing to travel.

OCTOBER

1 OCTOBER

TAKE THE TEAM WITH YOU

> HOSTESS
> Enjoy your trip.
>
> THE DOCTOR
> Oh, I can't wait. Allons-y.
>
> HOSTESS
> I'm sorry?
>
> THE DOCTOR
> It's French for 'Let's go'.

Midnight by Russell T Davies (2008)

● ● ● ● ● ●

'Allons-y' is the Tenth Doctor's rallying cry. Most people take it for granted when he says it: whether that's to Rose and Martha, to Queen Elizabeth I and Lady Christina de Souza, to people aboard the SS *Pentallian* and cruise spaceship *Titanic*, and with Jackson Lake.

The Hostess is the only person who asks him to explain it, when the Doctor is keen for the shuttle to depart on its journey across the diamond planet of Midnight. You can see why. It's a trip to see an enormous jewel the size of a glacier that reaches the Cliffs of Oblivion and shatters into sapphires at its edge to fall a hundred thousand feet into a crystal ravine. No wonder he wants to get a shift on.

As a call to action, the phrase encourages everyone to move together. It's not a command that people must obey; it's an exhortation to work together. Not 'Go' but 'Let's go!' You'll get people to do the right thing when you invite them to act with you as a team.

2 OCTOBER

COMPUTER SAYS NO

JANE GARRETT
We trust the computer. It is our strength and our guide.

THE DOCTOR
Not this time.

JAMIE MCCRIMMON
Well, why not?

THE DOCTOR
Because Jamie, the computer is faced with an
insoluble problem. Either way it risks destroying
itself and this it cannot do. It must play safe.

The Ice Warriors by Brian Hayles (1967)

• • • • • •

Far in the future, much of Britain lies under a glacier in a bitterly cold
new Ice Age. The team at Britannicus Base hope to slow the advance
of the ice by using a powerful ioniser. Then they're attacked by Ice
Warriors from Mars!

The Doctor suggests that the ioniser could be used against the
Ice Warriors' spaceship, but the computer at Britannicus Base rules
against the idea because it calculates a 50 per cent chance that it would
be destroyed in the process! The only way to stop the attack is to
ignore the computer – to the horror of the humans.

Since this story was first broadcast, computers, tablets and mobile
phones have become ever more important in our lives. Are we too
dependent on them? Spend some time today without using a digital
device of any sort, and you'll see.

3 OCTOBER

WHAT THE DOCTOR HATES

ACE
Don't you have things you hate?

THE DOCTOR
I can't stand burnt toast. I loathe bus stations – terrible places,
full of lost luggage and lost souls. Then there's unrequited
love, and tyranny and cruelty. We all have a
universe of our own terrors to face.

Ghost Light by Marc Platt (1989)

• • • • • •

In 1983, years before she meets the Doctor, a very young Ace sneaks into the ruin of Gabriel Chase, an old house in Perivale, and discovers that it's haunted. On hearing this, the Doctor is intrigued and takes an older Ace back in time to 1883 to learn the origin of this 'ghost'.

But he doesn't *tell* Ace where they actually are. When she finds out, she's furious that he's taken her to Gabriel Chase against her will – and says that he too must have things he doesn't want to face.

It's odd to hear the Doctor admit to hatred. But what he hates is very revealing. The 'terrors' he wants to battle are all things that have a negative impact on people's lives. Follow the Doctor's example and think about what you stand for – and stand against. What 'terrors' stand in your way? Recognising the challenge is the first step in making real change.

4 OCTOBER

HELPFUL EXPLANATIONS

LIEUTENANT-GENERAL LOGAN
They'll attack again at first light.
I don't know what to do. Help me.

THE DOCTOR
I'm going to need a pointy stick.

Flux: War of the Sontarans by Chris Chibnall (2021)

• • • • • •

A catastrophic attack on Sontaran forces in the Crimea sees Her Majesty's Army Light Division routed and leaves their commanding officer a broken man. General Logan previously rejected the Doctor's advice – why would he need it when he had Queen and Country on his side? Now his soldiers have paid the price for his mistakes, and he's begging for her help.

The Doctor swiftly outlines 'Project: Crimean Eviction'. It involves statistical analysis about the Sontaran rest cycle, data capture from field observations by a Jamaican nurse, an understanding of atmospheric influence, an explanation of alien armour and physiology and an appreciation of supply logistics, all explained in terms that combatants in a mid-19th century conflict will grasp quickly.

It's a lot for her audience to take in. Which is why the Doctor's instinct is to use visual aids in the form of maps and drawings spread across the table and wall of Mary Seacole's British Hotel, and direct their attention with a pointy stick.

There are so many occasions when it's better, clearer and more instructive to demonstrate rather than describe. Show, don't tell.

5 OCTOBER

THE VALUE OF WHAT WE MAKE

ROMANA
Precious stones?

DOCTOR
Very precious. In a geological sense,
more precious than diamonds.

Destiny of the Daleks by Terry Nation (1979)

• • • • • •

Arriving on a bleak, foreboding planet, the Doctor alights on what Romana initially thinks might be precious stones. In fact, it's gravel in a binding of something like limestone and clay.

Prompted by the Doctor, Romana looks more closely. Limestone, clay and water are used to make cement, and with gravel make concrete. We might think it odd that the Doctor considers this more valuable than diamonds. But what he and Romana have found has been *manufactured*, so is evidence of intelligent life on the planet.

Today, we have probes exploring the Moon and robots scouring the surface of Mars, but they're not looking for diamonds and rubies. Instead, they're searching for things that we have in abundance on Earth and therefore take for granted: liquid water and signs of life. The more we search space, the rarer these things seem be, and so the more precious they become.

Puddles, bacteria and bits of concrete – let alone everything else! We live on a world rich in wonders.

6 OCTOBER

SOCIAL LIES

THE DOCTOR
I'm the Doctor. I'm a Time Lord from the planet Gallifrey.
I stole a time machine and ran away and I've been
flouting the principal law of my own people ever since.
That wasn't quite what I was meant to say!

The Time of the Doctor by Steven Moffat (2013)

• • • • • •

The Doctor and Clara arrive on Trenzalore. It seems a hospitable enough place, and they give a cheery greeting to the first couple of locals they meet. Though they also say some unexpectedly candid things about their themselves and their feelings.

The town has a truth field, set up by the Time Lords before they vanished from the universe. It's designed to ensure the Doctor isn't lying when he eventually turns up and responds to a question only he can answer. Does that make life in Trenzalore a bit difficult? Well, yes and no.

Social lies are when we prioritise another person's feelings over truth: a child expecting the Easter Bunny, or when we politely enjoy an awful meal cooked by a relative. It shows gratitude, generosity and compassion. Don't let them become antisocial lies for your own personal gain.

7 OCTOBER

BACK-SEAT DRIVERS

THE DOCTOR

You can't rule a world in hiding. You've got to come out
onto the balcony sometimes and wave a tentacle.

Terror of the Zygons by Robert Banks Stewart (1975)

• • • • • •

Since at least the Middle Ages, a group of some six Zygons lived in
a damaged spacecraft in the waters of Loch Ness. Their armoured
cyborg Skarasen – whose lactic fluid fed the Zygons – would swim
about and occasionally be sighted. But otherwise the Zygons kept
themselves hidden while plotting the conquest of the world.

When the Fourth Doctor encountered the creatures, he mocked
their skulking ways, challenging them to step out into the open. In
doing so, he provoked Zygon leader Broton into spelling out all his
plans. But there's a broader point to bear in mind.

People will often comment on something from a position of relative safety, suggesting they know better. They might criticize someone's
driving from the comfort of the back seat. They might be a so-called
'keyboard warrior', posting aggressively but anonymously online.

But it's easy to snipe from the sidelines. If you're going to lead, you
need to be out in front.

8 OCTOBER

HOW TO BE REMEMBERED

ROSE TYLER
He thought you were brilliant.

DONNA NOBLE
Don't be stupid.

ROSE TYLER
But you are. It just took the Doctor to show
you that, simply by being with him. He did the
same to me. To everyone he touches.

Turn Left by Russell T Davies (2008)

• • • • • •

The Doctor has died in an alternative reality created by the Trickster's time beetle – so he's not around to prevent accidents and alien incursions that cause millions of deaths across the planet with cataclysmic effects on health, the environment, and social justice.

With the fabric of reality collapsing, Rose Tyler travels between the universes to find Donna Noble, the inadvertent catalyst for the catastrophe. Donna despairs that she is nothing. She can't believe that someone as special as the Doctor would want to travel with her. Rose reminds her that what the Doctor saw in her helped Donna reach her potential.

People won't necessarily recall the specific things you did in life. How busy you were, how hard you worked, the things you owned, the status you achieved. They will remember the time you spent with them, whether they could count on you, and how you made them feel.

9 OCTOBER

GET BOOKED UP

THE DOCTOR

We're in a library. Books – best weapons
in the world! This room's the greatest arsenal
we could have. Arm yourself.

Tooth and Claw by Russell T Davies (2006)

• • • • • •

In Scotland in 1879, the Doctor, Rose Tyler and Queen Victoria battle
ninja-like monks and a terrifying werewolf. Though the queen coolly
shoots down a would-be human assassin, the werewolf cannot be
defeated with weapons so conventional.

The Doctor, Rose and the queen take shelter in Torchwood
House, owned by Sir Robert MacLeish. It appears that his father and
the queen's late husband Prince Albert prepared the house for a potential werewolf attack a long time ago. The library contains clues to the
research they were doing: useful books on mistletoe and magic. From
these tomes, and from what Queen Victoria tells him, the Doctor
manages to deduce a method for defeating the creature.

As the Doctor says, the knowledge in these books together with
the plans Albert made, means that the prince is still protecting Victoria
nearly two decades after his death.

Through books, we can engage in the knowledge, experience
and wisdom of other people – even those who have died. With that
knowledge, we're better equipped to face life's challenges and don't
need actual weapons! Today, pick a good book to read and see what its
author wants to share with you.

(No, not this one – that would be too easy!)

10 OCTOBER

RESPECT PEOPLE'S CHOICES

MISSY
Chose it himself, you know, trying to sound
mysterious. And then he dropped the 'Who' when
he realised it was a tiny bit on the nose.

THE DOCTOR
Stop teasing her and focus.

BILL POTTS
Is she serious, though, Doctor?
Is your real name 'Doctor Who'?

World Enough and Time by Steven Moffat (2017)

• • • • • •

As part of Missy's rehabilitation, the Doctor lets her lead the investigation of a distress call. Missy says she's now 'Doctor Who' because she's pretending to be the Doctor and that was how she knew him when they grew up together.

The Doctor dislikes fellow Time Lord Drax using his school name 'Theta Sigma'. People sometimes ask him 'Doctor who?' when they're first introduced. The Doctor takes various aliases – John Smith, Dr Caligari, Dr von Wer – and only ever seems to tell River Song his original name, which we never hear. He wouldn't even reveal it when trapped on Trenzalore. And Tecteun, the woman who rescued and raised the Doctor on Gallifrey, never uses it.

We're each assigned our given name at birth. When we're older, some people may choose to change theirs. It's polite to respect that choice when we talk to them or about them.

11 OCTOBER

IMPROVE THOSE SOCIAL SKILLS (1)

THE DOCTOR
I'm trying to do small talk.
I thought I was doing quite well.

YASMIN KHAN
Needs work.

THE DOCTOR
Maybe I'm nervous. Or just socially awkward.

Arachnids in the UK by Chris Chibnall (2018)

· · · · · ·

We've all been there, usually with new people. We don't know what to say. Sometimes, like the Thirteenth Doctor, *trying* to do small talk only makes things worse because we say the first thing that comes to mind.

You could be like the Doctor and admit you're feeling nervous. If the person you're talking to is nervous as well, you've immediately made a connection.

But here's a good tip for taking the pressure off this socially awkward Doctor (and you). Simply flip the problem round and encourage the other person to talk.

Get them to talk about themselves. Listen, and be interested. Open up the conservation by asking them to expand on things they've just told you. It's a bit like playing tennis: you bat the conversation back to them to keep it going.

Other incarnations of the Doctor aren't nearly so awkward. In fact, they can be incredibly charming. How do they do it – and what can we learn from them? We'll find out tomorrow...

12 OCTOBER

IMPROVE THOSE SOCIAL SKILLS (II)

THE DOCTOR
Now don't tell me. Corporal Benton, isn't it?

BENTON
Sergeant Benton now.

THE DOCTOR
How do you do, my dear fellow? I haven't seen you
since that nasty business with the Cybermen.

The Three Doctors by Bob Baker and Dave Martin (1972–73)

• • • • • •

The Second Doctor can be by turns mischievous and irascible – and then he turns on the charm. How does he win people over, and can we do it ourselves?

Well, just look at this quick little exchange. This is a Third Doctor story and we're inside the Third Doctor's TARDIS. But the Second Doctor breezes in and strikes up conversation with UNIT's redoubtable Benton. Look how much he packs into just those few lines.

1. He uses Benton's name and remembers something about him – in this case, his military rank.
2. He listens to what Benton then says.
3. More than that, he expresses interest and delight in the fact Benton has been promoted.
4. He mentions shared experience with the Cybermen, inviting Benton to reminisce – and also bring him up to speed.

Benton is immediately won over, and for that matter so are we. What an entrance!

13 OCTOBER

HELP MAKE CONNECTIONS

CLARA OSWALD

An ordinary person wants to meet someone that they
know very well for lunch. What do they do?

THE DOCTOR

Well, they probably get in touch and suggest lunch.

CLARA OSWALD

OK. So what sort of person would put a
cryptic note in a newspaper advert?

Deep Breath by Steven Moffat (2014)

• • • • • •

Mancini's Family Restaurant offers the best dinner in Victorian London.
Clara Oswald and the Doctor each respond to a puzzling personal
advert in the newspaper: 'Impossible Girl. Lunch on the other side.'

Something doesn't smell right about the venue – and it's not just
the tramp's coat that the Doctor is wearing. They're about to discover
that their fellow diners are automatons made of clockwork parts and
human remains.

What has drawn the pair here? Estranged since the Doctor's
recent regeneration, each of them thinks that the other placed the
advert. Neither of them did. There's a woman out there who's very
keen that the pair should stay together.

If you know a couple are perfect for each other, but too shy to take
the next step, make the introduction for them. Invite them both to an
event with you so they can meet and get to know each other in the
trusted environment of your presence.

14 OCTOBER

WE ARE OUR EXPERIENCE

THE DOCTOR
I am being diminished – whittled away, piece
by piece. A man is the sum of his memories,
you know. A Time Lord even more so.

The Five Doctors by Terrance Dicks (1983)

· · · · · ·

The Fifth Doctor and his friends Tegan and Turlough take a well-deserved break on the tranquil Eye of Orion. But then the holiday abruptly ends.

All through time and space, the Doctor's previous incarnations are captured by a time scoop and transported to the Death Zone on Gallifrey to compete in a deadly game. The Fifth Doctor feels the loss of each of his previous selves as if he were being physically attacked. When the attempt to scoop the Fourth Doctor from his time stream fails, the Fifth Doctor is nearly pulled into the time vortex after him, where he too could become trapped.

The physical effect on the Doctor is a manifestation of a more philosophical idea: that who we are is the product of our experience. The good, the bad, the mistakes we make and the lessons we learn, all add up to make you *you*. So do your best to create good memories every day.

15 OCTOBER

LEVEL THE PLAYING FIELD

THE DOCTOR
No! Bo! Ho! Sho! Ko! Ro! To! So!
Bo Ko Do Zo Go Bo Fo Po Jo!

The Stolen Earth by Russell T Davies (2008)

• • • • • •

The Doctor first met a platoon of Judoon on the Moon. They are thick-skinned police mercenaries, brutish and single-minded, who take no heed of the unintended consequences of their actions.

He knows from that first encounter that their translators can cope with people who speak in other languages. Nevertheless, when he meets them now in the Shadow Proclamation, he chooses to address the Judoon using their own language and its idiosyncratic dialect. The Doctor shows respect without backing down. We can't be sure precisely what he's saying, but since the Judoon holster their raised weapons, we can be clear they approve.

In an unexpected confrontation, don't be intimidated by who you meet. Adapt your response to what they expect – whether language, terminology or culture. Establish from the outset that you're meeting on equal terms, and demonstrate your willingness to behave in that manner. The sooner you establish mutually acceptable ground rules and expectations, the more successful your encounter.

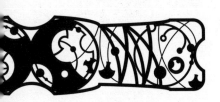

16 OCTOBER

SCEPTICAL JUDGMENTS

THE DOCTOR
You should read Pyrrho, my boy.
He founded scepticism – a great asset to your business.

The Keys of Marinus by Terry Nation (1964)

• • • • • •

On the planet Marinus, you're considered guilty until proven innocent, which is bad news when the Doctor's friend Ian is accused of murder and faces a sentence of death. Defending Ian in court, the Doctor advises the other lawyers to read up on Pyrrho.

In fact, no writings of painter-turned-philosopher Pyrrho of Elis (c. 365–c. 275 BCE) are known to survive. The earliest surviving account of Pyrrho's thinking is a very brief summary by Eusebius of Caesarea, written about 313 CE, some 600 years after Pyrrho's death. According to this, Pyrrho and his followers argued that we can't really be sure of anything, either through sense or reason, so we should always suspend judgement.

As the Doctor goes on to expose the real murderer, he surely doesn't mean we should never reach any judgement. But he wants the lawyers to question both the evidence and their own assumptions before making a decision. That's a good lesson for us all.

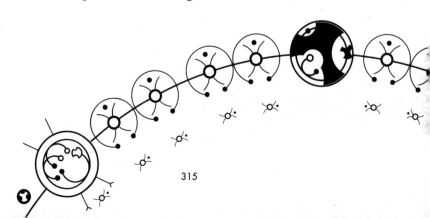

17 OCTOBER

ALTRUISTIC ACTION

THE DOCTOR
Without hope. Without witness. Without reward.

The Doctor Falls by Steven Moffat (2017)

• • • • • •

On a Mondasian colony ship dangerously close to a black hole, Cybermen make relentless progress as they kill or convert people throughout the entire vessel. They blast their way upwards, floor by floor, to confront the terrified humans.

The Doctor fails to persuade the Master and Missy to stand with him in an act of kindness, a final defence to prevent the Cybermen advancing any further. The Doctor sends Nardole off to an upper floor with a crowd of humans to protect. Bill Potts, already converted into a Cyberman, goes to defend another area.

Now the Doctor stands alone on floor 507, ready to trigger fuel lines and fusion turbos under the floor, spark an explosive critical failure that will eliminate the Cyber army, and die himself in the conflagration.

Kindness often means a choice to do something virtuous that puts other people's needs before your own. When you do it not to be noticed, and with no guarantee of receiving anything in return, the true reward is the boost to your own self-esteem.

18 OCTOBER

BATTLES IN THE OPEN

THE DOCTOR
As long as Morgaine's people are shooting at us,
she won't be using more obscure methods of attack.

Battlefield by Ben Aaronovitch (1989)

• • • • • •

At the bottom of a lake in the Carbury Trust Conservation Area sits an enormous spaceship. It has been there for 1,200 years, effectively a tomb for the legendary King Arthur – a real man who comes from another dimension.

Then Arthur's old enemy, the witch Morgaine, arrives in Carbury with an army of soldiers to start old battles anew. The Doctor's friends at UNIT are outgunned because Morgaine wields extraordinary powers, her advanced technology indistinguishable from magic. She can zap a helicopter out of the sky, kill people with a touch of her hand, and summon the world-devouring creature known only as the Destroyer.

So when the Doctor and his friends are attacked by knights with blasters and grenades, he is almost relieved. If he can see what Morgaine is up to, he knows she's not conjuring something far more deadly.

Don't be intimidated when you face problems or obstacles. Knowing they're there means you can do something about them. Not knowing about them is worse!

19 OCTOBER

MAKE, DON'T BREAK

THE DOCTOR
What pretty crockery this is. Sad really, isn't it?
People spend all their time making nice things,
and other people come along and break them.

The Enemy of the World by David Whitaker (1967–68)

• • • • • •

In a caravan outside the Research Centre at Kanowa, Australia in 2018, Giles Kent receives an unpleasant visitor. The oleaginous Benik is deputy to Salamander, the so-called 'Saviour of the World', who miraculously solved a global food shortage. But Benik uses his association with Salamander to bully Kent, instructing a guard to smash up the caravan.

Benik is unpleasant but the Doctor believes that his behaviour doesn't necessarily prove that Salamander is also bad. The Doctor, who happens to look just like Salamander, impersonates him to find out the truth... And it turns out that Salamander is evil after all, having caused the world food shortage in the first place.

It takes skill and effort to make things well, and to find real solutions to difficult problems. On the other hand, breaking things is easy – we can cause harm even without meaning to do so.

So always be wary of 'easy' answers or miraculous solutions – you might want to look a little closer.

20 OCTOBER

CARERS NEED CARERS TOO

THE DOCTOR
This is Clara. Not my assistant.
She's... er... some other word.

CLARA OSWALD
I'm his carer.

THE DOCTOR
Yeah. My carer. She cares so I don't have to.

Into the Dalek by Phil Ford and Steven Moffat (2014)

• • • • • •

The Doctor rescues a crew member on the hospital ship *Aristotle*, but is disconcerted by an unexpected encounter with a Dalek that wants to exterminate all other Daleks. He makes a quick trip back to Earth to fetch Clara Oswald for advice, and introduces her to the members of the Combined Galactic Resistance on their lone rebel ship.

Clara's sarcastic comment is about looking after the older man. The Doctor ripostes that she's there as his conscience, because of his brusque and unapproachable manner. We know that the Doctor has already shown his vulnerability to Clara, asking candidly whether she thinks he is a good man. In truth, they care for each other.

It's stressful looking after someone who is vulnerable. It could be a sick child, an elderly relative, or an adult with additional needs. Remember that carers require help, resources, emotional support and breaks. They need people to care for them, too.

21 OCTOBER

KEEPING SECRETS

RIVER SONG TO THE DOCTOR
Spoilers!

Silence in the Library (2008)
Forest of the Dead (2008)
The Big Bang (2010)
The Impossible Astronaut (2011)
The Wedding of River Song (2011)
The Name of the Doctor (2013)

• • • • • •

THE DOCTOR TO RIVER SONG
Spoilers!

Forest of the Dead (2008)
Let's Kill Hitler (2011)
The Husbands of River Song (2015)

• • • • • •

RIVER SONG TO AMY POND
Spoilers!

The Time of Angels (2010)
The Pandorica Opens (2010)

• • • • • •

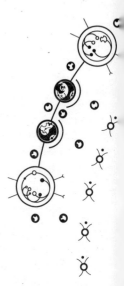

River Song's life with the Doctor is full of spoilers. He first meets her in a 51st century library at the end of her life. The adventures she's already had with him will be in his future. They're all documented in her handwritten diary because those encounters are already in her past.

To keep things on track from the outset, River succinctly cautions the Doctor about 'Spoilers!' — sometimes as a warning, sometimes just to tease.

It's natural that the Doctor starts to say it himself in their future conversations. Because each time we meet them together, River knows just that little bit less about the Doctor's future, and he knows more about hers.

Past, present, or future: keeping secrets from people you care about that would hurt or not help them — if withheld for the right reasons — can be an act of love.

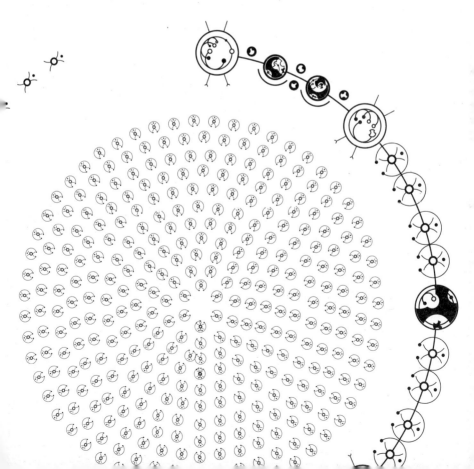

22 OCTOBER

ALTERNATIVE SOLUTIONS

PROFESSOR SORENSON
By taking material from this planet we can
refuel it and save our civilisation.

THE DOCTOR
I'm afraid that isn't the solution.
You must find an alternative energy source.

Planet of Evil by Louis Marks (1975)

. . . . . .

In the 372nd century, a group of humanoid Morestrans explore Zeta Minor – the furthermost planet in the known universe – in desperate search of a power source to replace that of their own dying star.

But the material they draw from below the planet's surface has unusual effects. When Professor Sorenson ignores the Doctor's warnings and plunders this resource, he becomes possessed by an entity composed of antimatter.

We can't really blame the Morestrans for being so keen to exploit this strange and powerful material; their civilisation is dependent on the discovery of a new supply of energy, after all. The problem is in that energy being sourced in a way that causes damage to the environment and life on Zeta Minor.

Rushing to solve a problem can often mean we make things worse. Consider your options, explore the alternatives, and look for long-term solutions that have the least negative impact.

23 OCTOBER

EVERYBODY HURTS, SOMETIMES

KUBLAI KHAN
Do you mock our afflictions?

THE DOCTOR
It's my back. It's broken!

Marco Polo by John Lucarotti (1964)

• • • • • •

The First Doctor was granted an audience in what's now known as Beijing with the great Emperor Kublai Khan. All who dared enter the presence of the 'Master of the World' were required to kowtow before him, kneeling prostrate and touching their foreheads to the floor three times. Failure to do so would mean instant death!

But the Doctor arrived in Beijing after months on horseback, trekking hundreds of miles. An old man anyway, the Doctor was sore and crotchety after the journey and struggled to get down on his knees.

While others tried to shush the Doctor's complaints, he moaned and grumbled – and so attracted the Khan's attention. In fact, the great Khan was also an old man suffering from aches and pains. Soon he and the Doctor had become the best of friends, even playing board games together.

Don't suffer in silence. Also, you never know what's really going on in people's lives; even those who seem like strong and confident people can have troubles of their own.

24 OCTOBER

OPINIONS VERSUS FACTS

THE DOCTOR

The very powerful and the very stupid have one thing in
common. They don't alter their views to fit the facts, they alter
the facts to fit their views. Which can be uncomfortable if
you happen to be one of the facts that needs altering.

The Face of Evil by Chris Boucher (1977)

• • • • • •

Many years ago, the Doctor reprogrammed a mission computer for
the Mordee expedition. Now he's in two minds about the wisdom of
doing that, because it has evolved into Xoanon, a living creature with
multiple personalities – including his.

His attempt to explain these facts to Xoanon fails, and his new
friend Leela rescues him. Unable to accept the truth about itself, the
very powerful computer wants to kill the Doctor.

Opinions are subjective – we each have our own. Facts are
objective – they can be verified. Stating your personal truth doesn't
make it true for everyone. Cherry-picking facts out of context to
support your beliefs is misleading and dangerous. Imposing your opinions on others isn't going to change their minds – and it's oppressive
to do so.

25 OCTOBER

DON'T GLOAT

JO GRANT
You felt sorry for him, didn't you? You wanted to
come down here and see that he was all right.

THE DOCTOR
Well, he used to be a friend of mine once.
A very good friend.

The Sea Devils by Malcolm Hulke (1972)

• • • • • •

The Doctor and Jo travel to an island off the coast of southern England to visit a castle guarded by armed personnel. Deep inside the castle, the Master is held prisoner in a maximum security cell.

The security arrangements are impeccable. For example, all staff have undergone rigorous training to resist hypnosis. But the Doctor isn't here to inspect the prison's safeguards. Nor does he seek to gloat over his old enemy.

No, he's here purely out of concern, even recognising the Master as a former friend. The Doctor is wary, not wanting to be duped by this most devious of adversaries, but he's genuinely keen to see the Master is well treated during his incarceration.

Don't kick someone when they're already down – even if they've behaved badly. Be better than them and hold yourself to a higher standard.

26 OCTOBER

USE WHAT'S AT HAND

ROBIN HOOD
Draw your sword and prove your words.

THE DOCTOR
I have no sword. I don't need a sword.
Because I am the Doctor. And this is my spoon. *En garde!*

Robot of Sherwood by Mark Gatiss (2014)

• • • • • •

Offered the opportunity to go wherever, whenever, anywhere in time and space, Clara Oswald asks to visit Robin Hood. The Doctor tells her that old-fashioned heroes only exist in old-fashioned story books. So he is every bit as surprised as Clara is delighted to materialise the TARDIS in 1190 CE and find himself face to face with the legendary heroic outlaw.

Robin claims ownership of the TARDIS as soon as he sees it, and unsheathes his sword. The Doctor refuses and brandishes his spoon. On a narrow river crossing, hand-to-hand combat ensues, like Errol Flynn fighting a Chuckle Brother. Robin is bold, but the Doctor dumps him in the drink.

You won't always have time to be perfectly prepared for any situation. Don't give up. Show some enthusiasm and have a go with the resources immediately at hand. It won't always require you to flatten someone with flatware.

27 OCTOBER

WISE COUNSEL

THE DOCTOR
Never be cruel, never be cowardly, and never, ever eat pears!
Remember – hate is always foolish, and love is always wise.
Always try to be nice, but never fail to be kind.

Twice Upon a Time by Steven Moffat (2017)

• • • • • •

Alone in his TARDIS, the Doctor faces the end of his life. His confrontation with the Cybermen on a Mondasian colony ship mortally wounded him, and his initial choice was to die rather than regenerate.

His decision changes when he meets a former self, immediately after his very first encounter with the Cybermen at the South Pole. That earlier incarnation candidly admits to him that he is scared about regenerating for the first time. Like him, the Twelfth Doctor accepts his future. One more lifetime won't kill anyone – well, except him. He's now ready to offer advice to the next Doctor, whoever that will be.

Apart from his jokey ban on pears (they're too squishy and they always make your chin wet), the Doctor's wise counsel for his successor is what he calls the basic stuff – as it can be for us. Like the new Doctor, we should be ready to laugh hard, run fast and be kind.

28 OCTOBER

ARTIFICIAL ART

THE DOCTOR
You've thrown the dice once.
You don't get a second throw.

City of Death by David Agnew (1979)

• • • • • •

The last of the cruel, alien Jagaroth attempt to launch their damaged spacecraft from a lifeless, uninhabitable world. But when Scaroth activates full power, the ship disintegrates, the other Jagaroth are killed and he is propelled into the future.

In Paris in 1979, Scaroth – disguised as a posh art collector (and human) – devises an ingenious plot to return to the moment before the explosion and stop himself pressing the button. But the Doctor realises that the explosion of the spaceship 400 million years previously did more than wipe out the Jagaroth.

The radioactive blast caused amino acids in nearby mud to form tiny cells, which eventually evolved into vegetable and animal life – including you and me. The Doctor can't allow Scaroth to go back and correct his error at the expense of all life ever on Earth.

The Doctor's point still applies to those of us who don't have access to time travel. None of us can go back and alter the hand that life has dealt us. All we can do is go forward and attempt to make a better future.

29 OCTOBER

ANOTHER TRUE STORY

THE DOCTOR
The unicorn appeared to be real until
you said it wasn't. Then we were safe.

ZOE HERIOT
But we believed in it, Jamie and I.

THE DOCTOR
Yes, that was just the danger.

The Mind Robber by Peter Ling (1968)

• • • • • •

After the TARDIS suddenly explodes, the Doctor and his friends find themselves in the Land of Fiction alongside characters from stories and mythology. When a unicorn charges right at them, the Doctor makes his friends say out loud that it doesn't exist – and the creature disappears.

In fact, the forces in control of the Land of Fiction aim to make the Doctor part of the story, and keep him and his friends from ever escaping. The lure of a good story could make them forget who they really are.

Stories can help us in our lives. Sometimes they guide us through difficulties; sometimes they give us a break. That's hopefully how this book can help too. But the Doctor is right when he says later on in *The Mind Robber* that we need to ensure we don't lose ourselves entirely in the comforts of fiction. We need to hang on to real life.

30 OCTOBER

STRONGER TOGETHER

THE DOCTOR
D'you know why this TARDIS is always rattling about the place?
It's designed to have six pilots. And I have to do it single handed!
Now we can fly this thing like it's meant to be flown!

Journey's End by Russell T Davies (2008)

• • • • • •

The Doctor escapes Davros's Crucible Vaults with all his friends safely inside the TARDIS. Now it's all hands to the controls in order to return Planet Earth back home.

There's Rose Tyler, Mickey Smith, Jack Harkness, Martha Jones, Sarah Jane Smith, Donna Noble and the Doctor's cloned doppelgänger. No role for Jackie Tyler, unfortunately. (Or luckily, depending on your point of view.)

The Doctor's connection to his TARDIS is more than the bio-imprimatur of most Time Lords and their ships. He can be a bit proprietorial about his space-time machine. River Song teases him that it wheezes and groans on landing because he leaves the brakes on. This time, however, he's happy to have trusted friends on hand to make this tricky trip.

Don't be afraid to ask for help when you need it. Assign tasks to others. Even if you're stronger than any individual member of your team, you're not better than all of them combined.

31 OCTOBER

EVERYONE'S IMPORTANT TO SOMEONE

THE DOCTOR
Do you know, in nine hundred years of time and space,
I've never met anyone who wasn't important before.

A Christmas Carol by Steven Moffat (2010)

• • • • • •

Businessman Kazran Sardick controls the electric skies above the planet Ember in the 44th century. The Doctor drops in to see him, requesting assistance to rescue a space liner accommodating four thousand passengers that's plunging into the atmosphere.

Abigail Pettigrew's family visits Sardick, begging him to release her from her cryogenic casket for Christmas. Kazran doesn't see Abigail as a person, only as security held against her family's debt – she's nobody important to him.

The Doctor arrived in the hope that Sardick would help. Now he sees what kind of person he's dealing with – though not yet why the businessman is like that.

We encounter new people every day. In the crowd, travelling on the bus, working in shops, driving down the road, posting online. We don't know them, and may never know them, so start out with goodwill. We don't know what's happening in their lives, and they are all important to someone. And when you feel lost in the crowd, remember you're important to someone else, too.

NOVEMBER

1 NOVEMBER

WE'RE IN THIS TOGETHER

SUTEKH
You are a Time Lord: what interest have you in humans?

THE DOCTOR
All sapient lifeforms are our kith, Sutekh.

Pyramids of Mars by Stephen Harris (1975)

· · · · · ·

In the 'mastaba' or burial chamber below a pyramid in Egypt sits an ancient god. In fact, Sutekh is the last of an extremely powerful alien species, the Osirans, trapped for eternity by his own people using a forcefield controlled from the planet Mars.

When an archaeologist stumbles into the burial chamber in 1911, Sutekh seizes on his chance to escape – until the Doctor gets in his way. The Doctor knows that if Sutekh breaks free, he will leave nothing but destruction in his wake, and no lifeform in the galaxy would be able to stand against him. Not even the Time Lords.

Sutekh can't understand why a Time Lord such as the Doctor would show such interest in the puny humans on Earth. The Doctor's reply is telling. 'Sapient' means intelligent or capable of thinking; 'kith' is a very old word meaning 'neighbours' or 'people from the same country'.

The Doctor is surely saying that there's a very old, even innate, bond between all thinking creatures. With intelligence, no one is alien or foreign. We are simply neighbours.

2 NOVEMBER

CALL HANDLING

• • • • • •

Hardly anyone in the universe knows the TARDIS phone number. Clara does – she was given it by some woman in a shop, though she doesn't know who that was.

Clara tells the Doctor to ignore an incoming call. She wants to get away for her hot date with Danny Pink without distractions. The Doctor isn't worried. Until the next thing either of them remembers is that they're in the galaxy's most dangerous bank, holding an alien worm that has wiped their memories ahead of a briefing on how to raid the vault.

Don't get annoyed or fooled by unwanted calls or texts:

- Hang up on automated, pre-recorded calls or human spammers calling indiscriminately – no point in discussing things.
- Hang up on unexpected calls that could be fraudsters, then look up the official company number to call back.
- Add your number to your country's 'Do Not Call' register to remove it from telemarketing lists.
- Block unwelcome caller numbers, and report them to your phone company.
- Let unknown numbers go to voicemail – real callers will leave a message.

3 NOVEMBER

YOUR ACTIONS DEFINE YOU

JACKSON LAKE
I am nothing but a lie.

THE DOCTOR
No, no, no, no, no. Infostamps are just facts and figures.
All that bravery – saving Rosita, defending London town!
And the invention! Building a TARDIS! That's all you.

The Next Doctor by Russell T Davies (2008)

• • • • • •

Jackson Lake is devastated to learn that he is not the man he thinks he is. A Time Lord, the Doctor, the one, the only, the best. He rescued Rosita at Osterman's Wharf, fought Cybershades with a lasso, tapped a wall with his sonic screwdriver, built a balloon TARDIS, and recalled his regeneration after facing down the Cybermen. All in all, a bit of a legend.

He is really a teacher of mathematics from Sussex who came to London three weeks ago. The Cybermen killed his wife, a memory he has suppressed while in a fugue state. The Cybermen's Infostamp containing their knowledge of the Doctor backfired and streamed all its information right into Jackson's mind.

Even if we stand on the shoulders of giants, it's what we then do that marks us out for distinction. Judge people's worth not by whatever flashy titles they may have, but on what they achieve and how they attempt it.

4 NOVEMBER

KNOWN UNKNOWNS

THE DOCTOR
Until we know who else is working for the
Intelligence, everyone must be suspect.

The Web of Fear by Mervyn Haisman and Henry Lincoln (1968)

• • • • • •

When murderous, robotic Yeti invade London, the Doctor and his friends help the army fight back from a base down in the tunnels of the underground train network. There, the Doctor and young scientist Anne Travers investigate the mechanisms controlling the Yeti and manage to get one robot to obey their commands.

This is an important breakthrough which could help stop the attack, but the Doctor is wary of telling anyone else what he and Anne have achieved. He knows that the alien entity controlling the Yeti, known as the Great Intelligence, can also control human beings. Any of the Doctor's friends could be under its malign influence – meaning that the 'secret weapon' might be discovered.

It's likely the Doctor's friends Jamie and Victoria would be hurt to be under the Doctor's suspicion, but with so much at stake, his uncertainty isn't a weakness.

Recognising what you don't know can help you avoid making mistakes. When something really matters, we need to be sure of those we can rely on.

5 NOVEMBER

EXPRESS YOURSELF

THE DOCTOR
Bow ties are cool.

The Eleventh Hour by Steven Moffat (2010)
Amy's Choice by Simon Nye (2010)
The Lodger by Gareth Roberts (2010)
Vincent and the Doctor by Richard Curtis (2010)
The Snowmen by Steven Moffat (2012)

● ● ● ● ● ●

The Doctors each have a distinctive style throughout their lives. Most often it's unspoken. The Third Doctor, for example, didn't comment on his frilled shirts and lined capes, even when someone like Squire Winstanley of Devil's End thought he was in costume and wearing a wig.

The Eleventh Doctor is more than happy to celebrate his own sartorial choices, even with his doppelgänger self at one point. UNIT scientist Osgood admires his look enough to adopt it herself. River Song dislikes his fez and Stetson so much that she shoots at them. But the Doctor loves bow ties, even if others don't always agree, and he isn't afraid to say do.

When you're no longer obliged to wear school uniform or standard work clothing, you can pick your own style. It doesn't have to be about brands and fitting in with everyone else. If you wear what you like to express yourself and don't care what others think, well, that's cool.

6 NOVEMBER

LOYALTY TO WHO?

SIR GEORGE HUTCHINSON
You speak treason.

THE DOCTOR
Fluently! Stop the games.

The Awakening by Eric Pringle (1984)

• • • • • •

On May Day 1984, local magistrate Sir George Hutchinson wants every man, woman and child in the village of Little Hodcombe to take part in war games being held to commemorate a fateful day in local history. On 6 July 1643, parliamentary soldiers clashed with a regiment loyal to King Charles I and both sides were wiped out. It might be an odd event to celebrate but Sir George believes that the war games will be a fun adventure for all ages.

The Doctor discovers that the battle in 1643 was exacerbated by a psychic alien, the Malus from Hakol in the star system Rifta. The Malus still dwells within the local church and will draw energy from the games, intent on making the mock conflict real.

When the Doctor tries to halt the games, Sir George accuses him of disloyalty, and the Doctor is unrepentant and proud.

It's right to challenge those in authority when they don't consider other people, or even risk doing them harm. We have a loyalty to everyone else and to stand up for those without power.

7 NOVEMBER

OPEN TO ODDNESS

THE DOCTOR

To be fair, I did have a couple of gadgets which he
probably didn't, like a teaspoon and an open mind.

The Creature from the Pit by David Fisher (1979)

• • • • • •

Responding to a distress signal, the TARDIS lands in the jungle of the
planet Chloris, where the Doctor and Romana find the ruins of high,
curving walls made from a semi-metallic material.

Some of the finest brains on Chloris have studied this strange
structure. One conscientious engineer, Doran, concludes that it is the
ruin of a temple. But the Doctor taps the walls with a teaspoon and
listens with a stethoscope, confirming that the low-frequency 'distress
call' emanates from what is really an enormous eggshell.

Doran scoffs that this is ridiculous, because a bird big enough
to lay such an egg would have a wingspan of at least a mile. But the
Doctor only nods at this, and soon enough succeeds in finding the
massive creature. While others on Chloris attack it, the open-minded
Doctor makes friends with the beast, discovering it to be a Tythonian
ambassador called Erato.

Life is often unexpected and odd, and things – especially people
– aren't always what they seem. But, like the Doctor, it's important to
always keep an open mind.

8 NOVEMBER

ADMIT MISTAKES

THE DOCTOR
Right, quick update. I made a terrible mistake.
We shouldn't be here. I'm going to fix it and get you
guys home, I promise. Soon as I figure out where we are.

GRAHAM
How are you going to do that?

THE DOCTOR
Not sure. Treating it as a chance to surprise myself.

The Ghost Monument by Chris Chibnall (2018)

• • • • • •

When you're the Doctor, doing everything, everywhere, every time, mistakes are inevitable. And the consequences can be deadly.

New friends Yasmin Khan, Graham O'Brien and Ryan Sinclair help her track her missing TARDIS using a machine she lashed up from Stenza technology and a microwave. Bad news: the machine dumped them all in the vacuum of space. Good news: they were scooped to safety by passing Albarian pilots. Bad news again: their rescuers dumped them on a barren planet.

When Yaz asks if the blunder means they'll die, the Doctor says that it comes to us all, but not right now — not if she's got anything to do with it.

When a mistake happens, be candid, state your objective and don't pretend you have all the answers immediately. Then you and your team can take positive steps to fix it.

9 NOVEMBER

DON'T BRING THEM DOWN

JACKIE TYLER

Let me tell you something about those who get left behind.
Because it's hard. And that's what you become – hard.
But if there's one thing I've learned, it's that I will never let
her down. And I'll protect them both until the end of my life.
So whatever you want, I'm warning you, back off.

Love & Monsters by Russell T Davies (2006)

• • • • • •

A dangerous elemental shade escapes from the Howling Halls and hides in the darkness of a family home. The Doctor manages to track down and stop this living shadow but not before it kills an innocent woman. The woman's son Elton Pope, aged only three or four, is a witness to the traumatic event and it haunts him for the rest of his life.

As a grown-up, Elton makes friends with other people who know about the Doctor. But under the influence of the beguiling Victor Kennedy, the group's enthusiasm becomes ever more obsessive and they go in search of the Doctor by targeting his friends.

Elton ends up meeting Jackie Tyler, who is lonely while her daughter Rose is away in the TARDIS. Elton befriends her – to get information. When Jackie finds out, she is hurt and angry.

Elton's behaviour is not excused by his childhood trauma or by his enthusiasm for finding out about the Doctor. We are responsible for our actions and the impact they have on others. As with Jackie, be mindful that other people have their own struggles, too.

10 NOVEMBER

WORK TO A SCHEDULE

THE DOCTOR

I'm split across multiple events, multiple time streams. I can't be constant. Multiple crises and I'm still trying to work out the plan. You're camouflaged here because this is where you belong. The best place to hide you all is in your own lives.

Flux: Once, Upon Time by Chris Chibnall (2021)

• • • • • •

Ever had one of those days? Daleks, Cybermen and Sontarans are about to wipe out humanity. Your friends are threatened by Ravagers in the Temple of Atropos. You're lost in thought about a time you can barely remember when you worked for Division.

The Doctor's solution is to jump into a time storm in order to hide the fam and herself in their own individual time streams. Then she can warn them what's going on by visiting each of them: Dan Lewis meeting his girlfriend; Yasmin Khan on patrol with her police officer colleague and playing video games with her sister; and the Doctor herself raiding the Temple many years previously.

When you take on lots at once, it's hard to pay full attention to everything, give your best or achieve your potential. Make an effective plan by scheduling dedicated time for each job – the better results will be well worth it.

11 NOVEMBER

BEING PART OF THE SHOW

THE DOCTOR
That's what you like, isn't it? Taking someone with a
touch of individuality and imagination, and wearing
them down to nothingness in your service.

The Greatest Show in the Galaxy by Stephen Wyatt (1988–89)

• • • • • •

The Psychic Circus on the planet Segonax claims to be the 'greatest show in the galaxy'. Its festival talent show is open to everyone – with big prizes to be won.

But the Doctor and Ace discover that those who can't sufficiently entertain the audience are brutally killed. And the audience members themselves aren't as human they appear. In fact, the circus is in thrall to three almighty Gods of Ragnarok, who exist concurrently in two different time spaces. The Doctor is initially forced to perform for them, then refuses to let them feed any more from his energy – and brings the show to a close.

Lots of companies depend on the enthusiasm, imagination and commitment of their staff. That's fine while employees are valued and enjoy the benefits of the workplace. But it mustn't be a one-way process. Your talent, your work – whatever that might be – is of value. Never tolerate being exploited.

12 NOVEMBER

IDENTIFY YOUR NORTH STAR

THE DOCTOR
Just think of them. Because that planet out there, all three suns,
wormholes and alien sand, that planet is nothing. You hear
me? Nothing, compared to all those things waiting for you.
Food and home and people. Hold on to that. Cos we're going
to get there, I promise. I'm going to get you home.

Planet of the Dead by Russell T Davies and Gareth Roberts (2009)

· · · · · ·

Ever had the feeling you're getting nowhere and can't see a way
forward? The number 200 bus has taken a bit of a detour from its
usual route through the Gladwell Tunnel and ended up stuck in the
sand on the planet San Helios.

The panicking passengers don't understand wormholes. They
only understand that they are trapped far from home and death is
coming. The Doctor calms them by having them describe where
they were going tonight: seeing a partner and teenage daughter;
visiting a friend; a night in with the telly; cooking a nice couple of
chops and gravy.

In an unexpected and worrying situation, you can lose focus, feel
overwhelmed and powerless. Focus on your desired outcome, your
destination, and things will come into focus.

13 NOVEMBER

ADMITTING THINGS ARE BAD
IS HOW YOU MAKE THEM BETTER

THE DOCTOR
At first we thought it was some sort of meteorite storm.

LEADER PLANTAGENET
And what do you think now?

THE DOCTOR
I think your shelters are totally inadequate and your
warning system does nothing but create panic.

LEADER PLANTAGENET
I did not ask –

THE DOCTOR
Your population has already fallen below critical value required
for guaranteed growth and you're regularly losing new lives.
I think – and you did ask what I think – I think your colony of
Earth people is in grave danger of extinction.

Frontios by Christopher H Bidmead (1984)

• • • • • •

Fleeing the imminent collision of the Earth with the Sun, one of the last surviving groups of humanity settles on the desolate world of Frontios in the Veruna system. There, they are regularly battered by meteorite attacks from an unseen aggressor. But young Leader Plantagenet will hear no mewling words of defeat; he is determined to win.

Plantagenet is so stubbornly defiant, he's blind to the many difficulties faced by his desperate, vulnerable people. He doesn't take too kindly to the Doctor pointing out their problems, either.

Unlike Plantagenet, if you're going to solve a problem, you first have to acknowledge it exists, then assess it objectively — even if it means admitting that things are in a bad state. Only then can you make a plan to overcome the problem.

14 NOVEMBER

RELATIONSHIP ADVICE

DANNY PINK

I don't need him to like me. It doesn't matter if he
likes me or hates me, I just need to do exactly one
thing for you. I need to be good enough for you.
That's why he's angry. Just in case I'm not.

The Caretaker by Gareth Roberts and Steven Moffat (2014)

• • • • • •

The Doctor goes undercover at Coal Hill School to track one of the deadliest killing machines ever created. A Skovox Blitzer's not something you want turning up unexpectedly in the storeroom.

Clara Oswald didn't expect the Doctor would turn up at her workplace today. Nor that he'd disapprove so much of her boyfriend, Maths teacher Danny Pink – who mistakes the Doctor for Clara's space dad. She loves Danny, but is that enough for the Doctor to go easier on him? When Danny bravely saves them from the Blitzer, the Doctor accepts that's a good start.

It's normal to want your parents to like the person you love. You're stuck in the middle if they do not. Discuss it calmly. They may be trying to protect you from what they feel is an unwise partnership, but at the end of the day your life and your loves are your own – the decision must be yours, and those that care will come to understand.

15 NOVEMBER

WHAT FRIENDS DON'T LET FRIENDS DO

'ROSE TYLER'
I'm perfectly fine.

THE DOCTOR
These people are dying and Rose would care.

New Earth by Russell T Davies (2006)

• • • • • •

In the year 5,000,000,023, the Doctor and Rose Tyler visit the planet
New Earth in the galaxy M87. They've received an anonymous plea to
help someone who's seemingly in Ward 26 of one of the planet's hospitals.
But when they arrive, the ward seems to be running smoothly – indeed,
patients seem to recover from illnesses that have no known cures.

Investigating further, the Doctor discovers a huge underground
vault known as 'intensive care', in which thousands of living humans
are being infected with terrible diseases as part of vast programme to
develop new treatments. The suffering of these people is the human
cost of the miracle cures in use upstairs.

The Doctor is appalled by this – and by Rose's seeming lack of
concern. In fact, her body has been possessed by one of the Doctor's
old enemies – the evil Lady Cassandra. The Doctor notices something
is amiss because he knows Rose so well.

A true friend won't ignore bad behaviour or acting out of
character. It's often a sign of something else being wrong – which, as a
good friend, we can help with.

16 NOVEMBER

NO ONE DESERVES *THAT*

DONNA NOBLE
I missed my wedding, lost my job and
became a widow on the same day. Sort of.

THE DOCTOR
I couldn't save him.

DONNA NOBLE
He deserved it. No, he didn't.

The Runaway Bride by Russell T Davies (2006)

• • • • • •

Donna Noble is about to marry her fiancé Lance Bennett in church when she suddenly finds herself aboard the TARDIS. It turns out she's been attracted to the ship because Lance has been feeding her Huon particles at the behest of his alien accomplice.

A human full of Huon particles is the key that the spider-like Empress of the Racnoss needs to unlock the heart of the planet Earth and release the dormant Racnoss sleeping within – who will then consume the entire planet.

When the Doctor rescues Donna, Lance is himself fed with Huon particles and released into the centre of the Earth. He has used Donna, been cruel to her and lied to her about his true motivations.

But she takes no pleasure in seeing Lance meet the fate he had planned for her, and she stops the Doctor revelling in his defeat of the Racnoss – saying he's done enough. This, we learn later, saves his life.

Donna's been badly treated but what sets her free is that she doesn't become cruel and cynical like Lance. Other people might be mean; you don't have to be.

17 NOVEMBER

PERSONAL PRIORITIES

THE DOCTOR

I didn't exactly come straight here. Had a bit of fun, y'know, travelled about, did this and that. Got into trouble, you know me. It was brilliant. I saw the Phosphorous Carousel of the Great Magellan Gestalt. Saved a planet from the Red Carnivorous Maw. Named a galaxy Alison. Got married – that was a mistake. Good Queen Bess, and let me tell you, her nickname is no longer... Anyway... what d'you want?

The End of Time Part One by Russell T Davies (2009)

· · · · · ·

The Doctor knows plenty of holiday destinations. The beaches of Halergan 3. Magnificent views in the Medusa Cascade. A picnic on Asgard. The Singing Towers of Darillium. Metebelis 3 (on a good day).

Ood Sigma doesn't understand why the Doctor delayed his journey to the Ood-Sphere. They called him because they've been having nightmares. He's been in no rush to turn up, because the last time he was there Ood Sigma said the Doctor's song would be ending soon. It's fair to say that he doesn't want to go.

Resist the temptation to drop everything whenever someone calls you out of the blue. You're not always on the clock outside work, and it's OK to say no sometimes, even to your friends. Decide your own priorities, and make time for some fun things while you're at it.

18 NOVEMBER

INTERFERENCE

THE DOCTOR
Of course we should interfere!
Always do what you're best at.

Nightmare of Eden by Bob Baker (1979)

● ● ● ● ● ●

Emerging from warp drive on its approach to the planet Azure, the interstellar cruise liner *Empress* materialises on top of another ship, the *Hecate*. There's no explosion but the two vessels are fused together.

Observing this from the TARDIS, the Doctor's trusty robot dog K-9 concludes that the areas of overlap are highly unstable, so passengers and crew are in danger. Romana is apprehensive about getting involved but the Doctor doesn't hesitate to plunge in.

Then he discovers that the ships have been joined together on purpose to enable a deadly drug called Vraxoin to be smuggled from one vessel to the other. The Doctor has seen whole communities and planets destroyed by the effects of this awful drug, so he involves himself in catching the smugglers and bringing them to justice.

'I don't work for anybody,' says the Doctor at one point. 'I'm just having fun.' We can have fun just like the Doctor, and enjoy helping other people where we can. But of course the Doctor also takes things seriously whenever there's a threat that people might be hurt or harmed.

19 NOVEMBER

LET YOUR HEART SING

THE DOCTOR
Klokleeda partha mennin klatch,
Aroon, aroon, aroon.
Klokleeda sheena teerinatch,
Aroon, aroon, aroon

The Curse of Peladon by Brian Hayles (1972)

· · · · · ·

The Third Doctor enjoys singing for his own amusement. 'Shine on Martian moons up in the sky,' he croons as he attempts to repair the TARDIS. 'Oh I do like to be beside the seaside,' he goes as he plots a course to the effervescent seas of Florana.

But singing also gets him out of a tight spot. When the stone gargoyle Bok attacks the Doctor and Jo in a barrow at Devil's End, the Doctor scares off the creature with a bit of a Venusian lullaby. 'Klokleda partha mennin klatch,' he explains to Jo, roughly translates as 'Close your eyes, my darling – well, three of them, at least.'

In the tunnels under the citadel of Peladon, the Doctor uses the same lullaby to soothe the royal beast Aggedor on more than one occasion. It doesn't matter what the words mean, or whether Bok or Aggedor can understand them. It doesn't even matter if the Doctor is a good or indifferent singer. The song still conveys the Doctor's meaning.

Today, listen to a piece of music that makes you feel good – and sing along.

20 NOVEMBER

IT'S YOUR TAG

GRAHAM O'BRIEN
Oi, whoa, whoa, whoa. What are you doing?
That is vandalism. We'll have to pay for that.

THE DOCTOR
Don't worry, special pen.

GRAHAM O'BRIEN
No, pack it in. You ain't Banksy.

THE DOCTOR
Or am I?

Rosa by Malorie Blackman (2018)

* * * * * *

An out-of-time impostor is skulking in an Alabama bus works in 1955. The Doctor is suspicious about his interest in local seamstress Rosa Parks, destined to become a vital activist in the civil rights movement.

The Doctor makes notes across a motel room wall on what they know about Mrs Parks. Graham is alarmed, and the Doctor jokes she may be the pseudonymous and anonymous street artist Banksy, best known for his graffiti in 21st-century Bristol, England, rather than 20th-century Montgomery, Alabama.

Fortunately, the Doctor's special pen isn't permanent. She has respect for property unlike River Song, who once carved the message 'HELLO SWEETIE ΘΣ Φ ΓΥΔϟ' on a cliff of pure diamond on the oldest planet in the universe, just to attract the Doctor's attention.

We all want to leave our mark but there are better ways of doing it than scrawling on a wall.

21 NOVEMBER

THE POWER OF 'I DON'T KNOW'

THE DOCTOR

I believe I haven't seen everything. I don't know. It's funny, isn't it? The things you make up – the rules. If that thing had said it came from beyond the universe, I'd believe it, but *before* the universe? Impossible! Doesn't fit my rule. Still, that's why I keep travelling. To be proved wrong. Thank you, Ida.

The Satan Pit by Matt Jones (2006)

* * * * * *

Hanging from a cable ten miles beneath the surface of the impossible planet Krop Tor, the Doctor muses on the claim made by a huge and fearsome creature that it is really the Devil. Science officer Ida Scott doesn't believe in the Devil, only in bad things done by people. The Doctor admits that, on the evidence available, he just doesn't know.

The striking thing is that this isn't an admission of defeat. In fact, the Doctor seems inspired by this uncertainty – and promptly takes a 'leap of faith' by unclipping his harness and falling away into the darkness, to find out what's really down there.

The first step to knowledge is to be conscious of our own ignorance. Then, with enthusiasm, we can venture forward by exploring, probing and deducing. That's how we make sense of the void.

22 NOVEMBER

FROZEN BY FEAR?

CLARA OSWALD
Doctor, this is dangerous now.

THE DOCTOR
It was dangerous before. Everything's dangerous if you want it to
be. Eating chips is dangerous. Crossing the road. It's no way to
live your life. Tell her. You're supposed to be teaching her.

Kill the Moon by Peter Harness (2014)

• • • • • •

Kids think it's a fun school trip if they go to Brighton. With the Doctor
as driver, they're more likely to end up in the Satanic Nebula or the
Lagoon of Lost Stars. In the case of Courtney Woods, Year 10 pupil at
Coal Hill School, today she's flying through space 35 years in her own
future. That will look good in her posts on Tumblr.

Her teacher Clara Oswald has a duty of care. Imagine completing
a risk assessment form for travelling in a space shuttle loaded with
nuclear bombs destined for a lunar mining base full of germs the size
of giant spiders while the Moon disintegrates.

Dimensions may be relative in the TARDIS, but so is danger. Don't
take reckless risks, but don't let fear hold you back from challenging
yourself to grow stronger and become better – whether it's making a
big job change or inviting that new friend out for a drink.

23 NOVEMBER

MEANT NOT SAID

THE DOCTOR
Well, where would you like to go?

JAMIE MCCRIMMON
I couldn't care less.

THE DOCTOR
I was fond of her too, you know, Jamie.

Fury from the Deep by Victor Pemberton (1968)

. . . . . .

A monstrous seaweed creature attacks the Doctor's friend Victoria Waterfield and, quite understandably, she screams in terror. But the monster immediately retreats – and the Doctor is quick to realise that Victoria's piercing screams are the key to defeating the menace.

Perhaps Victoria ought to be pleased to play such a key part in thwarting the monster, but in a quiet moment afterwards she admits to 'always' being frightened in her travels with the Doctor. When he asks if Victoria wants to leave the TARDIS, she says she doesn't know – but the Doctor understands what she really means. Then, when the Doctor and Jamie leave without her, Jamie is cross and sulky – and again the Doctor understands.

People don't always say outright what they really think and feel. They might be worried that their feelings will hurt someone else, or if they're really hurt or upset, they can lash out. A true friend tries to look beyond what someone says and tries to understand what they actually mean.

24 NOVEMBER

WISDOM OF THE AGES

THE DOCTOR
I'm older than you. I'm nine hundred and six.

WILFRED MOTT
What, really, though? Nine hundred years.
We must look like insects to you.

THE DOCTOR
I think you look like giants.

The End of Time Part Two by Russell T Davies (2010)

· · · · · ·

The Doctor and Wilfred Mott have teleported to a spaceship 100,000 miles above planet Earth. As the Doctor thwarts the Master's plan, old soldier Wilf learns from a Gallifreyan woman that this will be the Doctor's final battle: he must stand at arms, or lose himself and the world.

Looking down at the planet, Wilf reminisces with the Doctor about his army service; of skinny little Private Mott in Palestine six decades ago. He worries how the Doctor can stand at arms when he will not carry a gun. The Doctor expresses his admiration for humanity in general, and Wilf in particular, and learns from his conversation with the younger man.

Age may convey wisdom. The longer you live, the more chance you have had to acquire knowledge and apply it. Whereas the young have a fresh perspective unencumbered by preconceptions. You can learn from people, no matter what their age — even if you are much older than them.

25 NOVEMBER

BALANCING PLEASURE AND FUN

TEGAN JOVANKA

My Aunt Vanessa said, when I became an
air stewardess, 'If you stop enjoying it, give
it up.' It's stopped being fun, Doctor.

Resurrection of the Daleks by Eric Saward (1984)

• • • • • •

We tend to think of 'hedonists' as people who are relentless
pleasure-seekers but the word has a more precise technical meaning.
Hedonism is the name given to some Ancient Greek philosophies that
regard pleasure as intrinsically good.

The idea is most closely associated with Epicurus (341–270 BCE),
who dismissed the idea of an afterlife and believed in the supreme
importance of earthly pleasure. 'It is impossible,' said Epicurus, 'to live
pleasurably without living prudently, honourably and justly.' His followers
gave a name to the job of working this out: the hedonic calculus.

In speaking of fun, Tegan's not complaining that her recent
experience battling Daleks wasn't enough of a laugh. Hers is a moral
calculation. 'Too many good people have died today,' she says regret-
fully. On her first day in the TARDIS, she loses an aunt but also helps
to save the universe. On her last, almost everybody dies – but there is
a less obviously positive counterbalance.

26 NOVEMBER

BEWARE OF IMITATIONS

SARAH JANE SMITH
We are on Earth, aren't we?

THE DOCTOR
Well, unless someone's started exporting acorns.
Oak trees don't grow anywhere else in the galaxy.

The Android Invasion by Terry Nation (1975)

• • • • • •

The TARDIS lands near the Space Control Centre about a mile from the quiet village of Devesham. Sarah has visited before but there's something uncanny about it now.

For one thing, a dead soldier has coins in his pockets that are all brand new. The calendar on the wall of a pub shows the same date over and over. Stranger still, the Doctor's friends at UNIT don't seem to know who he is.

The Doctor soon learns that he and Sarah have landed in a *copy* of the neighbourhood round Devesham, part of a diabolical plot engineered by the rhinoceros-like Kraals from planet Oseidon.

While the Kraals make good copies, the Doctor notes what is unique. To the best of our knowledge, oak trees can't be found anywhere else but on Earth. It's true of all our plant life, and the animals, too. What a fascinating thought: whatever you're looking at right now, whatever your surroundings – they are unique to this one, small world.

27 NOVEMBER

CONFIDENTIAL AND CONFIDENT

> LADY PEINFORTE
> But I know your secrets.
>
> THE DOCTOR
> Very well, tell them.
>
> LADY PEINFORTE
> I shall tell them of Gallifrey, tell them of
> the old time – the time of chaos!
>
> THE DOCTOR
> Be my guest.

Silver Nemesis by Kevin Clarke (1988)

· · · · · ·

The fearsome Lady Peinforte uses black magic and advanced technology to journey from her house in Windsor in 1638 to the same spot 250 years later. She's in pursuit of a statue of herself cast from validium – a living metal with extraordinary destructive powers.

The Cybermen also want control of this powerful substance. When the Doctor won't surrender the statue to Lady Peinforte, she threatens to share his secrets, and those of the Time Lords, with the Cyber Leader. But the Doctor isn't concerned: the emotionless Cybermen don't care about the history of Gallifrey.

We're each the main character in the story of our lives. It's easy to think that our background, feelings and secrets are of great interest to everyone else. But they're the main characters in *their* stories, wrapped up in their own concerns. It's a liberating notion to ponder. Have the confidence not to worry what other people think about you.

28 NOVEMBER

CHOOSE YOUR WORDS CAREFULLY

THE DOCTOR
Don't you think she looks tired?

The Christmas Invasion by Russell T Davies (2005)

• • • • • •

The alien Sycorax have invaded Earth at Christmas time. Everyone with A-positive blood is under their control, held hostage in a trance-like state in order to force the rest of the planet to surrender to the ruthless invaders. When some of Earth's representatives attempt to negotiate peace, the Sycorax Leader brutally murders them.

The newly regenerated Doctor soon exposes the limits of the aliens' 'blood control', wins a sword fight against the Sycorax leader and finally sends the invaders on their way. However, Prime Minister Harriet Jones doesn't think this is sufficient retaliation given the number of people killed, injured and scared out of their wits. On her orders, Torchwood shoots down the Sycorax spaceship – even though it is retreating back into space.

The Doctor is horrified by Harriet's actions and won't entertain her attempts to justify what she's done. When she challenges him, he threatens to bring down her government with just six words. He carries out his threat, seeding doubt about her ability to continue in her role – a meme which spreads very quickly through the media.

We might not have the ability to bring down governments like the Doctor, but words are powerful nevertheless. They can do considerable damage. Before you wield them, remember that we must all live with the consequences of the things we say and do.

29 NOVEMBER

WRONGS MADE RIGHT

THE DOCTOR

Because I accused you unjustly, you were determined
to prove me wrong. So you put your mind to the
problem and, luckily, you solved it.

The Edge of Destruction by David Whitaker (1964)

• • • • • •

The First Doctor could be irascible and grumpy, and sometimes even
rather mean. On one occasion, things go wrong with the TARDIS
due to a technical fault – a tiny, broken spring inside a switch – but
the Doctor angrily blames Barbara and Ian, and tries to put them
off his ship.

Later, the Doctor seeks Barbara's forgiveness and recognises
that he hurt her deeply. His words leave her – and us – in no doubt
of his contrition. They become better friends after this because he
acknowledges what he did was wrong.

Barbara's reaction to the Doctor's bad behaviour is also important.
The injustice of it fires righteous anger inside her and she determines
to uncover what really happened to the TARDIS. In doing so, she saves
everyone's lives.

Things can go wrong. People can be mean and unfair. But sometimes how we respond can make things better.

30 NOVEMBER

MAKE NOTES

AMY POND
What's the book?

THE DOCTOR
Stay away from it.

AMY POND
What is it, though?

THE DOCTOR
Her diary.

RIVER SONG
Our diary.

THE DOCTOR
Her past, my future. Time travel.
We keep meeting in the wrong order.

The Time of Angels by Steven Moffat (2010)

• • • • • •

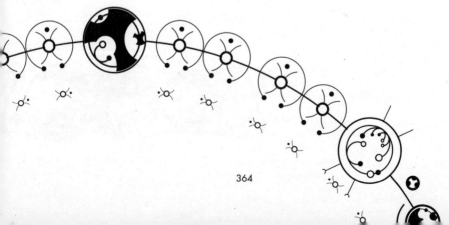

There's a beach on Alfava Metraxis, seventh planet of the Dundra System, a lovely spot spoiled only by the nearby smouldering wreckage of the Starliner *Byzantium*. And it's where the Doctor and River Song are catching up.

Amy thinks this is the first occasion she's met River. The Doctor and River know they have each met many times before. But those encounters were at different points in their respective pasts and futures, so they don't have the same memories.

The Doctor accidentally reveals that River will become a professor – whoops, spoilers! River is more cautious and checks her handwritten notes about whether they have done the Bone Meadows yet. The diary probably mentions Jim the Fish, too. (Not a topic for discussion here.)

You'll have bags of stuff going on in your life at different times. Whether you're planning a holiday, studying for a degree or doing the shopping, always make good notes. You can't remember everything.

DECEMBER

1 DECEMBER

EATING THE ELEPHANT

THE DOCTOR

Tiny actions, that's what Krasko's doing.
See, he's clever, I'll give him that. He knows.
He's not planning on killing, or destroying
or breaking history. He's planning to nudge
it just enough so that it doesn't happen.

Rosa by Malorie Blackman (2018)

• • • • • •

Time-travelling criminal Krasko was incarcerated in the Stormcage. He hurt thousands, so the secure prison facility placed a neural restrictor in his brain before his release. Now he cannot kill or injure living things. But his time inside gave him plenty of time to think, and he knows tiny actions change the world.

He plans to alter Earth history with minor interventions that build to a larger effect: modify a drivers' rota, damage a vehicle, block a road, discourage bus passengers from boarding. The Doctor and her friends counter this to ensure Rosa Parks gets an opportunity to make her own individual and extremely brave decision that invigorates the American civil rights movement.

Things sometimes seem too daunting: clearing the shed, writing a book, running a marathon. If you never start, you're guaranteed to fail. Tidy a small section, write a page, go for a jog around the block. Take that small but important first step.

2 DECEMBER

LISTEN TO THE HEART

THE DOCTOR
I made some cocoa and got engaged.
Don't giggle, my boy.

The Aztecs by John Lucarotti (1964)

• • • • • •

The Doctor is pleased with his cleverness in charming a wise, kindly Aztec woman called Cameca who helps him find a way back to his entombed TARDIS. However, he neglects to pay proper attention to what she says about the significance of sharing cocoa. He's very happy to make Cameca her beverage of choice – until he realises with a shock that he has just agreed to marriage.

It's a misunderstanding that the Doctor's friend Ian finds very funny. And yet this inattentiveness on the Doctor's part, which could so easily have been avoided, causes Cameca great pain. She is heart-broken to realise that the Doctor didn't mean his promise and will not stay with her. Luckily for him, she still helps him to recover his ship, but it's a salutary lesson: when a friend speaks from the heart, they deserve to be heard – and understood.

3 DECEMBER

GET OUT

THE DOCTOR
You're not saved yet. Come on, let's get out of
here before the whole place explodes.

The Horns of Nimon by Anthony Read (1979–80)

•   •   •   •   •   •

The Power Complex of the planet Skonnos is a labyrinth of ever-changing corridors. Those poor souls unlucky enough to be lost within it are soon captured by the bull-like Nimon who drain their victims of their life-force.

Soldeed, leader of the Skonnon Empire, has been tricked into condoning this practice. He thinks there's only a single Nimon, who he reveres as a god. When the truth is revealed, and the would-be victims rebel, Soldeed operates a control to destroy the Power Complex.

The young victims are grateful to be freed but the Doctor wastes no time in celebration. He understands the danger – to them and to himself – and quickly leads them to safety. The young victims then turn on one of Soldeed's people, but the Doctor and Romana urge them to get away and take cover. As a result, no one is hurt in the explosion.

Put safety first. Questions, explanations and recriminations can all come later. If you're in a bad situation, don't hang around – just get out.

4 DECEMBER

BE HONEST WITH CHILDREN

THE DOCTOR
You know when grown-ups tell you everything's
going to be fine and you think they're probably
lying to make you feel better?

AMELIA POND
Yes.

THE DOCTOR
Everything's going to be fine.

The Eleventh Hour by Steven Moffat (2010)

• • • • • •

A raggedy man investigates the scary crack in Amelia Pond's bedroom wall. A voice from beyond it says Prisoner Zero has escaped. To close the crack, the man must first widen it – and he doesn't like to worry the little girl about the risks.

Later he will say he has to leave for five minutes and be right back. Amy's heard people say that before. Inevitably, the raggedy man disappoints her by not returning for 12 years.

Being honest with a child is hard in situations like grief, separation, illness, or traumatic current events. It's important they can cope, that they can trust you, and that you don't ignore the stress they may be feeling. Depending on their age and maturity, be honest and straightforward, choose the right moment and don't make promises you can't keep. As they grow, it will help them understand and establish their own values.

5 DECEMBER

KEEP IT SIMPLE

ZOE HERIOT
Oh, it isn't a theory. You can't disprove the facts: it's pure logic.

THE DOCTOR
Logic, my dear Zoe, merely enables one
to be wrong with authority.

The Wheel in Space by David Whitaker (1968)

• • • • • •

The Phoenix Mark IV rocket *Silver Carrier* is found some 85 million miles off course but only carries fuel for around 20 million miles. Brilliant astrophysicist Zoe Heriot concludes that it must have been refuelled in space and – since it couldn't have drifted so far so quickly – was then purposefully piloted.

The Doctor counsels caution at relying solely on logic. Anyway, he's more interested in an odd lump of plastic found near a dead man's body. Zoe again applies logic to the problem but the Doctor suggests they X-ray the plastic to see if contains a clue to the man's death. This hadn't occurred to Zoe, who was too busy contriving elaborate theories. In response, the Doctor cites the famous legend of the Gordian knot: a tangle so complex it couldn't be untied until Alexander the Great simply cut through it with his sword.

We can get lost in complexity. Sometimes we make progress by keeping things simple.

6 DECEMBER

EMPHASISE THE POSITIVE

THE DOCTOR

Eustacius Jericho, proper scientist. Under siege from the impossible, doesn't even stop to be scared, just wants to understand what's beyond his comprehension.

Flux: Village of the Angels by Chris Chibnall and Maxine Alderman (2021)

• • • • • •

Weeping Angels have surrounded Professor Eustacius Jericho's house in the village of Medderton. The professor is conducting experiments in the basement, measuring the theta waves of a percipient called Claire Brown on an electroencephalogram.

The rational Jericho initially thinks the Doctor's talk of quantum beings is ridiculous. Nevertheless, he does not let the frightening events happening in his own home prevent him from evaluating the evidence. After all, during the war, he saw plenty of things beyond his comprehension when he helped to liberate the concentration camps.

He starts to understand that Claire's premotions are a symptom of something taking root within her mind and causing a genuine psychic manifestation. The Doctor spots Jericho making these connections and tells him she's impressed.

The best encouragement is to reinforce what someone does well, not just criticise when they make a mistake. Look for opportunities to tell people when you have caught them doing something right rather than something wrong.

7 DECEMBER

EXPECT THE UNEXPECTED

THE DOCTOR

Every great decision creates ripples, like a huge boulder
dropped in a lake. The ripples merge, rebound off the banks
in unforeseeable ways. The heavier the decision, the larger
the waves, the more uncertain the consequences.

Remembrance of the Daleks by Ben Aaronovitch (1988)

• • • • • •

A school in Shoreditch, east London, in 1963 is the unlikely field of battle for two rival factions of Daleks. Even more surprisingly, they're here at the Doctor's request.

Okay, he didn't expect two rival factions to turn up at once. His brilliantly devious scheme is to lure *one* lot of Daleks into a trap with the promise of an incredible prize – the 'Hand of Omega'. This legendary device is the remote stellar manipulator that long ago gave the Time Lords power over their local star, granting them mastery over time.

As well as *two* Dalek factions, the Doctor must contend with his friend Ace ignoring his warnings and running headlong into danger. The Doctor isn't even sure his clever plan will work – or whether there may be unintended consequences.

Even our best-laid plans don't always go as expected. Think about what might go wrong – and prepare for it. Be agile, adapt where needed, and your plan stands a better chance of success.

8 DECEMBER

MAKING CHOICES

THE DOCTOR
I didn't know if I could save her. I couldn't save Quell, I couldn't save Moorhouse. There was a good chance that she'd die too. At which point, I would have just moved onto the next, and the next, until I beat it. Sometimes the only choices you have are bad ones. But you still have to choose.

Mummy on the Orient Express by Jamie Mathieson (2014)

• • • • • •

Clara Oswald and the Doctor teleport to safety from the fiery destruction of a train that was traversing space along hyperspace ribbons. The Doctor discovered the train was really a disguised laboratory that used crew and passengers as expendable victims of the Foretold – an ancient soldier kept alive indefinitely by malfunctioning technology.

The creature killed passenger Professor Emil Moorhouse and train captain Hector Quell. The Doctor put passenger Maisie Pitt in danger without knowing he could save her – before taking her place to confront the Foretold.

A dilemma requires a decision with no guaranteed good outcome. Focus on the facts. When you're between a rock and a hard place, accept that not making a choice is a choice in itself – and that may be worse.

9 DECEMBER

MOVING ON

THE DOCTOR
Death is the price we pay for progress.

The Brain of Morbius by Robin Bland (1976)

• • • • • •

On the storm-ravaged planet Karn, the impossible dream of a thousand alchemists drips like tea from an urn. A particular flame burning beneath a particular type of rock causes oxidisation of the chemicals inside it, producing a liquid that can regenerate tissue and prolong life for millennia.

The Doctor makes use of this extraordinary 'Elixir of Life' but does not subscribe to the mysticism around it. He says that with a decent spectrograph one could probably synthesise the stuff by the gallon – but that the consequences would be appalling.

As he notes, the Sisterhood of Karn – who protect the elixir and take regular sips of it – are all perfectly preserved after centuries. But, as their leader Maren acknowledges, 'Nothing here ever changes.' There is no innovation, promotion or variety. Immortality is more curse than blessing; she and her people are trapped.

Death is a part of life. It will comes to us all. That can be hard to accept and gruelling to experience, but it's how we avoid stagnation as a species. An individual might die, but humanity itself moves on.

10 DECEMBER

THROW YOURSELF INTO IT

THE DOCTOR
The eject button.

AMY POND
How does a mouth have an eject button?

THE DOCTOR
Think about it. Right then. This isn't
going to be big on dignity. Geronimo!

The Beast Below by Steven Moffat (2010)

• • • • • •

Amy Pond (age 1,306) and the Doctor (age unspecified) discover that colony vessel *Starship UK* has evacuated humans from a doomed Earth on the back of a Star Whale. They're dumped six hundred feet via a high-speed air cannon into a rubbish dump in a squelchy cave full of slime and organic matter.

The cave is the whale's huge mouth, supplied with food waste through feeder tubes from all over the ship. At risk of being swallowed, and already awash in debris and drool, the Doctor vibrates the whale's chemo-receptors to reverse the involuntary reaction. They're about to be evacuated again – this time, on a tidal wave of vomit.

A false sense of dignity may hold you back. Fear of being too good for something, a reluctance to get involved because you're afraid of failure, or dreading how others may judge you – even when you know it's the right thing to do. So let your hair down, join in wholeheartedly and take the plunge. It may not be as bad as you think.

11 DECEMBER

SMILE THOUGH YOUR HEART IS BREAKING?

THE DOCTOR

What were these opportunities you gave them – a bag
of sweets, a few tawdry party games, bland, soulless
music? Do these things make you happy? Of course
they don't, because they're cosmetic. Happiness is
nothing unless it exists side by side with sadness.

The Happiness Patrol by Graeme Curry (1988)

• • • • • •

It's against the law on the planet Terra Alpha to be unhappy – on pain
of immediate death. 'Happiness patrols' roam the streets in search of
so-called 'killjoys' to capture and execute.

The Doctor and his friend Ace foment an overnight revolution
against this harsh regime, with the help of the native Pipe People and
a cool, blues-playing medical student, Earl Sigma. Sometimes it feels
good to be blue.

But the tyrannical Helen A remains unrepentant. When the
Doctor argues that she created a world with no compassion or love,
Helen A counters that there was at least control. But for all she's cruel
to other people, Helen A loves her pet Fifi, a predatory Stigorax. When
Fifi is fatally wounded, Helen A breaks down in tears.

We can't force anyone (or ourselves) to be happy. The best way
through sadness is with compassion and support.

12 DECEMBER

WHAT PEOPLE DON'T SAY

THE DOCTOR
Why have you never mentioned your home
planet before? Are you in trouble?

VISLOR TURLOUGH
What makes you think that?

THE DOCTOR
Instinct – and the fact I've never seen you so nervous before.

Planet of Fire by Peter Grimwade (1984)

• • • • • •

It's only as Turlough leaves the TARDIS after multiple adventures that the Doctor learns who his travelling companion really is. We learned in Turlough's first TV adventure, *Mawdryn Undead* (1983), that he's more than an ordinary, if naughty, schoolboy and that he's not even from Earth. Subsequent stories revealed his scientific and technological knowledge – far beyond that of a 20th-century Earth schoolboy.

But only in *Planet of Fire* (1984), his final full-length TV story, do we learn that Vislor Turlough is a junior ensign commander from the planet Trion. The fact he's revealed so little about himself is in itself revealing about his experience and feelings.

We often judge people by their actions and the things they say. But what they *don't* say or do can be just as illuminating about who they are.

13 DECEMBER

BE THERE

YOSS INKL
In honour of you both, I wanted to call him Avocado...
after the ancient Earth hero, Avocado Pear.

GRAHAM O'BRIEN
No, no, mate, that is a fruit... it's not a hero.

YOSS INKL
But we did it in school.
You mean the Gifftan history logs are wrong?

The Tsuranga Conundrum by Chris Chibnall (2018)

• • • • • •

Gifftan males give birth to male offspring and female Gifftans bear females. They don't hang about, either: pregnancy lasts a week. Just as well that Yoss Inkl is en route to a 67th century hospital to deliver his firstborn.

The Doctor explains she's a doctor of medicine, science, engineering, candyfloss, Lego, philosophy, music, problems, people and hope. But when Yoss is ready to give birth, the Doctor's away. While she prevents further deaths aboard the ship, Graham O'Brien and Ryan Sinclair step in as Yoss's birth partners.

They don't have to be perfect; they just have to be there. Just as well, because Graham's expertise comes from watching *Call the Midwife*, Ryan's only watched YouTube, and Yoss's knowledge of Earth history is flawed. A readiness to make an effort and learn by making mistakes is what's needed. And don't trust everything you read on the internet.

14 DECEMBER

IT'S BEHIND YOU

THE DOCTOR
Square one. That's where we've got to go if we
want to find out what Skagra's up to. Once we
know that, we know where to find him.

Shada by Douglas Adams (not broadcast)

• • • • • •

Dr Skagra is a geneticist, astro-engineer, cyberneticist, neuro-structuralist and moral theologian who steals the minds of other brilliant scientists. His ultimate plan is to cause the whole of creation to merge into one single, god-like mind.

When Skagra steals the Doctor's TARDIS and kidnaps Romana in the process, the Doctor is keen to get after him – but doesn't know where he is heading next. His solution is to look at where Skagra has *been*.

If we want to understand someone's behaviour, it often helps to learn more about their background. It's true of ourselves, as well. Psychotherapy often involves exploring the impact of past events in our lives to help us make sense of our present feelings and behaviour so that we are better equipped to deal with whatever the future might hold.

Think of a time when you were happy as a child. Got one? Now, what can you do today that could rekindle some of that feeling?

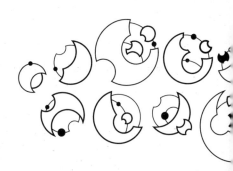

15 DECEMBER

HOPE INSPIRES

CLARA OSWALD
Lie to them. Give them hope. Tell them they're all
going to be fine. Isn't that what you would do?

THE DOCTOR
In a manner of speaking. It's true that people with hope tend
to run faster, whereas people who think they're doomed...

Flatline by Jamie Mathieson (2014)

• • • • • •

The Doctor is trapped in a shrinking TARDIS, unable to escape through its tiny doors. Investigating disappearances in Bristol, Clara Oswald takes his psychic paper, his sonic screwdriver and, while she's at it, his name.

Extra-terrestrial creatures from a two-dimensional universe reduce locals to shambling husks. The victims stalk Clara and a group of survivors through the subway system. Clara urges her group on to reach safety and keep them alive. She remembers how the Doctor's done this in the past: lying is a vital survival skill, albeit a terrible habit. But does it even still count as lying if she's doing it for someone's own good?

Hope helps us cope with adversity because it helps us manage stress and anxiety. Tell people that something is possible to motivate them. They have a goal to work towards, are prepared to solve problems and will decide it's worth making an effort.

16 DECEMBER

INACTION SPEAKS LOUDER THAN WORDS

THE DOCTOR
I know it is the way of Dulkis to discuss and to deliberate,
but the situation is urgent. Send someone to the
island to confirm what we've told you.

The Dominators by Norman Ashby (1968)

• • • • • •

The people of the planet Dulkis long ago banned warfare and their few remaining weapons are displayed in a museum to warn of the horrors of war. As part of their education, students are also taken to visit an island that is still radioactive 172 years after the last conflict.

But this means that when cruel, callous Dominators and their robot Quarks land on Dulkis, the Dulcians have no means with which to defend themselves. Their leaders are so used to debating peacefully, they struggle to understand even the *idea* of an aggressor. And it can take them months to make any decision.

But one frustrated young Dulcian, Cully, thinks there is more behind his elders' inaction: he believes they simply switch off when they encounter anything that they don't understand. The truth is that talk is easy and safe for these people.

It's not always easy to confront aggressive behaviour or to take action against it. But it gets worse the longer we delay.

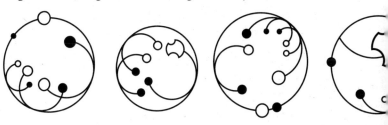

17 DECEMBER

FOLLOW YOUR INSTINCTS

THE DOCTOR
I don't know what you're up to, Professor, but whatever
they've promised, you cannot trust them. Call them
what you like, the Daleks are death.

Victory of the Daleks by Mark Gatiss (2010)

• • • • • •

One of the Doctor's oldest and deadliest enemies meekly serves tea in Professor Edwin Bracewell's laboratory. The Doctor is appalled that UK forces have accepted this new help as a servant and warrior in World War II. He insists that hate looks like a Dalek, and he's going to prove it.

He has suspicions about the professor, too. Did Bracewell's clever notions about hypersonic flight and gravity bubbles really come to him in the bath, or did the Daleks promise him something more?

The Doctor is proved right. Bracewell is uncovered as an unwitting Dalek android with a bomb inside him, and not a Scottish scientist who grew up in a Paisley post office.

Although you can't distrust on sight everyone you ever meet, their reputations will precede them. When you have your suspicions, ask polite but telling questions, and let them reveal their true nature to you and others.

18 DECEMBER

TEMPTING FATE

IDA SCOTT
Well, we've come this far. There's no turning back.

THE DOCTOR
Oh, did you have to? 'No turning back'? That's almost as
bad as, 'Nothing can possibly go wrong,' or, 'This is
going to be the best Christmas Walford's ever had.'

The Impossible Planet by Matt Jones (2006)

• • • • • •

The planet Krop Tor is in perpetual orbit around a black hole – which, according to the laws of physics, is impossible. A crew of human scientists studying the planet are dumbfounded by the arrival of the Doctor and Rose Tyler since it should also be impossible to have visitors on Krop Tor. But the Doctor is more concerned by samples of writing so impossibly old that the TARDIS can't translate them.

The crew drill down through solid rock to what they suspect is a power source some ten miles beneath the surface. When the drill stops, the Doctor and science officer Ida Scott head down to investigate. Ida is feeling confident, but the Doctor isn't keen to tempt fate as there may be danger ahead. He jokingly quotes the TV soap *EastEnders*, where disaster is never far off – especially when one of the characters happens to share a note of optimism.

Complacency makes us vulnerable. Whatever you're doing or trying to achieve, plan ahead and be prepared for when things to go wrong.

19 DECEMBER

THE KINDNESS OF STRANGERS

THE DOCTOR
I might regenerate, I don't know.
Feels different this time.

The Caves of Androzani by Robert Holmes (1984)

• • • • • •

The Doctor takes new companion Peri Brown to the planet Androzani Minor, where they come into contact with a fuzzy, sticky ball which gives them a strange stinging sensation. Unfortunately, they've encountered a Spectrox nest and the pair are now suffering from Spectrox toxaemia.

Symptoms of this deadly affliction begin with a rash. Subsequent cramp and spasms are 'followed by slow paralysis of the thoracic spinal nerve' and, finally, the so-called 'thermal death point'.

The Doctor learns of a potential cure – the milk of the carnivorous queen bat – which can only be found 200 metres down in the planet's underground system of caves. It's a perilous journey and even though the Doctor is ill, he succeeds in his mission.

Unfortunately, there's only enough milk to save Peri – someone he has just met – and his words suggest he's not even sure he can survive a regeneration. Put another way, he's willing to give up his own life for his new companion.

It's one thing to make a sacrifice for friends or family; it's another level of heroism altogether to do so for a stranger.

20 DECEMBER

LEAVING GRACEFULLY

SARAH JANE SMITH
Goodbye, Doctor, until the next time.

THE DOCTOR
Don't forget me, Sarah Jane.

SARAH JANE SMITH
No one's ever going to forget you.

The Sarah Jane Adventures: The Wedding of Sarah Jane Smith
by Gareth Roberts (2009)

· · · · · ·

Sarah Jane Smith is to marry the charming Peter Dalton. She's annoyed that her young friends are so suspicious of him. They have good reason to be: it's a trap set by the Trickster, an old enemy from beyond the universe, who wants to break into our reality and enslave her.

The Doctor arrives to stop the wedding and asks Sarah to make an impossible choice: defeating the Trickster means losing Peter.

With the Trickster banished, Sarah Jane thinks the Doctor will just sneak off and leave her – he's done it before, after all. But he returns in the TARDIS to say goodbye.

We tend to remember the first time we meet people, because we recall it every time we see them again. We rarely know if we are together with them for the final time. Cherish each moment when you are with a loved one, and things may be just a little easier should it turn out to be your last.

21 DECEMBER

JUST SAY NO

THE DOCTOR
No.

DALEK
Explain yourself.

THE DOCTOR
I said 'No'.

Bad Wolf by Russell T Davies (2005)

• • • • • •

In the year 200,100, the Doctor and his friends aboard space station Satellite 5 discover a hidden fleet of 200 spaceships poised to invade the Earth. Each ship is carrying more than 2,000 Daleks – about half a million in total – ready to exterminate humanity.

What's more, the Daleks have taken Rose prisoner. They warn the Doctor not to interfere with their invasion or they will exterminate his friend. As the Daleks say, the Doctor has no weapons, no defences and no plan.

Yet he tells them simply, 'No.' He will not stand idly by and let them wreak destruction. He goes on to say he'll rescue Rose, save Earth and defeat the Daleks. Just him saying so actually scares them.

It's not always easy to stand up for what's right, especially against anyone wielding strength or power. But have courage. And start by saying 'No.'

22 DECEMBER

SUPPORT FULL POTENTIAL

THE DOCTOR
Not easy is it, being clever? You look at the world and you connect things, random things, and think, 'Why can't anyone else see it? The rest of the world is so slow.' And you're on your own.

The Sontaran Stratagem by Helen Raynor (2008)

• • • • • •

Teenager Luke Rattigan is an inventive genius. Creating the Fountain Six search engine at the age of 12 made him a millionaire.

But the Doctor is suspicious about how he devised the ATMOS car device, and confronts him at the Rattigan Academy that Luke set up as a school for handpicked geniuses. The Doctor tests Luke by correcting a trivial grammar error. Luke looks for his chance to snap back at the Doctor, insisting he is right.

Gifted children develop cognitively at a much faster rate than they develop physically, emotionally and socially. Just as less able kids need additional assistance at home and school, so too do smart kids to avoid getting bored, discouraged and disruptive. Everyone deserves the encouragement and support to reach their full potential.

23 DECEMBER

DELEGATION, THAT'S THE THING

THE DOCTOR

(To Hardin) Have a baby. (To Romana) I think
we're redundant here. Let's go.

The Leisure Hive by David Fisher (1980)

• • • • • •

The Leisure Hive on the planet Argolis is designed to produce physical, psychic and intellectual refreshment. But competition from other worlds, which offer non-gravity swimming pools and robot gladiators, means Argolis faces bankruptcy.

Intelligent, reptilian Foamasi – the Argolins' former enemies – offer to buy the planet. But a young Argolin, Pangol, plans to start another war with them by using a machine to generate an army of clones of himself.

The Doctor and Romana help prevent this conflict, and Pangol's army turns out to be copies of the Doctor which then vanish one by one. When Pangol tries to use the generator machine again, it rejuvenates him into a baby.

The sense is that, second time round, Pangol might turn out better. But the Doctor never considers this to be his job; he promptly hands the baby over to someone else.

It's good to fix problems and prevent conflict. But not everything is your responsibility. Know when you're redundant and it's time to hand over control to someone else.

24 DECEMBER

SAY IT IN PERSON

THE DOCTOR
That's all I have. I'm sorry it's not more.
I'm probably worried for you if you're hearing this.
And I'm sure I miss you.

YASMIN KHAN
I miss you too.

THE DOCTOR
I know you do. I hope you said, 'I miss you too',
or else that bit's weird. Oh, hang on. Wait there.
I think you're calling me from the control room.

Flux: Survivors of the Flux by Chris Chibnall (2021)

* * * * * *

Yasmin Khan travels the globe in 1904 with Dan Lewis and Eustacius Jericho. Alone in the cabin of a transatlantic liner, she replays an adaptive hologram recording. The Doctor slipped it into her pocket the last time they were together and set it to activate two weeks later.

Yaz has played the message before — it's her briefing to discover the date for the end of the world. She knows from hearing the message again that the Doctor misses her but cannot convey her own feelings to the Doctor now they're apart.

Don't just rehearse in your head what you might say to someone about your hopes and fears, your achievements and disasters, your pride and love. You can't assume they will guess, so tell them —ideally in person.

25 DECEMBER

DREAM PRESENTS

THE DOCTOR
All of time and all of space is sitting out there.
A big blue box. Please, don't even argue.

CLARA OSWALD
Merry Christmas, Doctor.

THE DOCTOR
Merry Christmas, Clara Oswald.

Last Christmas by Steven Moffat (2014)

• • • • • •

Turkey dinner with all the trimmings. Pudding and mince pies. A glass or two of sherry. A cosy chair in front of a festive game show on the telly. No wonder you dropped off to sleep on Christmas Day.

Or were you seized by a dream crab? The Katrofarri attach themselves to human heads. They induce a dream state to keep victims happy while turning their brains into soup (even worse than watching game shows).

Among the victims, Clara dreams of returning to the TARDIS. The Doctor dreams he's missed Clara for decades. Everyone dreams of Santa Claus. Finally free from the Katrofarri, the Doctor offers Clara a gift too big to wrap: a return to travelling the universe with him.

Presents are one thing, but it's the consideration that counts. Today is a day to be considerate to others – what can you do to make their dreams come true?

26 DECEMBER

TRUE IDENTITY

BLON FEL-FOTCH PASSAMEER-DAY SLITHEEN
I spared her life.

THE DOCTOR
You let one of them go but that's nothing new. Every now
and then, a little victim's spared – because she smiled,
because he's got freckles, because they begged. And
that's how you live with yourself. That's how you slaughter
millions. Because once in a while, on a whim, if the wind's
in the right direction, you happen to be kind.

Boom Town by Russell T Davies (2005)

• • • • • •

At a nice quayside bistro, the Doctor has dinner with the deadly
Blon Fel-Fotch Passameer-Day Slitheen, who has adopted the identity
of a human she murdered – Margaret Blaine – and is now Lord Mayor
of Cardiff.

Blon tells the Doctor that she's changed and no longer a killer. But
the Doctor knows she's still murdering those who get in her way. In
fact, Blon is plotting to exploit the energy source of a nearby rift in
time and space, allowing her to escape from Earth – which of course
would be destroyed in the process.

As the Doctor shows, a person's character isn't revealed by individual things they might occasionally do – or not do. It's more about
what all their actions and deeds add up to – the balance of good and
bad. Before you judge someone, try to get a complete picture of them
first. You may end up modifying your initial impression.

27 DECEMBER

DO WHAT YOU CAN

THE DOCTOR

Stars implode. Planets grow cold. Catastrophe is the metabolism of the universe. I can fight monsters. I can't fight physics.

In the Forest of the Night by Frank Cottrell-Boyce (2014)

• • • • • •

Coal Hill School's Gifted and Talented group of pupils is on a field trip with Miss Oswald and Mr Pink. It's a shock to discover central London transformed overnight into a forest. It's even more of a surprise to see inside the TARDIS.

The Doctor's a scarier teacher than Miss Oswald or Mr Pink. The children are not reassured by his lesson about the solar flare heading towards Earth at a thousand kilometres a second. The coronal mass ejection is brewing up a solar wind big enough to blow the whole planet away. Miss Oswald hasn't mentioned this, because she doesn't want to scare them with something they can do nothing about.

The Doctor cannot control catastrophic events. On this occasion, the planet is saved by a life force in the trees. The children take the action they can: warning the world to stand back and leave the trees to do their work. You won't despair about things you cannot change if you work on those things you can influence.

28 DECEMBER

FOLLOW YOUR NOSE

THE DOCTOR
Let's concentrate on the Daleks. Have you noticed, for example,
that when they move about there's a sort of acrid smell?

The Daleks by Terry Nation (1963–64)

• • • • • •

The Doctor and his friends are taken prisoner by the Daleks and imprisoned in a cell deep in their underground city. Immediately, the Doctor applies himself to how they might escape – and he does so by using all his senses.

His first observation involves touch and hearing: the floors of the Dalek city are made of metal, he says. Then he notes the distinctive odour of the Daleks. His friends Barbara and Ian are quick to make the connection – Daleks smell like dodgem cars at a fairground. Soon, the friends have deduced that the Daleks in this city are powered by electricity drawn from the metal floors. Breaking that connection becomes the means of escape...

When we face what seem like insurmountable problems or feel as if we're trapped, it can help to take a moment and use all our senses. By orienting ourselves, by taking stock of our feelings, we can get a fresh perspective – and perhaps find the way out.

29 DECEMBER

DON'T FEED THE TROLLS

AMY POND
Three. Doctor, it's coming. I can feel it. I'm going to die!

THE DOCTOR
Please just shut up. I'm thinking. Now, counting.
What's that about? Bob, why are they making her count?

ANGEL BOB
To make her afraid, sir.

THE DOCTOR
OK, but why? What for?

ANGEL BOB
For fun, sir.

Flesh and Stone by Steven Moffat (2010)

· · · · · ·

Amy stares at a Weeping Angel as it climbs from a screen, and since the image of an Angel is an Angel, now it's in the vision centres of her brain.

The Angels have stripped the cerebral cortex from a clerical combatant called Bob and re-animated a version of his consciousness to communicate with the Doctor. Angel Bob's voice sounds calm and reasonable over the radio link. But his words taunt the Doctor about being trapped. The Angels are laughing at their victims, trying to make them answer, and frightening them for the sake of it.

The Doctor chooses when to talk to Angel Bob and when to throw away his radio. If people say things just to upset you for their own enjoyment, you can choose not to feed the trolls.

30 DECEMBER

DON'T SUFFER SUFFERING

THE CONTROLLER
People have never been happier or more prosperous.

THE DOCTOR
Then why do you need so many people to keep them under
control – don't they *like* being happy and prosperous?

Day of the Daleks by Louis Marks (1972)

• • • • • •

Soldiers from 22nd century Earth travel back in time to assassinate a politician who they believe must be prevented from starting a global war. The Doctor and Jo Grant pursue the soldiers back into the future and soon see for themselves the terrible results of this conflict.

The human 'Controller' of the ruined Earth is really a servant of the Daleks. What he describes as a 'rehabilitation centre for hardened criminals' is actually full of old men and women, even children. The Controller tries to argue that some people will always need discipline and that Earth has never been more efficiently or economically run. Of course, the Doctor's not having any of that.

Some people will try to excuse the suffering of others. That it's good for them. Or that they deserve it. Or that if they only worked harder or were more resourceful, they would suffer less.

That's easy to say when you're not the one who is suffering; it's an unacceptable excuse not to help.

31 DECEMBER

MAGICAL MOMENTS

THE DOCTOR

I want you to remember everything. Every single day with
me. Every single second. Because your memories are
more powerful than anything else on this planet. Give the
Memory Weave everything. Every planet, every face,
every madman, every loss, every sunset, every scent,
every terror, every joy. Every Doctor. Every me.

The Sarah Jane Adventures: Death of the Doctor
by Russell T Davies (2010)

• • • • • •

The Shansheeth trap Sarah Jane Smith and Jo Jones in a Memory
Weave device. By making the two women visualise the TARDIS key,
the alien vultures will gain access to the Doctor's time machine. The
Doctor urges his friends instead to overload the Memory Weave with
all their memories of their adventures with him.

Sarah remembers Bellal, dinosaurs, Davros and the Daleks,
Sontarans, Hieronymous, Harrison Chase, Zeta Minor, Sutekh,
UNIT, Zygons, Kraals and Eldrad. Jo remembers Daleks and Ogrons,
Spiridon, Kronos, Sea Devils, Skybase One, Draconians, Drashigs, the
Dæmons and the Master. They each remember Peladon. And they both
remember their Doctors.

You never forget meeting your first Doctor. Perhaps with your
family seeing a new episode broadcast on the telly. With friends
watching a repeat on a streaming service. Or a Blu-ray collection or
novelisation bought as a present. That magical first moment that started
all your lasting memories of *Doctor Who*.

Remember the effect it had on you. Use that power to do something good, and make the Doctor proud.

SAYING GOODBYE

THE DOCTOR
And so, my friends, our story is at an end.
The TARDIS is waiting and I must move on to
another time, another place. Perhaps some remote
corner of the outer universe. But wherever it is, we
shall meet again. We *shall* meet again. Goodbye.

The Pescatons by Victor Pemberton (1976)

• • • • • •

Saying a firm goodbye is a means of achieving closure. Closure may
also be achieved by finishing a book and placing it back on the shelf.
   It's time to give that a try.

DEDICATION